WHEN I PAINT MY MASTERPIECE

Copyright © 2022 by Daniel Loveday

All rights reserved. No part of this book may be reproduced in any manner whatsoever without written permission except in the case of brief quotations embodied in critical articles and reviews.

First Printing, 2022

WHEN I PAINT MY MASTERPIECE

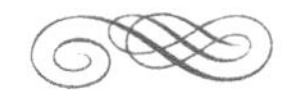

DANIEL LOVEDAY

Bobwire Books

'From the River Rhône to the hills of Vence,
From the sea below to the high Durance
The land of perfect refuge
Is carousing and sorrowless.
There among that noble people
I have left my heart rejoicing
With the one who makes the others smile.'

From Peire Vidal, *Ab l'alen tir vas me l'aire*

I

Town's only hill was silken and wavy and it glowed vermillion red in the late afternoons of the summer, when its shadow stretched long across the roads and wagons and homesteads that it overlooked. Upon it there was almost always sat Willie Bridger, an old man who had no telescope and who painted nebulae and supernovae and stellar formations in his spare time. This was despite the arthritis in his hands and the hunching of his back, the both of which told that he was entering the winter of his years, and for this reason he seldom ventured down from the hill. He would have built himself an outhouse up there if he wasn't so brittle. He already had his daughters and their husbands building a planetarium in town so he didn't think he'd fare well asking them to build him a toilet too. And the other folks in town wouldn't do it knowing that his twice-daily shuttle down the hill to use the honkytonk restroom was often all they got to see of him during the week.

On the hill he slept under the shade of his fishing hat during the day and watched the sky at night. It crossed his mind that he ought to be crass and ill-mannered whenever he spoke to any of the folks in town because that would give them a reason to build him an outhouse. But poor Willie didn't have it in him to be discourteous and, if somehow he did, it was unlikely that anyone would believe it to be anything more than an act. And anyway Willie was often lonely and this he measured by how far away from the stars he felt on any given clear night. When they shunned the gazing pleas of his eyes - as he often experienced in the midst of a melancholic stretch of perceived isolation

- he would begrudgingly ascend the broad cairn across the hill's crown. It was barely a whisker taller than ten feet and yet atop it Willie often found that his celestial devotions would be better reciprocated by the twinkling audience.

Every day the climb up the hill got harder and harder. It was partly because his house was a quarter mile across town that Willie had begun sleeping on the hill; he was already panting by the time he got to the foot of it. The dust and haze from the passing prairie schooners also caused his lungs great distress, though not as much as the flivvers had when they'd been all the go in town. But always the clear night sky was waiting for Willie Bridger when he got to the top of his hill, and so always was his collapsible chair. Somehow a crude Aeolian harp had found its way up there in recent years - a gift, perhaps? - and it too had become a fixture on the cairn. But there was never a telescope because Willie Bridger never had the money to buy one. When his son-in-law Jon got back from the War he brought a pair of military binoculars with him as a gift to Willie, but Willie's arthritic and excitable hands meant they didn't last the first trip up the hill. Still he sheltered under the umbrella of routine and still he kept studying the sky.

The prospective planetarium demanded that he knew every nook and cranny of it like he did the back of his stiff hands. He researched thoroughly despite that his old eyes didn't thank him for heavy reading. Always he had essays by Leavitt and Hubble and especially Annie Cannon, whom Willie thought was simply the smartest person who ever walked the earth. He met her once when he was of middle-age, at a convention in Taranto. She had signed his copy of *In the Footsteps of Columbus* and discussed Betelgeuse with him at great length. Years later she had invited him by letter to Arequipa where she hoped he might study the skies of the southern hemisphere with her. But, much to his daughters' chagrin, Willie Bridger decided to stay in town. Peru was a long, long way away.

Despite that Betelgeuse was his favourite star Willie's favourite constellation was not Orion - it was Gemini. His favourite planet was Earth. Because Willie was so revered for his intelligence in town folks often asked him what he was building aside from the planetarium. They regularly assumed it would some kind of an interstellar vessel or train or stagecoach, but Willie would laugh them away and say that he had enough trouble getting from A to B in town, let alone outer space. But he would remind them that his planetarium would bring the stars to them, so that they wouldn't ever have to think about venturing out into such a frightening, beautiful place. Night after night he looked up before he fell asleep in his collapsible chair, where then he dreamt all about building an interstellar vessel or train or stagecoach.

Naturally his vacation time was dictated by cloud cover. When the clouds came in and the rolling thunder with them Willie often sauntered down to the Pig's Itch and chewed the fat awhile with July Slade the proprietor. The Pig's Itch was the old estate built by July's ancestors, but was now an impromptu boarding house and speakeasy. Old Willie didn't much like to wet his whistle in public but his arrival at the Pig's Itch always brought a flurry of customers who doubled or sometimes tripled July's typical nightly takings. People simply wanted a chance to catch up with Willie. In the same way that a red sunset tells that tomorrow will be dry and pleasant, an overcast night in town told that the Pig's Itch should expect booming business. Dawn would come and Willie would head back up the hill to his collapsible chair, leaving everyone else to stumble on home, satisfied at a rare encounter.

Mostly people felt safe when Willie was around. He carried with him a protective aspect despite that he was rarely very tender. His sympathy and his care was carried and displayed in his big, brown, unfrowning eyes; considered and decadent and paternal and the open pages of his character. Willie might have walked naked into the Pig's Itch and it would have taken a minute for anyone to notice, such was the expressiveness he held in his eyes. Furthermore, everything he did was slow and considered, including the words he spoke and the expressions he made. His stories were lyrical and charismatic and yet they were unflamboyant. Seldom was he over-impassioned and always was he temperate, and little goes further than that combination to relaxing a people. The folks in town were drawn to him like moths to a flame.

Sourpusses and rays of sunshine alike were pulled into Willie's circle of security. It meant that his trips to the Pig's Itch were something of an event in town.

Willie had family that he neglected to see. He had three granddaughters now and all of them liked to sass him because he was rarely around. His daughters' names were Maggie and Mary. Maggie was married to Charlie Bellingham and Mary to Jon Harper. They often acted as their father's envoy to the rest of the town when he got a little too immersed in his studies. It was made known to them that Willie was missed during his long tours on the hill, and so the burden fell on them to reassure their people that he would return to the masses as soon as either his brandy-soda cravings or the clouds came back. Willie suspected that his daughters resented this responsibility but he was loath to make changes to his stubborn routine at such an eyes. Maggie, who was the eldest, was often very flippant with him. Mary was softer and gentler, but Willie, perhaps deeply insecure, hated to be patronised. It was far preferable to be sassed by Maggie than sweet-talked by Mary.

All three of his granddaughters belonged to Maggie. Their names were Doc, Elsie and Hattie. Old Doc the eldest daughter was Willie's secret favourite and the only one of the girls who ever sat with him on the hill, despite that she was mostly taciturn and antisocial. She was his favourite because she - unlike Elsie and Hattie - never forgot what he looked like no matter how long he stayed away and because she too liked the sky. Maggie, Mary, Charlie and Jon all tutted or sniggered or rolled their eyes when Willie started talking a blue streak about the stars. And Elsie and Hattie would vanish lickety-split. Not Doc though. Doc loved to hear about them. Often Willie wondered if little old Doc just loved to learn pure and simple, but then he noticed how quickly she grew bored of the bugs she studied underneath the boardwalk. Even novels or encyclopaedias or slapjack or checkers or game of graces or cat's cradle couldn't keep her attention long. Only in the picture shows and the sky and herpetology could she become truly lost, and Willie loved that about her. He knew that she was the most like him. Doc also did very little in the way of looking after her appearance and so consistently upheld a smelly shabbiness – something else that Willie respected. Always her overalls were plastered in dirt and her face mucky as heck.

(ii)

Doc was always keen to help her grandfather out in some way or another. Often Momma wouldn't let her because she believed it encouraged Willie to stay up on the hill while the kid ran his errands for him. So Doc learned to keep it a secret when she did. She was currently carrying messages to and from the post office for Pop-pop because he was corresponding with Edwin Hubble himself over the possibility of having a star named after one of town's most well-respected alumni. They had enlisted the help of the telegraph operator. His name was Sidney and he was responsible for directly communicating with the observatory in San Manassas where Edwin Hubble was currently working. Sidney had a belle and she was the lady who worked at the telegraph station in San Manassas, so he was always waiting either patiently or impatiently for correspondence.

On a hot Friday afternoon Doc went for an update at the station. Last week Doc had again left her Mary Janes by the livery stable when fixing to pet one of the mares. She'd forgotten to collect them afterwards and they had been eaten by a thoroughbred called Barnes. Now Doc was barefoot again – the shoes had lasted less than a month - and because it was very hot underfoot Doc had to walk on the tips of her toes. She was tall and bony for her age, creaking with every move but by no means was she weak. Once she fought the schoolhouse bully and bust his tooth despite that he had two inches on her. She carried an enviable carefreeness so disastrous that she often got caught in the nude when collecting the paper on a morning. For her most days began and ended with a clumsy attempt at an arabesque or a turn-out in front of her bedroom mirror, and if she was feeling particularly excitable then she would do a stretch of the black bottom while humming *Kansas City Kitty*. She had an unconventionally handsome face and handsome hands, and could be identified from a hundred yards by her loping gait and swinging long arms.

Sidney was punching letters into the telegraph machine and listening to a record on the phonograph. He looked thoroughly disorientated.

'Hidy-do, Sidney,' said Doc, finally able to put the balls and heels of her feet down as she pushed into the office. 'Any news for me?'

'Naw,' said Sidney.

'Still nothing from the observatory?' asked Doc.

'Nothing, not even from the station to tell us to hold tight. It seems Miss Grimes ain't got much of a desire to reply to my electrical signals. Do you think that means she's got her designs on up and leaving old Sidney?'

'You should follow up,' said Doc.

'I did. I told her she's leaving me with no choice but to sulk.'

'On the *star*, Sidney.'

'Let me alone. I don't have time to be pushed around by a kid-girl with no shoes.'

'Fuhgeddaboudit,' said Doc.

Doc left the telegraph station and began to bounce on her tiptoes again. In the post office next door she purchased the latest copy of *The New York Times* for a dime. The dime spent was one taken from the swear box that her mother kept in an attempt to manage her temper. She flicked to the astronomy section on page two for anything of note to report to Pop-pop. Doc had begun to worry that Hubble had died, but there was nothing on that in the paper, so she thanked the shop-keeper Earl and headed back out into the sun. It was sweltering out but Doc knew that it would get much hotter over the next couple of months and so she lamented herself for her low pain threshold. Being so footloose could be a drag sometimes.

Pop-pop's hill was on the west side of town and always had delightful views of the sunset, which he typically woke up in time for. So Doc headed that way and wondered if she might ask him to take her to see a picture at the nickelodeon in Laguna. She had one dime left but wasn't perfectly willing to part with it, yet knew that Pop-pop wouldn't pay her admission, unlikely even his own. He liked the pictures but he preferred the sky. Doc was undecided on which was better. The sky was bigger than a picture screen but a picture moved more than the sky did. The sky made her feel great awe and an intense, reflective melancholy that she didn't quite understand. But the pictures made her feel a great many different emotions - you could never predict how you'd feel at the pictures. *The Chechahcos*, for example, made her heart beat and bounce around so much that it almost flew out of her crazy mouth. And anyway what was better than both was amphibians. Doc had her sights set on studying herpetology in Boston one day.

Though the dark of the evening was fast approaching Pop-pop was still sleeping in his collapsible chair. The sun was so low that his fishing hat was doing nothing to shield his eyes, so Doc stood watching in wonderment at the old man's ability to keep asleep despite this obvious hinderance. Not wanting to wake him she removed the little floorcloth from her satchel and covered the dirt chair that she had made with a shovel years ago. It was built into a little rise in the earth opposite the collapsible chair. She sat down and tilted her ballcap low over her face and settled into a sleeping position, humming a piece that she had heard through her father's gramophone earlier that day. He had told her it was by Lang and Venuti.

Sundown came around and Doc was well-tuned enough to wake up of her own accord around the same time that her Pop-pop did. He was already rubbing the sleepies from his eyes and clearing his throat. The wind had picked up a little and the Aeolian harp touched Doc's hearing with a wistful purr.

'Let's get a fire going, kid,' Pop-pop said.

'Sure thing.'

Doc stretched, yawned big and wide and then began gathering some tinder while Pop-pop got first his bearings and then some timber. They liked to build the fire away from the chairs so as to prevent the light from smoking up their view of the sky. Once it was ready to be lit Doc remembered that she needed to ask about the picture show, for if she left it any longer the thought would surely vanish from her mind entirely; replaced for the hours to come by the contents of the twinkling dome above. The sky was simply that distracting.

'Pop-pop, will you take me to the nickelodeon?' she asked. 'I've a dime right here from the swear box,' she pulled the coin from her overalls pocket and proudly held it aloft.

'Ain't that your ma's?' asked Pop-pop.

'She says she's saving it for a rainy day. But it rarely rains here and when it does everyone stays inside. What can you buy inside your own house?'

'What's on?'

'I'm not sure, Pop-pop. Half the excitement is not knowing.'

'I'm too old to waste my hours on a shoddy picture,' said Pop-pop.

'Even with a smidgin of old Doc thrown in?' said Doc.

'I've a huge hallelujah for the folks that do but I am too conscious of time. I can almost see it these days - the time. My eyes may be going but *that* I see more clearly than ever.'

'But you ain't even got a clock up here, Pop-pop.'

Pop-pop struck a match and carefully ignited the tinder nest. He put his arm around Doc and guided her back to the collapsible chair and the dirt seat opposite it. They would return to the fire as soon as it got chilly and toast some marshmallows. It was a good way for them to stretch their legs intermittently.

But tonight the clouds came out and the gales with them and Pop-pop was forced to concede that they go to the Pig's Itch. He put little-big Doc on his shoulders and he grunted and he wheezed but Doc laughed and patted his head and messed with his ears and gave him some wet willies. Old Pop-pop had once had metal pieces in the lobes of his ears and they had sagged as a result, leaving old Doc with no choice but to flick them whenever she was sat on his shoulders. This she did all the way down to the Itch as the heels on the end of her long, gangling legs bashed against Pop-pop's hips.

(iii)

Mademoiselle Mélanie Celestine was in the Itch. She was married to Lester Monroe so she wasn't really a mademoiselle anymore, or a Celestine. But Doc, like most around town, regarded the name with such fondness that she resolved to secretly keep it for the nice lady. And Lester was never around so it was easy to forget that he existed. Mademoiselle Celestine was from Provence and was very fashionable, although she often turned up her nose at the flappers and dappers in town. Many of the latter had tried their hands with Mademoiselle Celestine over the years but she was stubborn and often belligerent in the face of favour-seeking men. It took a great deal for her to succumb and she had only done so twice since being in California: once with her previous fiancé July Slade and then with this Lester Monroe. He was a sailor and right now he was possibly on his way back north from Cape Horn.

What pleased Doc was that the wonderful Mademoiselle Celestine and her old beau July apparently felt comfortable enough in one another's presence for Mademoiselle Celestine to visit the Itch and for July not to tell her nome. But Doc saw clearly that July was looking at Mademoiselle Celestine so longingly that she thought his eyes might tilt into the corners of his mouth and his bowed head pull him down to the ground. And Mademoiselle Celestine barely saw him. Almost as soon as Pop-pop lifted Doc off his shoulders and onto the nearest barstool did Mademoiselle Celestine swoon over in her cloche hat and swaying silk gown of blue and black, brushing shoulders with July on her way but taking no notice of the collision.

'Doc! *La fille qui dort sous les belles étoiles,*' she said, giving the girl a big squeeze. Not many people dared to hug Doc but Mademoiselle Celestine thought improper to do otherwise, which Doc appreciated – a rare acceptance of intimacy. 'No muscle, no? Arms down to your ankles but no muscles on them? Look at these!'

Doc lifted her stronger left arm and flexed her piteous biceps.

'Hidy-do, Mademoiselle Celestine,' she said.

Mademoiselle Celestine clapped and delighted at this alleged revelation. 'I was wrong!' Then she waltzed off looking for some other feller to charm. No one else much fancied giving Doc the time of the day because in truth they were all scared of her. Only Mademoiselle Celestine and Pop-pop, but there was little chance that either of them would spend the evening with her and so Doc went and exchanged her dime for two nickels at the register, which was run by Mr Cricket.

'Ordering anything, kid?' he asked, peering over his monocle. He was coloured like Doc, only with hammock eyelids and a very gentle gait and posture. He lived on a bedroll on the balcony of July's bedroom because there had been no available space when he had arrived, and since some had eventually opened up he had already become too comfortable.

'All drinks on me if I win at the Liberty Bell,' lied Doc. She doubted that Mr Cricket would hold her to her promise as he too was a little afraid of her, and anyway he was still newish in town. Off she went to the fruit machine with her two shiny nickels, the first of which she duly put in the slot. She pulled the lever and it *whirred* and *grirred* hammer and tongs and then the reels span like there was no tomorrow. Doc watched with wide and glowing eyes as it did, but it gave her only a horseshoe and two spades. No payout. She held up the second nickel. Either she would go bust, come out with enough for a single nickelodeon ticket, break even or make enough for numerous trips. The prospect was tantalising.

Two horseshoes and a star appeared on the reels. Doc took her new dime and sighed, deciding that only pain would meet her if she continued on this daring endeavour. So instead she pulled a barstool with one hand and carried a spittoon with the other and found a nice corner from which she could observe and possibly sleep. The spittoon she kept because she knew it would keep the drunks from trying to talk with her later in the night. She thought of it as her own protective shield of sorts. And the irony of it was that it was the sight of her holding a container filled with the sots' own spit that kept them from wanting to go near her.

Awhile she sat and was bored. All that interested her was the wistfulness in July Slade's glistening eyes, but Doc didn't feel much up to being sad tonight. Instead she watched the throng build around Pop-pop as he greeted his people and answered their questions and shook their hands and somewhat clumsily received their compliments. Perhaps it was her boredom but this was the first time that little Doc had ever noticed that Pop-pop was looking older now. Most of the time she spent with him was at night and out on the hill, and starlight didn't do much to reveal the tightness of skin around a man's bones or the ridges in his forehead. He looked thinner than ever. The kerosene lamps did an unnervingly good job of showing it all.

So Doc moved her attention back to Mademoiselle Celestine who would never bring her sadness. Mademoiselle Celestine was unlikely capable of ageing or feeling sad or drunkenly making Doc feel uncomfortable. Mademoiselle Celestine was always ethereal and nebulous and floaty. Her dark brown hair was cut into a long bob of which she tucked half over her left ear. Her nose was so thin and narrow and delicate Doc wouldn't dare flick it like she flicked Pop-pop's ear lobes, out of fear she would snap the pretty thing. She used a delightful combination of rouge and pink-tinted salve on her long lips and there was a brightness to her eyes that Doc suspected were thanks to the use of belladonna drops. Once Doc had tried to achieve the same effect in her own eyes by raiding Ma's little showcase. But the drops hurt her eyes so much that she had screamed and confessed to the crime right there on the spot, crying like a little baby.

July Slade might have been equally handsome if he didn't look so sorrowful and wretched. He sat and he sulked and he stooged all evening long. Pop-pop always said that July Slade owned the happiest place in town that wasn't a cathouse, but not even that affected his mood. When he and Mademoiselle Celestine had been engaged to be married there had been such life in the Pig's Itch that one might have become disorientated - perhaps even overwhelmed - if they had stayed too long. Whenever the place became too quiet the couple organised a great fandango built around the phonograph or the piano that July had once owned. Always there was time to dance to *Crazy Blues* or Fiddlin' John Carson. Sometimes they had organised large group visits to the picture house in Laguna. They had sold penny dreadfuls behind the bar for the kids to read while the grownups hoedowned. Now July and Mademoiselle Celestine shared the premises as proprietor and customer respectively, rather than fiancé and fiancée respectively, and it made for sad viewing indeed.

When day broke old Doc was woken up by Pop-pop and he slapped her back on his shoulders to be carried home. Doc pleaded that Pop-pop let her sleep in the dirt seat but Pop-pop insisted that she be returned to her mother, lest Maggie have Pop-pop's guts for garters.

'Can Pop-pop come in for some coffee?' Doc asked Momma as she stumbled wearily from the old man's shoulders. It seemed that she had slept on the short walk.

'Sure thing, if he wants to,' said Momma. 'Go and put the kettle on while I talk with Pop-pop.'

Doc trotted into the kitchen where her insufferable sisters were sat around the table eating breakfast. Like always they sniggered at her and teased her for her boyishness and for her dorkish obsession with astronomy. Doc wanted to ignore them but couldn't help herself.

'I don't only like stars and the sky and space and stuff,' she said.

'Frogs?'

'*Amphibians*! Not just frogs, Elsie!'

'How are you gonna manage at the schoolhouse with no sleep?' asked Hattie, who had asymmetric ankles and an ugly scar on her collar from when Elsie bit her in a squabble. After nights up on the hill or down at the Itch Doc liked to play hooky from school and go and sleep in the meadow nearby. On a warm day it was delightful and she was determined to be able to sleep in the direct light of the sun just as Pop-pop did. This of course she did not want to get back to her parents, so she kept it from her likely traitorous sisters. Instead she stole a rasher from Hattie's plate and darted from the kitchen back out towards Pop-pop, but the door was closed and the old man was gone. Momma was sat on the window seat and looked sadly at Doc, who sighed and ambled on over, reaching out for Momma's hand as she knelt down next to her. Through the window they watched Pop-pop all the way down the street and up the hill until he was safely back in his collapsible chair, fishing hat pulled low over his face.

2

It had been a long time since July last had the old man come down to the Itch. Tonight he brought with him his mulatto granddaughter on his shoulders. Her spindly frame had grown plenty since July had last seen her. Her neck, arms and legs were all very long now and her head had grown disproportionately large. All of her was more than before except for her torso, which July figured a big feller could wrap a single hand the whole way around if he needed to move her off a barstool. She looked like a malnourished starfish. And she was often barefoot and always dirty, though only the former tonight. Doc was the only guest that July had ever asked to put *on* their shoes so as to make less mess on the carpet, which July did not see the funny side of. Infants were mostly nuisances to July and he knew very little about them.

But having the astronomer come to the Itch was a good distraction from Mélanie, whose arrival that evening had really turned July sore. On hearing earlier in the evening that his old bride-to-be would be shortly appearing, July had fetched Mr Cricket to the register. Mr Cricket was one of the newer boarders upstairs and he, like July, had no real job and was living off of old money, so he seldom refused the offer to busy himself. Any anyway July let him sleep on the balcony which was gracious enough in and of itself. With Mr Cricket behind the register July was free to go outside and thrash his quirt against the corral's tie rail over and over until he was beat. Then July threw up from nerves, waltzed back into the Itch and thanked Mr Cricket.

'She's that goddamn hussy you're always airing your lungs over?'

asked Mr Cricket, gesturing off to a place that July couldn't bear to look. 'Ain't much less than an angel to me.'

'Get out of here,' said July.

'I figure I'll stay.'

Mr Cricket scratched on his goatee and leant down on his elbow so that he could relax as he stared. Upon his return from the corral July had refused outright to even look at Mélanie, but now he was almost sweating from the resistance. He looked up and his body contemplated failing him for a fraction of a second. Any longer and his heart would have stopped, his legs given out and his bowels emptied. There was nothing to say that wasn't already encapsulated in Mr Cricket's description of Mélanie Celestine. Straight away she met July's eyes with her own that were pitiful and tender and July felt drowned in. But he couldn't look away and suddenly she was gliding towards him and he could smell peonies and hyacinths floating through the air with her.

'How are you, July?' she asked.

'*Ça va*, Mélanie,' said July. 'Yourself?'

If Mélanie's new husband had returned triumphantly from his voyage and made his entrance then and there July would never have noticed him. He doubted that anyone would have, and that was no slight on old sailor Lester – though July was never loath to slight Lester. When July had first introduced Mélanie to his parents she had worn no powder or rouge or lipstick on her face and had been nervous about it, but she had flattened them all the same. And now whenever July saw her she was delicately painted and she flattened people still.

'I expect we shall see the strange girl, no?' said Mélanie. 'The sky is overcast and she is often up the hill with Willie.'

'If woe betide us,' said Mr Cricket dreamily.

'I like her,' said Mélanie.

'Likely she will sit in a corner with a bowl of spit and watch us all,' said July.

'She keeps us honest,' Mélanie said.

July's frustrations with Mélanie were brought back to him and threatened to bubble right below his right eye. He saw her watching that very spot on his face, knowing that their talk was over and that she ought to move on. She smiled sadly at him once more and then said goodbye. When Mr Cricket's eyes fell to Mélanie's fanny he wolf-whistled and July clapped him over the head.

'How can you look at her in that way?' July said.

'How could you look at her any other way?' Mr Cricket said. 'Say, how does one get to look like that, you think?'

'Her mother sang songs about the sunshine to her when she was a little girl,' was July's best and only explanation.

When they first became itemed July and Mélanie had tiptoed around the bedroom rather than diving into the sheets. July had been nervous, plain and simple, and he expected that it was the same with Mélanie.

'I ain't never seen dog days this hot,' July had observed one morning, gullying his lip with a finger nail and feeling a tremor in the morning sun. He had never known such a sultry September. 'Dang right we slept in separate beds!'

To relieve themselves of the discomfiture they had small-talked about menial things like mayonnaise. Mélanie loved mayonnaise and claimed it was a French cuisine, but July was certain it was invented by the Hellman family. Neither of the two believed in the holy sacrament of marriage - at least not to the extent that they be restrained from fulfilling their desires until they left the altar. July believed in God, sure, but why would He care if July shared a nooky with Mélanie before they were married? July never had any doubts that she would be the only one he wanted to be with from the moment he laid eyes on her, and yet a bedding took a very long time to materialise.

What stopped them from that vulgar dance was that July couldn't bear to see her in that way. Mélanie didn't mind that, but July doubted that she understood. How could she understand that deep, unnatural fear he had: a fear of losing her through the ultimate act of togetherness? What an irony! To him Mélanie was a painting that not even the Louvre could afford. To take off her clothes would be to peel off the colours or to scratch on the canvas. Or perhaps July worried that Mélanie would feel that about him if she were to bed him. It was difficult for him to know. Neither did he know how any loving couple could gladly bed one another. How was the same problem not universal? And if it wasn't, then was Mélanie truly an angel of some kind?

As the months of their engagement waned the nookies or lack thereof became a trouble that weighed on the very air around July. The magic of the early affair dwindled and his customers winced or shuddered for reasons unknown to them as they walked through the door of the Itch. Food and drink lost its taste to July as his *joie de vivre* was sapped. He spent hours in the distillery making the moonshine stronger to ease his nerves. He had to visit Dr Wagner when his fingertip became septic as a result of his chewing his nails to pieces. It came to a day when he could barely be in the same room as Mélanie because he was so deeply ashamed of himself. And yet Mélanie seemed happy and committed to July and planned carefully for the future. They would move to a Provençal town, she said, live in a timberland *chaumière*, grow onions and visit the dance hall on Friday nights. France would be cold in winter but Mélanie would teach July to sew and July would teach Mélanie to chop wood. They would always be warm. His impotency affected her not at all. The weight in the air was felt only by July and his decreasing clientele.

And yet Mélanie never mentioned any children that they might have, which caused July's heavy heart to swell further hot with shame. He purchased some aphrodisiac from a travelling salesman who claimed to be a university-educated botanist. July scoffed at such an endeavour but the potion worked and suddenly he was ready. Though he did not enjoy the thought of sharing a poke with Mélanie he knew that it was a matter of need rather than want. If he wanted to keep her then he had to bed her, surely. Even if Mélanie made no implication that this was the case then there was the insecurity inside July that was almost overwhelming. He convinced himself that there was no future without consummation.

And they did indeed share nookies irregularly thereafter. And then the relationship fell apart, leaving July flummoxed. Within a month came a day when Mélanie was crying and July was crying and there was coffee and moonshine and tobacco and screaming. Mélanie made July feel a real scamp. At the summer soirée July believed he could reconcile things but Mélanie drunkenly told him that the engagement was indeed over and that she would be giving her hand to Lester Monroe for reasons that she was unwilling to divulge. July ought to have left town then and there. Mélanie had been his sole reason for remaining until then, but he couldn't face the idea of losing the sight of her forever. Often now he wondered if seeing her on the odd occasions, such as tonight at the Itch, was actually more painful to him than never seeing her again ever could be. Often July was just confused. The old katzenjammer headaches had long been replaced by a tight chest that resulted from the anger he got when drinking, and his persistent drinking itself had caused his memory to devolve into a kaleidoscope of cartoonish figures and landscapes. He feared Mélanie too would become a comic book frame. Everything was a muddle. July's melancholy hadn't even done him the courtesy of romanticisation: the type that painters and laureates have. It was just a drag.

(ii)

As predicted the astronomer's granddaughter went and sat in the corner with her spittoon. First she broke even at the slot machine. July found her funny and irritating but he would not pay her any mind while Mélanie was there - contrary to his initial optimism - though Doc fell asleep pretty quickly anyway. The sight of the cloudy sky brought the masses to the Itch and July had to fetch a couple other boarders from upstairs to help out at both the distillery and at the bar in order to keep up with demand. A Ph.D. student from the University of Chicago was staying in Room 1. In Room 5 was a canvasser working for some politician running for state senator. In Room 6 was a trio of queer lumbermen.

July did not charge a fee for staying at the Pig's Itch. In truth he enjoyed the company nowadays despite that he often appeared surly. What he did ask of his boarders was that he could cash in any favour of any kind and at any time and at his own convenience. He had found that prospective female boarders especially did not like the sound of this and when they turned away he often thought to himself, *If only they knew!* and went on thinking about Mélanie. As for those who took the deal July rarely cashed in his favours as he could usually take care of himself well enough, but every so often July found himself in a bind and took advantage of his system.

All other boarders were off-premises. July sighed as he left the attic room and returned slowly to the din that grew impetuously with every step he took down the staircase. It sounded not dissimilar to the noise of a shepherd's flock. Yet in and amongst and above the racket July could still somehow hear the silence of Mélanie, who seemed to become omnipresent when July was reminded of her.

He lured Willie Bridger out from the gaggle surrounding him with the promise of a free drink. Willie was not an avid drinker but he was economical and enjoyed a brandy and soda.

'How is your sister?' asked July.

'Keeping well as usual, I believe,' said Willie.

'Is the girl taking after her?'

'Who? Doc? How do you mean?'

'There are only two people who enjoy privacy more than those two. Doc hangs around you now but she is just turning into her great-aunt. Someday she too will hide away in her house, if you are not careful.'

'*You* try making friends with crazy arms like hers.'

'It's about how weird she is in her personality, not her physique.'

'I think she plays hooky. Doesn't get much of a chance to socialise,' said Willie. 'Got need for a pair of extra hands here?'

'At the Itch?'

'Yes.'

'Well, I ain't too sure about that, Willie.'

'Think on it.'

'Look, Willie, the girl's already asleep and it's not yet ten. How do you expect her to cope with work at the Itch?' said July.

And July was a cantankerous veteran with a familiarity with

violence that Willie did not need reminding of. The fields of Nord-Pas-de-Calais lived in his mind as much as the sand and mesquite of home did, and the battlefields hadn't yet devolved into some satirist's artistic impression as much of July's more recent memories had. Willie turned around, leant back on the bar and smirked to himself as he watched the long girl with a spittoon tilting onto her overalls, ready to spill.

'Her momma don't let her drink coffee after midday,' he said. 'Sure, she's not the blue-collar hero you're after, but she'll work cheap and she can reach any shelf you ask of her.'

'That I don't doubt,' said July. 'I expect she can tie her arms into figure-eights.'

'Heh,' said Willie.

'But Willie, what about when old Uncle Sam comes for the Itch? If she's on the payroll then she's liable for prosecution, don't matter that she's a kid. She'll be implicated.'

'Don't put her on the payroll. In fact, you don't even need to pay her out of your own pocket. I'll give you her wages from mine and you can make like they're your own.'

'You want to pay me to pay her to do work that won't do anything for you?' asked July.

'You were right before,' said Willie. 'She'll wind up alone. I just want her to have friends. There's not much worse than a lonesome child. I want her to have some security in her life, otherwise I worry that she'll up and leave the first chance she gets.'

By the witching hour there was fiddling and dancing and singing. Fern Davenport had brought her accordion as well, which she persuaded Mélanie to have a little play on. Cigar smoke began to perfume the air and choke the town into a merry slowdance. Mélanie and some lucky dreamer gently swayed from side to side, his face buried in her shoulder and her chin resting on his, her eyes glassily staring out into nowhere in particular, July unable to discern exactly what she was thinking. He did not like to see her eyes so dim but he got a strange sense of optimism from it.

Willie, a little disorientated from all the drink he'd been bought, found himself back at the bar and once again looking at Doc. As a man of almost constant sobriety it was inevitable that Willie would attain a certain loquaciousness on the back of a few drinks, and tonight was no exception to that rule. After cornering July behind the bar and binding him to his standing place with eyes holding such a subtle sadness, Willie confided in him that he thought his sister would have committed suicide in the time following her only child's death. July didn't want to get into it. Death July had seen a lot of over the years and it had taken a lot of goddamn work to keep it out of the Itch, especially in the days when he had first started rotgut alchemy. He'd seen men spew more blood than he ever knew possible and yet he'd somehow kept the corpses at bay. And Willie's sister Alma wasn't dead, so why the hell did the forgotten prospect of her suicide need to be brought up?

'We all worried,' said July, 'but you and her are made of something different, ain't you. You've both proven it. Nothing can kill the Bridger twins.'

Willie had a few drags.

'Thing is,' he went on, 'the better I know Doc the sadder I get.'

'She got a mean streak in her?'

'Don't be foolish,' Willie said. 'What I mean is that she becomes more and more like my own daughter and I can understand more and more what my sister went through when she lost hers. With every moment of pride or affection I have for Doc comes a consequent moment of pain.'

'Shouldn't you have already known how much it hurt her? Excuse my intrusiveness, of course, but I thought twins felt each other's feelings all the time?'

'No, July, I'm afraid it doesn't work so conveniently,' said Willie. 'But I know what you're trying to say, and I think that that it's true in some circumstances. But pain like that... I think it's too great and too personal to transcend one's own experience. Even if I was capable of feeling her feelings there would be no way of understanding it. Not until I got to know Doc, anyhow.'

'You talk of the kid like she's a pal,' said July.

(iii)

At sunup July rolled himself a cigarette and sat on the portico with his feet swinging from it. The Itch was in need of repair and he was presently reminded of this by a sharp sensation in his rear as he tried to make himself comfortable: a sizeable splintering in the floorboard. Eventually, he figured, there would need to be some renovations made. Rooms 2 and 3 had loose door handles, Room 4 had urine stains in the corner behind the odds-and-ends cupboard, the carpet in the reception was faded and dirty, there were scuffs and scrapes on the walls, cracked windows, leaky chamber pots, rotting basins and a growing feeling of ruin.

But how to afford renovations? Sure, July had his late father's money in the bank, as well as spread across a number of stocks. The man on KDKA said only last week that both Sears and General Motors were doing well, and July had mailed his buddy in New York City to corroborate this by checking the movie ticker. It had occurred to July to go himself to New York City and make a holiday out of it but he found the place to be too busy for his liking. The thing was that he was saving that money for prospective attorneys. When the Prohibition Unit came for him and the Itch - and they inevitably would - he would need the best attorneys going.

But less and less people were coming to stay at the Itch. It didn't seem to matter much that it was of no monetary cost to them – July sometimes worried that this actually created a sense of distrust amongst travellers. Couldn't a sucker do his fellow sucker a favour without injecting capital into the equation? Apparently not without wary eyes following his every move. July resolved that he would have to make the Itch a palace because no way was he going to start charging rent. But which stocks to sell and which savings to pull? July stomped on the cigarette and went back inside, followed the stairs up to Room 1 where the Ph.D. student Mr Hoyt was staying. Mr Hoyt was a budding economist and likely of the nouveau riche, judging by the extravagant width of his hatband ribbon that July had glared at many times through old money eyes. Presently July rapped loudly on Hoyt's door, hoping that the poor man hadn't yet dropped off to sleep.

'Mr Hoyt? Say, Mr Hoyt?'

'Yes?'

'It's July. Can I interest you in a sit in the sunshine?'

'Haven't you already cashed in your favour, Mr Slade?' Mr Hoyt sounded very dreary. 'I am exhausted.'

'This is no official favour I am asking of you, Mr Hoyt. I am appealing to your kindly nature.'

The door opened and Mr Hoyt stood there with his top button undone but otherwise dressed as he had been downstairs. That stupid trilby was still on his head.

'It's fast waning,' he said.

They went and sat outside together. Mr Hoyt brought with him a canteen and guzzled from it.

'Don't forget, if'n you stay past ten days I get to cash in another favour,' said July.

'I intend to move on,' said Mr Hoyt. He was a wiry fellow with small, crooked teeth and shaggy dark eyebrows. He wore a suit well, July begrudgingly decided; even in the heat of the morning he did not look to be breaking a sweat in the three-piece. 'Have you something in mind?'

'I need money help,' said July.

'Everyone needs money help,' said Mr Hoyt.

'Not that I've seen.'

'They all will in time. Send me a telegraph in five years and you can cash in this favour or good will or whatever *then* for some money help.'

July shrugged. Mr Hoyt pursed his lips and then chewed on his nails awhile. He asked for a drag of July's cigarette and took liberties with it before passing it back. As Hoyt stood up July realised that the son of a bitch had a little clipboard on him, which made July as mad as a march hare. He wanted to slog Hoyt on the spot.

'Say, are you working for the government?' he asked.

'No,' said Hoyt.

'Then who are you filling out a report for?'

'The economy's changing, Mr Slade. That's why I'm here. I'm keeping notes on it and I'm making preparations for the future, is all.'

A chuckwagon pulled by a palomino stud came into view down the road. Holding the reins was a young woman with pimples and dimples and silver hair and next to her was a man asleep under a large Stetson. Something about them reeked of Texas.

'Is this the Pig's Itch?' the girl asked, pulling up.

'Sure, this is the Itch,' said July.

'You're the proprietor?'

'Sure, I'm the proprietor.'

'You've boarding?'

'Sure, we've boarding.'

The girl nudged the sleeping man with her elbow and he snorted in his disorientation. Squinting as he awoke, he got a feel for his surroundings and listened confusedly as the girl explained to him where they were and what they were doing. He might have been asleep for a week judging by how muddled he was.

'We'd like to stay,' the girl finally said. 'Are we all right to check in now? I don't want to rush anyone.'

She gestured to Mr Hoyt, who was stood watching obnoxiously, looking a real square.

'Naw, don't worry about him. He's got a whole town to rile,' said July. He gestured to the new arrivals that they followed him inside and he explained to them that they could drop the palomino off at the livery stable for the duration of their stay. Maud who owned it would be more than pleased.

'It's all automobiles, trains and stagecoaches these days,' said July. 'No one comes by with their own horse no more. It's too easy to get here, there and everywhere and I ain't too pleased about it. That's not to say that I think people shouldn't come here, no, sir. *Au contraire*, I worry that it makes it too easy for people to *leave*.'

He got them to give their names and sign in.

'We'd like to know how you found out about us,' said July. 'Word of mouth? Telegram? The papers? The radio? Tick as many boxes as is necessary.'

'Sure,' said the girl whose name was Sunrise, taking the pencil.

'Is it your real name - Sunrise?'

'Sure is.'

'Where you folks from?'

'Rockwell. But we've come just now from the north country. We went across the border and then came back through Seattle, Portland and Salem.'

'That's one helluva journey. I thought you looked Texan.'

'Sure was, but we heard wonderful things about your town. I wanted to show Walter what all the fuss was about. We've undergone some real hardscrabble times the last year or so. I thought it an idea to get out somewhere nice.'

'A doomsayer is he, eh?' asked July.

'You don't know the half of it,' said Sunrise.

'Well, this place is full of lonesome folks, broken hearts, would-bes, has-beens and so forth. He'll fit right in. It's pretty rare that we get a troupe like yourselves. It's a nice change, although I'm not so sure that *you'll* fit right in, Miss Sunrise. A happy disposition in here? You might as well drive a motorcar into a meeting of the Amish. You'll have to turn that upside-down frown upside-down if you want to avoid suspicion from the other boarders.'

'That's all done,' said Sunrise, sliding the form back across the counter to July and beaming as widely as she could. 'Now, what do we owe you?'

'A favour,' said July.

'Excuse me?'

'Just a favour. At some point during your stay I get to cash in a favour and you're obligated to help me with whatever I need. It's more fun than a monetary transaction, don't you think?'

'Well, it does sound exciting, but I also know what some fellas are like when it comes to fresh angelicas staying near them.'

'You're a lovely lady but my heart lies with another,' laughed July. 'Besides, the old man looks plenty capable of protecting the two of you. Not that he'll need to.'

'We've come all this way,' admitted Sunrise, 'and we were told it was this or the cathouse, so what the hell. Do you have any canned goods? I've a hankering for some beans and haven't been able to get hold of any in years. I thought we could find some in Laguna but the factory shut down.'

'Heinz?'

'Please.'

'I reckon I could source some for you.'

'Will we have to owe you an extra favour?'

'Only if you stay past ten days. Call the beans a welcome gift.'

'Well, bully!' said Sunrise, and she and the old man followed July up to the room. July showed them all the amenities and then bid them good morning, feeling a delirious sense of elation as he traipsed back down the stairs. He put it down to the sleepless night and promptly went to bed.

3

Little ado was made about very much in town, but nonetheless there was a young lady who sought to dispel any nervous zephyr that she caught in the air. Responsibility for general wellbeing and upstandingness fell upon the keen shoulders of one Bitsy Powell, for she was one of the few who knew that Willie Bridger's protective sphere of influence only wound so far from up on his hill. She, like all others, was grateful for his presence and was surely comforted by it, but Bitsy was steadfast and thought about things mechanically. It was no use pretending that the lights of Willie's eyes would solve the tariff war, or rescue the town's barley farmers from the clutches of destitution, and sharecroppers would not be bailed out by the old man's merciful aura any longer. So Bitsy saw to it that the domestic troubles in town were solved to the best of her ability, and generally made her assistance available to any man, woman or child who sought it.

Mélanie Celestine was already at the site of today's crisis by the time Bitsy loped in on the back of her Choctaw. This horse's name was Marcus and he had been given as a foal to Bitsy by Alma Bridger - Willie's sister - who had initially mistaken him for a mustang when she found him not far off a farm in New Mexico. He was willowy and elegant but never made short work of anything, and there was no less affectionate horse in all the land, though he was never surly. It suited Bitsy down to a tee. There was also something modest about him which always intrigued her, as though he didn't quite know how to receive compliments or reward without falling into a bashful playfulness.

'One of the greyhound jockeys has escaped,' Mélanie explained.

'Is it still in town?' asked Bitsy.

'Most likely. He's a homely one, supposedly. He'll just be disorientated.'

Bitsy scratched her head and gave Marcus a sugar cube from the saddlebag. They had arrived on the boundary of the Snake Run Cattle Outfit Ranch, which by now had been grazed to an endless pasture of mostly dust, sand and cacti. Once it had been divided by a pronged wire which kept the Snake Outfit's cattle in its place, but it seemed that last night's winds had done a good job on tearing the posts from the ground and ruining a mile's worth of rope. The cattle had been remarkably stationary considering the furore.

The two of them were joined by the head of the Snake Run Cattle Outfit, Babe Vicks. Never once had Bitsy seen Babe up and around before midday despite the demanding nature of his work, but today he was looking sharp and it was not yet nine. Though one might assume this was because of the worry of possibly losing his herd, Bitsy reckoned it was more to do with the arrival of Mélanie than anything else. She needed only look at his wandering eyes to figure this. He was plump, portly and pernickety in character, and there were always too many firearms on his belt for Bitsy's liking.

'It's a notoriously aimless monkey,' said Babe Vicks of the greyhound jockey. 'Who knows where he might have gotten to. My wife reckons he stole some of her things, so keep an eye out for that. Jewellery and powder and such like.'

Babe's latest endeavour was monkey racing. He had imported a bunch of capuchins from Honduras and had been breeding greyhounds in preparation for bringing the sport to town. But the coupling of monkeys and greyhounds had proven a tall task for Babe and he was likely to give up on the endeavour any day soon, which would leave him a rancher with a surplus of apes and dogs. Not one race had been held yet, but two hounds had been sent to the veterinary surgery across town with infected fang bites.

'We'll find him,' said Bitsy. 'And in the meantime we'll just need to borrow a couple of line riders to fix up the bob-wire before the cattle go a-roaming.'

'If it's all right with y'all I'd like to stick around with you ladies.'

But Bitsy refused because she needed to speak privately with Mélanie. The two had decided to become co-executive co-ordinators for Bitsy's campaign and they needed to iron out some details, such as what exactly she was going to campaign for. That was today's agenda. She did not much fancy a grubby, irritable rancher leering at Mélanie all day long. But Bitsy was quick to thank Babe for his coming to her for help and promised him that she would spend all the time she had figuring out how to get his missing monkey back.

'Hm,' said Babe Vicks.

The interlude with Mélanie was brought to a close almost as it began when Bitsy remembered a favour she was owed by an old friend.

'I keep the law off you, remember?' she said to July Slade, joining him for a cigarette as he sat on the hitching post outside the Pig's Itch. She had skipped the pleasantries entirely, as was her prerogative. Mélanie had found an excuse not to join them. 'They had a warrant on you, July.'

'Yes, yes,' said July, barely awake despite the time. It appeared that he had been up all night after the arrival of Willie Bridger at the Pig's Itch. Old Bitsy had had to throw stones at his window. 'What is it you want then?'

'For you to cash in your favours,' said Bitsy.

'Huh?'

'Cash in the favours you got saved up from your boarders.'

'I thought you was cashing in *your* favours, Bitsy,' said July.

'I am. And your favour to me is cashing in your favours.'

Bitsy explained to July that the wire around the Snake Run Cattle Outfit Ranch had been torn down and that some cowherds were required.

'Can't I just do the roundup alone? I'd quite like to keep my favours.'

'Naw, it's dang near the whole boundary. We'll need a few cowherds. It's about twenty miles' worth.'

July knew as good as anyone that a deal's a deal, and he nodded painedly through his twitching and grunting.

'I'll have them up there by tomorrow at sunup,' he said.

'Thank you,' said Bitsy, then adding, 'also, I'm doing my campaign with Mélanie as a running mate of sorts. I'd appreciate it if you didn't run your mouth off to the folks around town anymore about how you reckon she's a flirt.'

'I only said that she's French!' said July.

Bitsy didn't like to put her fingers in other people's pies but this kind of hanky-panky simply could not be permitted if she and the people were to take her politicking seriously. Thus far any infamy that Bitsy had come to know was as a result of her enabling a bootlegger's honky-tonk malpractice, so it stood to reason that her future engagements ought to be free from controversy. It was obvious to her that July liked to spin tall tales about Mélanie because he was still sore, but there was no time for sympathy in politics. That was what her senator father had told her. He had lived his whole life in Montgomery and his politics reflected that. They did not quite agree with Bitsy but she endeavoured to replicate his practicality and resolve. There was never a more ruthless man in all of American history, she reckoned. And it was he who had friends in the Prohibition Unit and thus he that kept the heat from the Pig's Itch, though on Bitsy's consistent requests.

Joining Bitsy and Mélanie that afternoon was Hampstead, the young son of the local seamstress. Hampstead was not on the payroll of the campaign - no one but Mélanie was - but he had been promised three Abba Zabbas for every banner he sewed, which was apparently more than enough to tempt him. Mostly he just worked and thought about candy, though every so often when the day was hot and long he would find himself irreparably distracted by some menial detail that the municipal center had to offer. Then he would be out of commission for the rest of the day and there was nothing that Bitsy could do to put him back in line, so she would have to let him bump gums about whatever the hell it was until he tired himself out. Even Mélanie, who Bitsy had once thought had the power to sooth any man living, could not bring his focus back around. They had resorted to buying him a fan and Mélanie brought her crystal radio from home in order that he might keep cool and entertained respectively.

But today Hampstead was not hard at work as he usually was by the time Bitsy and Mélanie arrived. Instead he was sat with his arms folded behind the desk, alone in the wide, echoey hall. He looked a little impatient, perhaps even scathing.

'What's all this?' asked Mélanie.

'Good morning, kittens,' said the ten-year-old. 'How can I get my Abba Zabbas unless I finish this banner?'

'You can't,' said Bitsy.

'Exactly,' said Hampstead, 'so can you please decide on what you want me to write?'

'We're figuring that out today,' Bitsy turned to Mélanie, 'that's the last thing we need: a ticking clock.'

'One who can't tell the time,' added Mélanie. 'Hampstead, why don't you go and sit on the flagpole for a while?'

'What is there to see? Shebas, maybe?'

'Sure, plenty of shebas out today.'

Hampstead abided by Mélanie's suggestion.

'I ain't seen such a wannabe lounge lizard in a long while,' Bitsy said, pulling out a chair for Mélanie and then one for herself. They sat and looked at the banner which had been slovenly threaded to say:

VOTE FOUR BITSY. SHE WILL

And there was plenty of empty space on the right side where Hampstead would fill out the rest of the manifesto. It seemed that he had also tried his hand at sewing a rose into the bottom corner but had strayed too far on one of the petals, leaving it somewhere between a minimalist interpretation of the bombastic Andy Gump and a bumblebee.

'It'll do,' shrugged Mélanie. 'But considering he always talks of how he is a "words kind of kid", I'm not impressed.'

'Are there no literate sewers in this town?' cried Bitsy. 'And besides, what the hell are people supposed to vote for exactly? Why did he decide to write about voting? I haven't even begun a political career and I'm already cheating the town. Whatever will they think of me?'

'They are having a star named after you! You are the reason that July's can stay open,' Mélanie said dismissively, offering a comforting embrace and squeeze. 'Listen, we have the whole afternoon. Let us decide what it is we want to do; where it is we are going, no?'

Bitsy desperately wanted to cry at how ridiculous the whole thing was, and Bitsy rarely felt emotional. Mélanie withdrew a small canteen from her inside pocket and took a sip before wincing, then handed it over. Bitsy took some and thanked her. It was chartreuse. Bitsy hated every droplet of the stuff on her tongue but equally hastened to retrieve Mélanie from the slings and arrows of a moonshine hail. Bitsy took as much off Mélanie's hands as her immature, obnoxious palate would allow.

'I ought to be a communist,' said Bitsy, 'but I can't grow a beard, so I would look a fool.'

'Zinoviev doesn't have a beard,' said Mélanie. 'And Lenin's widow doesn't either.'

'And anyway I'm not interested in Bolshevism because I don't wish to be haunted by my grandfather's ghost. What is it around town that people are lacking? What is it that they need? What is possible for a person to obtain for their people that has not yet been obtained?'

'I would say likely much of the good things in life.'

'How could we make town better?'

'I do not know. I love town, in truth.'

'So do I. I ought to explore the rest of the country for something to improve. There really isn't much doing in town. My help is wasted here.'

'Where would you go, Bitsy?' asked Mélanie.

'I don't know. I doubt I'm ready to go anyway. I'm not like you, Mademoiselle; I can't just up and leave my home at my earliest convenience.'

'You can, Bitsy, but I'm glad you won't.'

Everyone looked at Mélanie as though she had one of Eden's coves hidden away in her eyes, or occasionally in her backside. Rooms fell silent when she entered them. Everyone who saw her wanted to bed her, men and women alike. But not Bitsy. Bitsy just thought that Mélanie was a tremendous asset. Because of her skills as a mimic and forger Mélanie had tricked her way into getting numerous grants from congressman and senators for the campaign when Bitsy's father didn't respond promptly to Bitsy's letters. Any handwriting could be replicated by Mélanie and any voice and mannerism could be mimicked despite that thick Provençal accent. Bitsy would rarely be without her but she would not goggle and gawk like the rest, and Bitsy expected that this was behind Mélanie's choice of best friend. Occasionally Mélanie played discs on the crystal and they danced the shimmy together. Sometimes they danced the Lindy Hop too, but mostly they just liked to shimmy around to Ben Bernie or Nat Shilkret & his Orchestra. Sometimes they shimmied so much that they fell about laughing.

It was a beautiful friendship because Bitsy had never seen Mélanie touch another human soul in such a way as she did Bitsy when dancing, not even Mr Monroe. She knew what they had was special and that it suited the both of them down the ground and below. But perhaps what was lacking from the relationship was the discussion of anything other than the trifling matters that they both experienced. What was peripheral to them both became important when they spoke, but not away from that. Bitsy was not a naturally curious person. In fact she had been reluctant to ask Mélanie anything even when Mélanie left Mr Slade. When Bitsy had later gone into the Itch for some giggle juice and a jaw with the clientele Mr Slade had burst into tears and started running his mouth about Mélanie. So Bitsy went home to sleep. At the time she was sleeping on a crude little palette because her bed had begun to rot, and yet it was still preferable to hearing old July daisying around.

It was no surprise then that Bitsy was so fond of old Hampstead. He didn't like to whinge about personal things much either. Bitsy had her little triumvirate and she was very pleased with it. Every day it occurred to Bitsy to go and thank Alma Bridger despite that she already had a thousand times and that Alma liked to be alone more than anyone else in the world. It drove Bitsy mad not being able to deliver manners where they were due. Often she posted letters through Alma's letterbox to keep the old broad informed on how everybody was doing, but Alma had stopped replying to these letters years ago. Nowadays Bitsy was just banking on that Alma appreciated it despite her lack of correspondence.

Bitsy had been acquainted with Alma's daughter Florence-Louise when they were in the same grade at school. They had looked alike: they both had blue eyes and freckles, as well as knobbly knees and dainty hands. They were about the same height. They were both independent and audacious. They both liked to dress like Marlene Dietrich and wear hats like Colleen Moore despite that *Flaming Youth* was a little reckless for Bitsy's liking. But Bitsy was beginning to suspect that Alma couldn't bear the sight of Bitsy because she reminded her of Florence-Louise. Bitsy had made a real effort to stay close with Alma after Florence-Louise's death but things had steadily declined and now there was virtually no correspondence from Alma's attic. Still Bitsy knew the old dame was still up there, and that gave her a great feeling of security, just as knowing that old Willie was sat up on his hill.

(ii)

Hampstead had seen not a one good-looking sheba in his time spent atop the flagpole. On another day he might have clocked out early and meandered down to the bleachers at the college football field and cast about for the college girls from up there, but it was just too hot to make such an odyssey. Instead he relaxed as best he could and hoped for a tan despite that his mother always told him that his skin wouldn't get blacker if he bathed in hot tar. He saw the girl Doc out and about, her arms swinging low and her legs creaking with every step she made. Hampstead often saw Doc around the schoolhouse but never spoke to her because in truth she frightened him. He was two grades her junior and he liked to keep out of the way of the older kids at the best of times, most of all when they were half a foot taller than him and capable of strangling him with a thumb and forefinger. Fortunately he was safe up on the flagpole because - as far as Hampstead knew - he was the best climber in town. The only person who was ever higher up than him was the old crank Willie Bridger, Doc's grandfather, but he had a hill all to himself. What was better about the hill was that it didn't give you sore buttocks.

So, sat on the flagpole and feeling mightily proud of himself as he always did from this vantage point, Hampstead called out to the aimless Doc and pulled up his shirt to show her his belly and his nipples. He wondered what kind of reaction he would get and felt thoroughly deflated when Doc simply cocked her head to one side at the sight of Hampstead's exposed torso, then carried on ambling. She was some kind of ponderous nymph and more mysterious still to Hampstead, not least because she was black and also white at the same time. Other than Doc and Doc's sisters there were no mixed kids in the whole town yet. But there was a zaniness to Doc outside of her melanin and this only added furious wildfire to the flames of Hampstead's intrigue.

He had also noticed in recent weeks that Doc was something of a truant. Hampstead often saw her swerve by the front gates of the schoolhouse on a morning, dark shadows under her eyes and dread in her very gait, before scuttling away down the road and into one of the alleys a few blocks down. Hampstead figured she was up to no good so fixed to follow her one time, but his mother caught him by the collar and shouted at him real and true in front of the whole schoolhouse. It made him so mad that he endeavoured to hate Doc Bellingham thereafter because it was definitely her fault in some way or another. Whatever skylarking Doc was up to, old Hampstead would get to the bottom of it or ruin her fun trying.

But for now he was stuck up on the flagpole outside the town hall when he could have been at Book Club with his pals. At Book Club there had originally been only one meeting per week, and through its three-hour duration Hampstead and his friends Tuna and Hector had gathered to read quietly and then discuss loudly. Now they had to separate the reading and the discussion because the debates had gotten so fiery that it tainted the whole reading experience. That was how the infamous Suds War had begun. Tuna had brought some Palmolive soap in preparation for an argument about *Tarzan of the Apes* and the three of them were caught in a brutal skirmish which ended only when Hector vomited from all the suds that Tuna had forced him to swallow. After that Tuna became the de facto leader of the group and they created Debate Club as a separate entity to Book Club. They moved it to the only day that they could get Ounce, the illiterate kid who lived in a shebang out near the railheads. Big Ounce was employed as the moderator because he was nearly six feet tall despite that he was only ten years old. They paid him in vocabulary and spelling because he liked to learn and because Tuna – who was now kind of the big boss of the posse – insisted that it was more valuable than currency.

Before long Hampstead was thinking about Abba Zabbas again.

'It ain't looking so sturdy,' he heard someone call from below. It was Bitsy, her hand on the foot of the flagpole, gently pressing against it.

'Hell, I'll fall!' Hampstead shouted down.

'Get down,' said Mélanie, whom Hampstead rarely refused. He clutched onto the pole and slid down, landing as gracefully as a gymnast and then brushing himself off.

'*Oui*, Mademoiselle,' he said. Then he turned to Bitsy. 'What the hell's wrong with you?'

'You're gonna break that pole,' she explained, giving it a push.

'Don't take away my flagpole time,' said Hampstead.

'*Je suis désolé*, Hampstead, I thought it was safe. But on closer inspection it clearly is not,' said Mélanie. 'Besides, even if you don't get hurt when it falls, the town will have still lost a flagpole.'

'But Shipwreck Kelly did it for thirteen hours. Can't I get half an hour every now and then? Have you decided what your angle is? Did you like my banner so far?'

'We shouldn't be letting you damage public property,' said Mélanie. 'No, we have not got an angle yet, Hampstead.'

Once Hampstead had had a gait that consisted usually of a hop, skip and jump, and sometimes even a lope. Now it was seldom so joyous and often more resembled a lonesome traipse, and it was all because of that she-devil Bitsy.

They got to arguing about the prospect of vandalism until finally the ladies became tired of Hampstead's stubbornness and they all lay down in the long grass together. Mélanie smoked her pipe and did her best to hide her drinking from Hampstead, though Hampstead was no schmuck. Although they agreed to go and visit the planetarium construction site Bitsy's mind was working fast and hard. It seemed to Hampstead that the squeaking flagpole and talk of vandalism had got her thinking, such was how taciturn she was.

4

It was midmorning the next day and Doc was sat in the Itch again, this time in the entryway, but she had nonetheless procured a spittoon once more and was clutching it tight to her chest in the empty hall. Her head was facing down and she observed her grip, which was notable for its white puddles on typically dark knuckles.

'Hello,' someone said.

Doc looked up. There stood a silver-haired girl with dimples and pimples and warmth breathing around her. She had quietly come down the stairs behind the secretaire and was smiling. Judging by her face she was young, perhaps twenty, but there was an aggressive agelessness about her or something curious that Doc couldn't quite put her finger on. And too was there a diffident understanding in the lakes of her blue eyes, one that conveyed itself without pressure on Doc, who felt that this new person perceived her in exactly the way that Doc wanted to be perceived, whatever that was. It was clear that the stranger believed that Doc was brimming with capability and promise, but no more than Doc herself was aware of – and always with trepidation. The entryway momentarily became a narrow ravine between the two of them.

'Hello,' said Doc.

The girl introduced herself as Sunrise Livingston, one of the new boarders from upstairs. Doc introduced herself as Doc, plain and simple.

'What are you up to, Doc?'

'Just looking at my arms,' Doc said.

'Your arms?'

'Sure. They're mighty long, don't you think? People assume I'd be used to them by now but they still catch me off guard every once in a while. Once I gave my big fat Uncle Jonas a hug and I nearly had a heart attack when my hands met behind his back. Pop-pop said that if I had had a heart attack before big fat Uncle Jonas did he would have been real mad about it.'

'Is that a spit jar?' asked Sunrise.

'Sure is.'

'Why's that? Is it empty?'

'Nome, got plenty of spit in it from last night, I expect.'

Sunrise went and sat down on the chair on the opposite side of the lobby to Doc, then raised an eyebrow at her.

'What's your angle?' Sunrise asked.

'No angle, I swear,' said Doc.

'You just carry around a spit jar?'

'In the Itch, I guess. Not at home. Momma would kill me.'

'No one goes near the girl with the spit jar.'

'Mostly not.'

'What are you doing here?'

'I have an interview.'

'With Mr Slade?'

'Yessum.'

'Right,' Sunrise got up, walked over to Doc and gently prised the spittoon from her long arms, then took her ballcap from her. 'I'll wait out here with your cap,' she said, putting it on her own head and then placing the spittoon down on the bureau.

'You look plenty smart and ritzy,' Sunrise went on, giving Doc a good up-and-down. 'Yeah, you scrub up real good in those glad rags, but they can't belong to you. They're too small. Or maybe you're in a spurt?'

'My little sister's,' said Doc. 'They're awful tight, even though I'm thin and frail.'

'What's the interview for?'

Doc shrugged, brushing the kerosene lamp on the bureau as she did so, almost knocking it over.

'Would you like me to do some practice questions with you?'

Doc very much wanted to say yes.

'I ain't too trusting of strangers,' she murmured habitually.

'I figure,' said Sunrise.

So they sat a while in comfortable quiet, the only sounds disturbing them the growing footsteps of one of the boarders directly above them upstairs. Every once in a while it made Doc start and twitch. Her stomach churned a few times and a cold aching filtered its way up to her ribs. Then the tips of her fingers went tingly and her knees wobbled despite her attempts to steady them. The growing powerlessness gave way to a grave feeling in the back of her head and she felt that chill in her chest lather itself under the skin of her whole body in but a few moments despite that it was nearly a hundred outside and that there was no breeze in the hall. A certainty of imminent death followed presently. Doc had never known a feeling like this before and it was horrible, just horrible. Then the breath completely went from her lungs and all resistance against frantic movement faltered. Her terrified eyes met Sunrise's and Sunrise sprang into life, although Doc barely noticed. She couldn't articulate anything and her vision fogged and spun.

But less than a minute passed and she was drawn back into consciousness by a gentle hand on her back. She began breathing normally again and could see straight. She was breathing in for four, holding for four and breathing out for four. Breathing in for four, holding for four and out for four. Breathing in for four, holding for four and out for four. It was strange to Doc that Sunrise was commentating on Doc's every movement, until Doc realised that she was actually following Sunrise's instructions, and that it was Sunrise's hand slowly stroking her upper back. It made her tickle but in a pleasant way, and besides it was distracting from the anxiety.

In her free hand Sunrise was holding the ballcap, which Doc suddenly had a hankering for. She was about to ask for it back before the door to the bar opened and July came through, bumping his head on the lintel as he did. He was tall as heck. Doc did not want to have an interview right now and her stomach whirred like the slot machine next door, but Sunrise stood up before Doc had time to think of a way out.

'Mr Slade!' said Sunrise. 'I have had some of my possessions stolen from our room. Would you please come and help us figure out who, when and why? I'm feeling hysterical about the whole thing.'

'Oh, Christ,' said July. 'What things?'

'Too many to name right at this moment,' said Sunrise, 'I'm very disorientated.'

'I'll come with you,' July assured her. 'Doc, would you wait around?'

'It's a great many things that have gone missing, Mr Slade. I don't expect this to be a matter completed in but a few minutes, I'm afraid.'

'Right, right. O.K. Doc, you run on to school and I'll send word for when we can rearrange to. Let's go, Miss Livingston.'

July led the way up the stairs and Doc said a nonchalant huh to herself.

(ii)

Doc was under strict instruction to return to the schoolhouse as soon as her interview had finished, but she was in such a muddle that she thought she ought to walk it off. Though she'd seen nothing troubling that morning in the Itch there was still a slight sense of lingering trauma that she couldn't quite wrap her head around. She kept up the four-four-four technique that Sunrise had given to her and she felt the feeling gradually return to her fingers and toes as she made her way through town. It was calming her down all right, but she knew what would make her real hunky-dory and that was Pop-pop, only it was barely midday, so he would be fast asleep in the collapsible chair.

What she wanted was to get out of the lousy glad rags she was squeezed into and get back into her trusty overalls, but Momma would not abide by her stopping by at the house. So restricted and short was the prairie skirt that there was hardly enough room for Doc to move her legs to walk right. There was so much ankle and shin showing that her teachers would think her an exhibitionist. In moments she felt a red shame envelop her and she wished she still had her ballcap to cover her face, but in the commotion back at the Itch it had been taken upstairs in Sunrise's hand.

Then Doc remembered that she had a dime still from the other night. There was a haberdashery near the river and it was much, much cheaper than the local boutique. Doc liked wearing men's clothes anyway. She purchased some Hercules knicker pants and a mariniére shirt, and because the haberdashery had no changing rooms she was forced to get redressed behind a trash receptacle around the back of the shop. To get there she had to slide through an uncomfortably narrow alley that only someone as slender as Doc could hope to get through. She then came back around onto the street and peered at herself in the glass of the store window before doing a little twirl. She looked like a French golfer. With the shame ebbing away she decided that she also ought to take off the t-straps and go it barefoot as she accustomed to, even on the hot ground.

But what to do with her day? The last thing Doc felt like doing was nothing. She wanted to ignore the horrible anxious breathlessness of earlier and distract herself. She still had three cents from the ten she had gone into the store with. The only Liberty Bell in town was at July's and there was no way in hell she was ready to go back there yet, so gambling with it was out of the question. She'd recently got into smoking cigarettes but they threatened to dent her pockets even further. She had three cents and three cents only. It would be enough to get to and from the nickelodeon in Laguna with a penny to spare, but that one remaining was still four pennies too short to actually get into the picture house. Doc looked at the alley from which she had just emerged in her new attire and wondered if she could repeat the feat of suppleness in some hidden crevice around the back of the nickelodeon. The prospect was tantalising. If she could manage it then there would be nothing to stop her from going to the pictures every week.

Because the bus was not a local one Doc was told curtly to sit at the back. She chewed on her lip with anticipation from the moment she got on, half expecting to have nibbled all the way through to the bottom of her chin by the time they arrived. She was like a little jackrabbit-Doc, gnawing away. The excitement that she was feeling was a welcome change from the sickening nervousness she had barely gotten over before departing from town. Some of the folks sat around her gave her irritated little glares whenever Doc's foot-tapping became too rapturous, but Doc barely noticed. She didn't even really notice the capuchin monkey perched behind the false front of the mom-and-pop grocery store that was on the road out of town.

In Laguna she caught a few bewildered eyes fall on her as she strolled nonchalantly towards the nickelodeon. It was hotter here than it was back home and the ground beneath the balls of Doc's bare feet knew it, and yet Doc had no desire to reach into her satchel for the ugly t-straps. Even if she hadn't been wearing boys' attire she would have looked funny. But drawing attention on the street was fine; what mattered was keeping inconspicuous around the picture house, though this would prove tricky. Doc did a quick lap of the block to get a feel for the security. There was only the girl in the ticket booth and she was eating an ice cream as she watched the street. She had noticed Doc but didn't give her the eyebrow or anything. On the marquee above the booth it said:

CHARLIE CHAPLIN IN... 'THE GOLD RUSH'

There was a trash alley behind the building, and Doc could see a door if she craned her long neck at the right angle. What Doc needed was to look so thoroughly uninterested in the nickelodeon that no one would ever suspect her of wanting to buy a ticket, let alone of sneaking in. Jasper was a travelling newspaper vendor and came to town once or twice a year. Mostly he found himself in Laguna because the papers in Doc's town were usually purchased from the post office. He would unlikely recognise Doc but Doc couldn't miss him because he had a huge tumour growing out the side of his neck, which apparently wasn't malignant, but Doc wondered how the heck a sucker could keep his head up with that growing out of the side of it.

He often sat by the sorrel pots near the barber shop, and this was exactly where Doc found him, not a quarter-mile from the picture house.

'Hey, newsie,' said Doc.

'Hey, kid,' said Jasper.

'Got anything for me today?'

'What you interested in?'

'A paper.'

'Yes, but which?'

'Any. The cheapest. I've only a little money.'

'Here you go.'

'Thanks. Here you go. Good luck with your tumour.'

She tossed him one of the two remaining pennies.

'Good luck with your feet,' said Jasper.

Then Doc strutted off and buried her face in the newspaper without reading a single word of what was on it. She didn't even read the headlines; she just wanted to look circumspect. It occurred to her that she should just act like the Tramp did in the pictures. Things often worked out for him, after all. Sort of. After tripping a couple of times, taking two wrong turns and bumping into a particularly pregnant and irritable woman, Doc found herself back outside the nickelodeon. She put on her most concentrated expression and stared at the newspaper as she made her way past the front and round the corner, where she hastily discarded the paper and threw herself into the alley. It was a delicate matter but Doc was surprisingly good on her tiptoes as a result of sneaking out of her house to go to the hill on so many occasions.

Doc waited next to the door on the side that it would open to. After twenty minutes a concierge from the hotel aside came out with a bunch of bedsheets, muttering vexedly about obscene fluids and stains that Doc didn't much like to hear about. Reaching out to stop the door from closing by itself as the concierge carried the sheets to the trash cans, Doc saw her moment and took it with great stealth. She strutted through the back office that the door opened into, through the corridor and into the lobby outside the picture room. Again she was faced with a predicament: there the ticket attendant was stood by the door. Doc had to wait around again, but she figured that she could stay in the picture room as long as she pleased and rewatch the picture again and again so it didn't matter that she might be missing big chunks of it. And soon enough the attendant had to use the restroom.

(iii)

All Doc wanted to do that night was see Pop-pop. She wanted to tell him about the picture and to ask him why that creep Hampstead had showed her his belly button and stuck out his tongue. Sure she had seen the kid once or twice at the schoolhouse, but Hampstead was two years younger and six inches shorter than her. What business had he got showing her his belly button, other than that he was a little rascal? Maybe he liked her, but that would be rare enough. Doc was almost as excited to chew the fat with Pop-pop as she had been on the bus to Laguna.

But Pop-pop wasn't happy to see Doc. In fact he barely spoke as he took her hand and dragged her down the hill back to her house. Doc began to cry as they went because she had never seen Pop-pop so despondent. She wasn't having the same experience that she had had in the Itch but she wished that it would come on because it would be better than the horror she was feeling at the sight of Pop-pop so enraged. His eyes were very cold and white.

'Pop-pop, please talk,' Doc cried.

'Not now,' said Pop-pop.

When they got to the house Momma was furious.

'Give those to me!' she said, pulling the t-straps from Doc's shaking hand.

Principle Brookes had followed up on Doc's absence on the advice of an unnamed student, and this had led to hysteria in the Bellingham household. Even the neighbours had been involved. Maggie had gone up the hill half expecting to find her daughter asleep in the dirt seat, and that was when she woke up Pop-pop. They'd been out searching all afternoon and into the early evening. Pop-pop had gone up the hill suspecting that Doc would come there first if and when she came back.

When the door to the house shut behind her Doc realised that Pop-pop had not come in.

'What in tarnation have you been doing all day? You're in for one hell of a whupping, do you hear me?'

'I went for a walk,' said Doc.

'All day, Doc?!'

Momma hit Doc with her palm and Doc cried some more. She was taller than her mother but she feared her ropy hands.

'I bought some clothes.'

Doc wanted to speak to only Pop-pop about her trip to the nickelodeon.

'Well done, you look like a peasant boy from Europe. Where are Elsie's things?'

'I gave you the shoes already,' said Doc.

'The rest of them, Doc!'

Doc's stomach sank as she remembered the prairie dress behind the trash cans at the haberdashery.

'I'll go fetch them,' she said. 'I know where they are, I swear. The boys' clothes store.'

'You'll do no such thing. I'm not letting you out of this house. Your father will fetch them. Go on upstairs now. I don't want to hear from you, O.K.?'

'O.K.,' said Doc, hanging her head low as she ascended the stairs to her room. When inside she got back into her overalls and lay on her bed crying for awhile. She thought she might ruin the mattress if she wasn't careful. Then she heard her parents coming up the stairs and the door creaked open just an inch, so Doc scrunched up her face real scrunchy and held in her tears and pretended to be asleep. Then the door closed again and she heard her parents talking away in their bedroom until it went silent. She opened her window, clambered onto the portico roof and jumped onto the street, angering her ankles. She ran all the way to and up the hill and threw herself into Pop-pop's arms at the top of it.

'They're awful mad at me,' sobbed Doc.

'And rightfully so,' said Pop-pop. 'You know, Doc, you can't just wander out of town by yourself.'

'I only went to the -'

'The picture house, I figured. But you can't do that on your own. You can't play hooky and then go to another town without telling anyone. It's not safe.'

'I'm big.'

'You're big like how bamboo is big. You grow stupid quick but you could get snapped into pieces in the instant someone else big gets a hold of you.'

'But who else would I go with? I've no real friends, and you were asleep.'

Pop-pop rubbed his eyes and breathed very slowly.

'How was your interview at the Itch?' he asked.

'I didn't do it,' said Doc.

'Why not?'

'I got a funny feeling and I had to run away.'

'A funny feeling how?'

'Like I was about to die.'

Pop-pop rubbed his eyes again.

'Don't worry about the interview,' he said. 'I'll talk to July and you'll be able to start work without doing one.'

'How?'

'Maybe you'll make friends with the boarders or the fellers that work in the kitchen or the distillery.'

'All right, Pop-pop,' said Doc.

'Did your mom hit you any?'

'Yeah. I reckon you'll be able to see it come sunup,' said Doc. 'I'll have a real bruise right here below my eye. Momma can be real scary when she wants to be.'

'Damn straight. She scares me too.'

'For real?'

'Well, sure. She's the big cheese in your house, ain't she. That means that she's got Charlie Bellingham and all three of his daughters doing her bidding. That's some woman.'

'She does care an awful lot.'

'That she does. Even goons care sometimes.'

'She says that she's most like Great-Auntie Alma,' Doc said.

'There's similarities,' Pop-pop mused.

'She won't ever go into hiding like Great-Auntie Alma?'

'No, I doubt it, but I wouldn't call what Alma is doing "hiding". She is recovering.'

'Like, from being sick?'

'Grief, yes. In the same way that influenza is contagious, Alma is aware that sadness can be too, and she thinks therefore that she is better served protecting the town from up in her attic than she is out amongst her folks.'

'You do the same a lot, only it's from your hill.'

'I suppose I grieve for Alma, but also I am old and aching,' said Pop-pop. 'All of me aches nowadays, Doc.'

'Oh, Pop-pop,' said Doc. 'You're such a goof.'

The hours ticked on that night and the stars came out in their herds. Pop-pop finally sighed and turned down to look at his Doc.

'Was it a good picture, kid?' he asked.

5

When Doc arrived at school the next day Hampstead began to feel real bad about the whole thing. Doc looked awful tired and to have had a soft beating on her cheek. It was very red and Hampstead regretted telling the principle about her being a truant. He didn't even know why he did it was the strange thing. Sure he told himself he hated her but he didn't feel that in his heart. He knew what hate was; he had felt it for Tuna after the Suds War, and what he felt about Doc certainly wasn't the same. But he was used to doing all in his power to avoid the principle's office and yet yesterday he had moved faster than he had ever moved before to spill the beans to him. He worried that people would find out. If Mélanie found out then she would surely hate him because she really liked Doc. So Hampstead decided to keep the whole thing bottled up and hoped that the guilt would fade away in time. He ignored the thought of old Doc all day and kept his head down when they passed each other in the hall. Hampstead even took the long route out of the building at home time so as to avoid Doc's classroom. It made him five minutes late home and he got a scolding, but who cared.

That evening Hampstead went and sat outside in the honey sunlight and re-read *Huckleberry Finn* in order to keep his mind occupied. Hampstead was a lover of all things Mark Twain and liked to think that he shared a character with Huck, though it was more realistic to say that he was a Tom Sawyer-type. Often Hampstead would lament himself for not being able to shirk his sensibility. He wanted to be a rogue like Huck but the awful truth was that Hampstead was just too responsible for any of Huck's tomfoolery. And Hampstead was a dreamer like Tom too; dreaming dreams formed in the bowels of a bookshelf and its many enticing inhabitants. In order to placate these frustrations Hampstead would simply drown himself in *Adventures* and pretend like he was living there for a time. The first time he read the series he did it in one sitting, missing supper in the evening and breakfast the next morning, though not out of choice - he was simply to engrossed to hear his mother calling for him.

Once he had tired himself out with reading Hampstead went to bed, but found that he couldn't sleep despite that it was quite a cool one and he was wearing his favourite pyjamas. He was always an excellent sleeper - to a fault, perhaps. Tonight, however, he tossed and he turned and he sweated and he couldn't shake the picture in his head of old Doc looking glum as gloop. Tom Sawyer and his friends had done little to maintain his distraction. Hampstead had never experienced a feeling like this before. Something was eating him up from the inside and he resolved to get rid of it once and for all, even if it meant addressing his crimes and owning up to it. He would seek advice from Bitsy after school tomorrow and go from there. Bitsy was pretty practical and non-judgemental, unlike Mélanie who would probably burst into tears if Hampstead owned up to her. Bitsy was the one he would ask. He would remind her that the only payment he'd been getting for his art was an Abba Zabba here and there, and that the least she could do was make him feel better about himself.

So the next day of school came and went and again Hampstead took the long way out of the building. Some of his friends were going to the field to play baseball with the white kids but Hampstead resisted the temptation to join them. He traipsed to the municipal hall and pestered Bitsy and Mélanie about their campaign but still they were useless, so Hampstead fixed up the flower that he had butchered in the corner of the banner and turned it into a sort of steeple topped by a cupola. Who cared. Then Bitsy had the terrible, terrible idea to go and check on the progress of the planetarium across town, which frightened Hampstead to no end for reasons as follows: firstly, it was Doc's father that was leading construction of the dang thing. Second, Hampstead just got a real queer feeling whenever he walked past it, like it was forbidden. That was strange because one day soon the whole town would be invited and it would be a swell time, leading Hampstead to adopt a rare introspection in order that he might understand his chary rationale. It had gotten him to the butt-end of nowhere but he remained in no mind to go.

'Not a chance,' he said.

'Well, we can't leave you here,' said Bitsy.

'Why not?'

'Because you're unsupervised and it's not our building,' said Mélanie. 'Why are you always so contrary?'

That stung old Hampstead and he caved right away. They made the trip to the planetarium and bought some ice cream as they went, which Hampstead was very grateful for. It gave him a spring in his step and nearly forgot about old Doc altogether until the construction site came into view and Doc's sweaty father approached them.

Charlie Bellingham was the first black to marry a white after he, Willie Bridger and Willie's sister Alma gave the town cops the bum's rush. Because of this he was renowned throughout town, though not as much as the Bridger twins were. He carried himself like a revolutionary, Hampstead's mother often remarked, mostly because one could not deny that there was purpose in his stride. Every part of him moved in unison and with resolve. He was muscular and tall and unmissable. He was soft-spoken despite that he was battle-hard. On his neck he had old burns from a noose and under his eye was a long, pink scar, both obtained during his battle against the deputies.

'Afternoon, all,' he said, shaking all their hands and giving Hampstead a big old pat on the head with that big old bat of a hand that he had.

'How's it coming, Charlie?' asked Bitsy.

'Mighty good,' said Charlie. 'Ahead of schedule, actually. It's gonna be something special when it finally opens.'

Hampstead got a good look at the site. It looked like a pile of crap to him. It was all rubble and timber and hammers and sawdust. What the hell was all the hullabaloo about?

'Does Mr Bridger not come down to help?' he asked.

'What, and come off his hill? Let me ask you this, kid: how would you feel if you looked up at that hill and he wasn't up there?'

'Not so good,' said Hampstead.

'Say, Miss Bitsy, I hear that Edwin Hubble himself is naming a star after you.'

'I think that's right,' Bitsy blushed.

'Ain't that something,' smiled Charlie. Mélanie smiled proudly at Bitsy, who nodded and grinned like a kid. Hampstead was beginning to feel bored, but before he knew it Charlie was explaining the mechanics of how the planetarium would work.

'Why are the stars different colours?' asked Hampstead, out of courtesy more than anything else.

'Planck's curve,' said Charlie, and that was enough on the matter for Hampstead.

'My momma likes your shoulders,' he remembered.

'Heh, that right?'

'Sure.'

'Give her my best.'

'Yessir.'

Hampstead liked Charlie a lot. He reminded him of his late father, only Charlie seemed like the kind of man that was incapable of succumbing to a fever like Hampstead's father had been. He reckoned Charlie was one hell of a pitcher too.

'Say, Hampstead,' said Charlie. 'Once I've finished work on the planetarium I figured I might start work on a brand new school for Negro children. How would you feel about that, kid?'

'I sure like going to school with white kids,' said Hampstead.

'Sure, but it wouldn't be a permanent switch. It would be for a few years at most, maybe just a couple semesters, then you would go back to the mixed school. You would come and learn classically. I would invite Booker Washington and Mr Du Bois to speak and teach if they so desired. And other coloured fellers with bright minds. *The Souls of Black Folks* would be the core text that we would learn from.'

'What would be the point in all this?' asked Hampstead.

'The betterment of the Negro race, kid.'

'Things are pretty good for the Negroes in town, ain't they?' said Bitsy.

'Here they're better than they were, for sure,' said Charlie. 'But we still have a great many things that could improve yet. It is very easy to think the race is run when you've eaten up a hunk of track, but I won't be doing that, nome. I would like to educate our children about education. I do not want them lulled into a sense that things are as good as they could be, which they might if their educational routes are not expanded. I want full and unchallenged integration of us folks. Have you read *The Negro Problem*, Miss Bitsy?'

'No, sir.'

'I would thoroughly recommend it.'

'But look at you, Mr Bellingham. You are a fully integrated member of this society. Look at what you do for everyone and how revered you are.'

'I toil and I labour, sure, but that is not how the perception of us folks will improve in the eyes of white men. And without positive perception we cannot hope to have influence. I believe this will only happen through lucrative opportunities and general inroads into the economy, which are only possible through better education. That is where it will all start: education. Sadly this is the cost of our society: that economic success is crucial for betterment. Morality is a sidenote, but one that will be included in this curriculum, should it ever come to fruition.'

'You're a fine man, Mr Bellingham,' said Mélanie.

'I'll think about it,' said Hampstead.

Then they left old Charlie to his works and Hampstead's mind began circling with thoughts of the spooky planetarium again. The talk of a new school had zipped through one ear and out the other, just as a great many things liked to do.

'This all seems mighty pointless,' he said. 'Why don't folks just look up at the night sky?'

'Well, some people like to sleep at night,' said Mélanie. 'Children and old people and even people in between. Myself, for example, well, I like to sleep at night.'

'That's true,' Hampstead sighed, 'but it just seems like an awful waste of time and resources and manpower. Old Charlie is a miracle of a man and he is slaving away on that dumb project. What gives!'

'You'll see once its ready.'

But Hampstead did not like it one bit, even if trusty old Charlie was on the job. Something just felt very off about the whole thing, but there were more pressing matters at hand: making amends to Charlie's daughter.

(ii)

Bitsy also could not figure out why the planetarium was necessary, but she thought it was good for the town at large to have such an experience to look forward to. This was said to be Willie's magnum opus and his paintings might have been up in a showcase with *The Boulevard Montmartre* and *The Starry Night* if he had been less humble, so this was sure to be a spectacle. Back at the hall Bitsy was asked by Mélanie to play on the piano for Hampstead and her. Mélanie loved listening to live music and was obsessed with the idea of seeing an orchestra play something, particularly Gershwin's *Rhapsody in Blue*. Bitsy was a novice pianist and scoffed when Mélanie first asked her to play *Rhapsody in Blue* because for starters there were about a million different instruments all being played at once. The piece had premiered the year before in New York and Mélanie had done all in her power to get tickets but had eventually decided against going when Bitsy sprained her ankle and had to give up hers. Bitsy had been desperate for Mélanie to go but Mélanie simply refused.

Mélanie also loved Scarlatti's *Sonata in F Minor*, which Bitsy was capable of playing at an awkwardly slower pace than the Philharmonic did. So when they got back to the hall they threw the sheet off the piano and Bitsy did her best while Mélanie and Hampstead sat on the stage together and listened quietly. Bitsy felt Mélanie's eyes on her but didn't want to meet them for fear of become disorientated. Hampstead she expected was staring aimlessly into space, enjoying the music but more concentrated on the prospect of his next meal or snack. When Bitsy finished she looked up gingerly and saw that Mélanie was cooing like a ringdove as she watched.

It was how they had met. Mélanie had been a knocker-up and Bitsy an early bird, and dawn was when Bitsy most liked to play the piano, which back then had been a crude and rickety old Wurlitzer. One day Bitsy had spotted Mélanie in her peripheral as the latter moseyed down the road to the next block of houses, only she had stopped by the window and listened as Bitsy played. Bitsy pretended like she hadn't noticed. Then Mélanie kept coming back, day after day, always listening through the glass and thinking herself unnoticed. It was free radio for her. And one day later she plucked up the courage to come in and listen awhile. Then they got to talking and then they were colleagues. Mélanie admired the playing but Bitsy admired the piano. To her it was a dusty, monolithic marvel, capable of allowing a person to transcend the typical bounds of emotion - which, to be fair, were restricted in Bitsy's view - and find themselves risen above. To see an orchestra was something she thought would be enjoyable, though she still prioritised her politics and career over any of that frivolity.

'Would you like me to teach you?' asked Bitsy, but Mélanie just shook her head. This perplexed Bitsy and annoyed her slightly. Was she a performing monkey to Mélanie?

'I'd like to learn it,' said Hampstead.

'Fix that stupid house you've made on the banner first.'

'*Damn*,' said Hampstead, pulling Mélanie out of her blissful trance and into a state of outrage. She was dumbstruck, as was Bitsy, though Bitsy found it quite funny.

'Are you for real?' asked Mélanie.

Hampstead lowered his head and looked ready to cry. He was far too young to be cussing like that and he knew it.

'I've got a lot going on right now!' he shouted, jumping from the stage, running past the piano and out the main doors on the opposite side. Bitsy didn't much feel like talking to Mélanie and so followed Hampstead out and found him up the flagpole again, his eyes a little glistened and a certain hangdog look about him. He looked a lonely schmuck.

'Hey, Hampstead,' said Bitsy.

'What do you want, Bitsy?'

'I ain't angry about you cussing.'

'Mademoiselle Celestine is, though.'

'Say, would you mind climbing down? I've got a favour to ask you.'

'I don't much feel like doing more sewing; I'll only ruin it further, Bitsy.'

'It's not that. It's actually quite a fun favour. I'm gonna give you permission to do something truly outrageous, Hampstead.'

Mélanie's indignation at Hampstead swearing, coupled with the damage that the boy was doing to the flagpole, had given Bitsy an unsettling but frankly remarkable idea. The boy clambered down and looked up curiously at Bitsy, who was a good foot taller than him, so she decided it would be better to ask him this favour on her knees. She needed him to trust her.

'Give me your ear,' she said, duly receiving it. '*What's the rudest cuss word you know?*'

Hampstead's eyes opened wide and his jaw swung a little. For a few moments he stared at Bitsy, apparently scrutinising her face for any signs of a trap, but he knew Bitsy too well to conclude that she was tricking him. She wouldn't betray the devil would old Bitsy, he hoped.

'I ain't speaking it out loud,' he finally said.

'Will you write it down?'

'No. I'll say to you the letters, though, and you can rearrange them. I ain't having nothing to do with that word coming into being, and I'm a bad speller so no one can say I spelled it deliberately.'

'How many letters?'

'Four, I reckon.'

'And you know what they are for sure?'

'I think so, but no one needs to know that.'

'Okay, that's swell. Come on, I'll buy you some lunch as a reward. Run and tell Mélanie that I'm taking you home, will you.'

'Swell!'

They walked to the European restaurant a few blocks away. It was called the Two Crows. As written upon the bill of sale posted in the foyer the place was owned by the German immigrant Elias Franke and his Hungarian friend Viktor, who were both made solely of skin, bone and cigarette smoke. Elias, Viktor and Bitsy got along terrifically, not least because Bitsy had a real taste for European cuisine. Among other things served was roast beef stew *(sauerbraten)*, pork knuckle (*schweinshaxe*), potato dumplings (*kartoffelkloesse*), goulash (*gulyas*), sweet bread (*kurtoskalacs*), stuffed cabbage *(toltott kaposzta)*, grilled sausage (*bratwurst*), potato pancake (*kartoffelpuffer*), cherry soup (*meggyleves*) and an aphrodisiac dish of vanilla custard dish topped elaborately by fresh meringue and some mysterious berry. This was only served on Friday evenings.

Hampstead took one swooping look at his surroundings and decided that the Two Crows would not do despite Bitsy's incessant banging the drum for it. It was too near the church for him to be involved in such shenanigans. God could be watching, he said. They walked a quarter-mile further and arrived at the beanery owned by Ally Brown and her brothers. It was called the Pie House but was always short on pies. Hampstead followed Bitsy in and they ordered themselves some dry sandwiches and Bitsy bought Hampstead a Coca-Cola. He guzzled on it like there was no tomorrow and finished it before even touching his food. Then he complained that he had nothing to water down his sandwich with, so Bitsy bought him another can. He drank it and then threw up a little bit in his mouth.

Once they were finished their meals the time came for Hampstead to fulfil his side of the bargain, only he looked petrified and had a sweat on all of a sudden.

'You just gotta spell it, kid,' said Bitsy.

The beanery was mostly empty but Hampstead looked so nervous there might have been a hundred eyes on him.

'I want something else,' he finally said.

Bitsy groaned.

'What?'

'I need your help. I did a girl dirty and I want to know how to fix things with her. You're smart and you know what's right and what's wrong, so I figure you'd be the best to ask. You ain't prone to judging, neither.'

'Which girl?'

'It's a secret.'

'What did you do?'

'I snaked her to the principle even though she didn't do anything to hurt me. Then her parents got real mad at her and hit her some. I swear I've got the heebie-jeebies all the time. You know how good I am at sleeping, right? Well, I barely got a wink in last night.'

This did not tickle Bitsy's fancy in the slightest, but she saw an opportunity to cover her back.

'This sounds like something you gotta figure out by yourself,' she said. 'But here's the thing, Hampstead: snaking out a friend ain't ever the right thing to do, you dig?'

'I know,' said Hampstead. 'But ain't there something you can do to help me fix things with her? She ain't my friend or nothing; I just want to do something for her that will make her happy. It don't need to be much, honest.'

'Why do you care so much if you ain't her friend?'

'I guess I just feel bad for her. She's lonely and I reckon she's probably the cat's pajamas. What do you reckon I should do?'

Bitsy explained that the fates would align to bless Hampstead with fortunes aplenty should - and this was essential - he never make the same mistake again. It was a necessary condition of his future successes. Ratting out friends would likely ruin his life.

'Anything else?' he said.

'Kid, I bought you lunch and two cokes. Let's leave it at that,' said Bitsy, feeling impatient. 'Now,' she pulled from her pocket a pen and a napkin, 'get spelling.'

An argument was brewing at the planetarium building site as it boiled in the beating sun of mid-afternoon. One could hear a bubbling violence in the shrill chorus of a half-dozen voices clamouring for some kind of meaningless and very temporary supremacy, and it was this violence that drew the attention of a passing Mélanie Celestine, but Mélanie drew inevitable leers more than she did penitent whimpers. So Mélanie fetched Bitsy, and Bitsy came to make sense of the brouhaha, and with an animated intention of solving it.

The main players involved in the dispute were two men and a river birch tree, all three of whom were gathered in the trickles of the town creek. The tallest of the two men and thus he with the shortest length of sodden ankle was Padhraic, a sullen Irishman with hands wider than they were long. He was an invaluable asset at any construction site because of those hands' slab-elevating qualities. Across from him was Hiram Bates, named not for nor descended from the Phoenician king, but named rather for Hiram Walker, the esteemed whisky tycoon from Ontario. Bates's parents had been barley farmers, and neither he nor they had fared well since the Volstead Act. And as for the tree, it seemed to Bitsy that it was more the subject of the argument than it was a participant - unlike how Mélanie had described it - but perhaps her original intentions had been lost on the nuances of a Provençal tongue. But as Bitsy involved herself more and more in the quarrel it became apparent that it was not specifically the tree that had caused such a commotion, but rather its shade.

'This is my tree and I ought to get to sit here for these two hours in the afternoon. That's how it's been since we started,' said Hiram.

'You can sit in exactly the same spot by the tree for two hours,' affirmed Padhraic, 'that goes without saying. I get to sit next to you is all.'

'Right, you see, this is where he thinks he's being all clever with his words,' Hiram said. 'He'd make a damn good attorney but this jury ain't falling for none of it. You see, Miss Bitsy, as is the peculiar relationship between the earth and the sun, it is inevitable that the shadow cast by this tree will move as the day goes on. So either Padhraic is in retard of the rest of us in basic astronomical knowledge or he wishes for me to lose out on some of the shade that I'm typically entitled to. I wish to move with the shade as my two hours go on, but his antics will prevent this from happening.'

'What are you talking about, "*entitled to*"?' scorned Padhraic. 'Do you own this particular plot of land? I should be able to sit.'

'I've been working with Charlie Bellingham since the very start of this job,' said Hiram. 'You started *this week*. I get the privilege of leaning up against whatever part of this tree I feel like and at whatever given time. *You* have to *earn* that privilege.'

'All I'm saying is that this is the only tree near the dome where a man can dip his toes in the creek. We do the same work so I figure it's only right that the shade be split between whoever needs a bit of it.'

'Why has no one else complained?' inquired Bitsy.

'None of the other fellers burn like I do,' said Padhraic from County Cork, and Bitsy nodded.

'As the day goes on I'll be moving with it,' said Hiram, whose finality was laced with apprehension.

'Bitsy?' said Padhraic.

'Ain't this something that can be sorted by a few bucks?'

'You wish for us to commodify shade now? What a goddamn stupid thing to say,' said Hiram. 'Someone get Charlie.'

'He's working,' said one of the other labourers.

'He hasn't stopped in days! Go and give him a reason to!' Hiram snapped back.

The labourer darted to the dome and Bitsy turned her attention back to Padhraic, who was somewhat stooped in order to have his menacing glare received by the squinting Hiram. There was a little rivulet of blood dribbling down from his scalp.

'Did you fellers actually throw hands over this?' said Bitsy.

They both turned at her and scowled.

'Do you mean to say that you came all the way here thinking that we were just having a little war of words? You didn't come because we grappled?' said Hiram.

'Well, I guess -'

'Do you think every argument requires your intervention or something? Cos you better not, not with how useless you've been anyhow.'

'I heard there was a conflict and I came to see if I could help put an end to it. I got the feeling, what with it being adults like yourselves, that it could escalate.'

'By sticking the suggestion of capital into it? Since when does that help?'

'I don't know, *Christ*.'

Bitsy's stomach was filled to the brim with the rubble of a Honolulu sandwich and it was perhaps the lemon juice that was making her sour. She was surrounded by men but she didn't care none. She booted the dirt and spat into he water at Hiram's feet. From experience she had learned in recent years that she presumably possessed some kind of natural aura that would cow even an angry audience into silence. Perhaps it was the voluminous hunches of her shoulders, the pointed lines of her face or the skeletal protuberances of her feet that burgeoned between the leathers of her two-straps. Perhaps it was more animalistic; that, not unlike how Bitsy was taught to be when chancing upon a bear, she stood up tall and unafraid when facing the possibility of violence. Perhaps it was that she was of six feet in height.

'Something to say?' she said to Hiram.

'I ought to step to you,' he said, scowling at the small circle of spittle passing his ankles.

But whether or not he was willing to, as was doubtful to Bitsy,

Charlie Bellingham presently arrived with a stride full of restiveness and hands full of implements.

'Settle this dispute,' said Padhraic, proceeding to explain the situation in somewhat biased terms, with regular corrective interjections from Hiram. Charlie listened pensively despite his shuffling feet, then broke his silence by handing the victory to the Irishman.

'Fine,' said Hiram. 'Take your goddamned shade, Padhraic. Bitsy, keep your goddamned nose out of other people's business. And don't stand too close to the old man. We know his track record for corrupting white women.'

He stalked back to the dome and a great many eyes followed his tracks, but only out of a collective unwillingness to avoid one another. Charlie Bellingham breathed slow and heavy, not so much a festering anger in his stature but rather a clearer resolve. After a few moments of awkwardness had subsided he turned back to his men.

'Any of you ever had to marry a woman you didn't love?' he asked.

No one said anything.

(ii)

July's happiest memory was a muddled one and one that also made him pensive and melancholic. It was peculiar because his memories of the War made him feel empty but this memory made him brim and swoon. He had been sat playing the piano one morning in summer, minding his business after a night of misperforming in the bedroom for Mélanie. July had learned to play when he was a boy and was quite deft with the keys - although his bashfulness would have many believe otherwise - by the time he reached his twenties, but usually played only when he felt wretched and needed an escape or a distraction. He couldn't remember what he had been playing that day. All that he remembered was that he thought he was alone until he wasn't. A pair of arms came over his and he felt Mélanie embrace him from behind, her chin resting on his shoulder and her breathing slow and steady in his ear. July may well have loused up the rest of the song - whatever it was - but in truth it didn't matter and he wouldn't have been able to tell because he was so lost in his little bliss. He felt he was truly united with Mélanie for the first time on that rare day of wine and roses.

A week after he became a bachelor again July donated the piano to the municipal hall which had been crying out for a replacement for the tumbledown Wurlitzer. The sorrow he felt when looking at his piano had been painful and yet addictive, so he did right by himself and gave up the thing. He knew that Bitsy was running her campaign from the hall and that made him wonder if Mélanie thought of him when she looked at it. Maybe it was something else that made her think of him but he hoped there was something. If she wasn't thinking about him then he felt smaller than he could articulate. One day she would come into the Itch with a bump on her tummy and his heart would shatter because from then on she would have no time or reason to think of him. That day scared July as much as anything. He hoped the piano would keep her thinking about him and maybe one day bring her back. The elegy to it on the floorboards was a pale square of sun-starved wood.

When July had finished explaining the marks on the floor to Sunrise he felt odd. He had told her everything and it hadn't taken her a word of please or come on to persuade him to do so.

'I must be blue,' he said.

What had been stolen from Sunrise's room on the day of Doc's interview was an apple peeler and some of her penny dreadfuls. July didn't understand why Sunrise cared any about them but he had promised to keep some extra security by the door in the meantime: Doc Bellingham herself. July had skipped her interview at her grandfather's behest and had instated her as a 'utility girl' within the Itch. For now this meant that she would sit and report on any comings and goings from Sunrise's room, and July had designs on making her a fulltime informant on all guests in the future. Doc was not only supple and unassuming, but also willing and enthusiastic. The sense of purpose that she seemed flushed with when given her post filled July with optimism for her future value.

'There's something very curious about you,' July said to Sunrise.

'How can someone so young have eyes that are so old? An old soul perhaps? I have one of those too.'

'And yet you have very young eyes, but a face that's ageing comparatively quickly around it. I wonder what that's about?' said Sunrise.

'I ought to start wearing powder, I guess.'

Sunrise finished her whiskey and tried her best to conceal a belch, but to no avail. She grinned sheepishly and asked for another. It was barely two o'clock.

'So why did you bring that old feller?' asked July. 'You two are awfully mysterious, I must say. I'm filled with questions every time I lay eyes on you and I'm not naturally inquisitive. I like to keep myself to myself; eyes down, no questions asked. It's simpler that way, I find. That's why I'm suited to looking after travellers: I don't ask no questions, I don't pry and I don't judge. I just sit and ask for a favour here and there.'

'It's a long story, Mister.'

'It is?'

'So long that I reckon you would have to cash in your favour if you wanted me to tell it.'

'You drive a hard bargain.'

'This old soul knows that a good story comes with a good price,' said Sunrise.

'Let's hear it,' said July. 'Consider the favour cashed in.'

Sunrise sniffed and breathed and tucked her hair over her ears.

'Back home I grew up next door to a group of labourers from the Philippines. It was such a pretty house. Everything was embroidered so delicately. There was shining rattan furniture, waterfall tapestries, impossible palettes and lots and lots of energy. The people that lived there had formed the first Filipino farm labourers' working union in California, but they also used the place as a small poultry farm and the profits from that paid the union dues. I loved the place so much but no one trusted it so much because the growers associations and the big sugars in town were all on the ropes. No one knew whether to take the labourers to court or to pick up their pitchforks and deal with themselves. One day all these white fellers were sitting there with their brimming pockets, and then the next their immigrant workers were driving around in flivvers.

'The labourers called the house the Roost. Oftentimes I would see guests coming in and out, you know, guests of *notoriety*. Victoria Woodhull, Du Bois, Alice Paul, even Harriet Tubman once. They all came to talk and drink with the labourers. The feller in charge was Angelo, and he apparently had once met Fitzgerald in Salinas but Fitzgerald was mighty hard to pin down and rarely replied to Angelo's correspondence, let alone accept an invitation to the Roost.'

'I read *This Side of Paradise*,' said July. 'Big deal!'

'Anyway,' Sunrise continued, 'I lived next door with my parents. Pa owned this little carpentry store with chisels and claw hammers and such like, while Ma worked in the label department of the Heinz factory in Las Lunas. I was almost out of school at this time. I played in the yard with Angelo's son Nathaniel, which sort of scared old man because there was this rumour going around that Angelo had one of Kamenev's books hidden away upstairs. I did a little investigating of my own into the matter and found that there was no Soviet book of any kind in that house. There was a *painting* by Lev Kamenev, but there are two Lev Kamenevs, you see. One of them was a painter.'

'I never heard of either of them.'

'Pa liked to read the foreign section of *The New York Times* and had been quite disturbed by the February Revolution, but anyway I kept on being friends with Nathaniel because he was real cute and I wanted to go with him, you know. And anyway the rest of the labourers in the Roost didn't care none for turning me into a socialist. Mostly Nathaniel and I kept to the yard where we could play dress-up or dance the black bottom and Charleston. Nathaniel had this crude little pogo stick which we tried fixing up together. He read me all these crazy Greek stories. Sometimes I gave him a kiss and he would get all red and then I gave him baked beans from the factory. He chopped us wood in the winter and picked me flowers in the spring. The labourers started to like me.'

'What was Nathaniel's deal?'

'He wanted to be a writer. He would bury himself in Whitman and Hardy and the Brontës and then he would recite his favourites to tell me. He'd tell me stories like Echo and Narcissus, Apollo and Daphne, Orpheus and Eurydice. I would just sit and listen like you are doing now, July. And I was in love with him.'

July stiffened up a little.

'*That* ain't like me though, right? That ain't what you're insinuating?'

'Of course not,' smiled Sunrise. 'When it rained I would go with his ma and we would sew garments using her lockstitch machine. Later my own ma joined us. Together over the course of six months we made a bodice with leg of mutton sleeves and embroidered lace on the front closing. It didn't fit a single lady in the house and no one in the village was willing to buy it from the Roost, so Nathaniel's uncle Piolo took apart the top of a chiffonier and built a frame for it. We placed it above the fireplace and would often sit and look at it. Nathaniel was diagnosed with some disease and told he had a year or so to live. A motor disease I think they called it.'

'Like, for a car?'

'Naw, not for a car. But he wanted to marry me but he couldn't speak too well no more and he hadn't even told me that he loved me yet because he was frightened. We spent less and less time dancing as he lost control in his legs, you know. They went all goofy.'

'I saw plenty of goofy legs in France,' said July.

'Nathaniel's were plenty goofy, that's for sure,' said Sunrise. 'He would just sit and watch while his ma and I sewed. He persuaded his pa to sell his flivver so that he could buy a ring, but no one in the whole wide world wanted to buy an automobile from a bunch of alleged socialists from abroad, so my pa bought the thing as a favour to Angelo, even though he barely had the money or the need for one.'

July's eyes fell to the delicate breadstick of a third finger on Sunrise's left hand and saw that it was adorned with neither gold ring nor pale halo.

'Wait, wait!' he said, manically shaking his arms, anticipating a tragedy. 'Drinks. Drinks! I ain't doing this sober.'

He fixed up two sidecars with extra Armagnac, placed them on the counter, then downed them both.

'What can I get you?' he winced.

'Southside?'

'Naw,' July mulled for a second. 'We need some absinthe. This is a honkytonk after all. Two corpse revivers, then six or so more.'

They drank quietly awhile.

'I'll tell you,' said July, 'I love a good yarn. Always have. Anyone who can spin a good one, well, they're worth keeping around, I'll tell you as much. Take you, Sunrise, fuhrinstance.'

'Naw,' said Sunrise, 'I just had some crazy things happen to me, Mister. That don't make me a good storyteller. A good storyteller would be someone who had nothing crazy happen to them but they can still spin a good yarn.'

'Or it would make them a good liar. Proceed.'

Sunrise sighed plaintively and curled her fingers around her cup, whitening her knuckles and disquieting her drinking buddy.

'There came a day when he couldn't tell the cook whether he wanted his eggs fried or boiled. His ma told me to go over to the Roost that evening because he was going to propose. She wanted it a surprise but he'd gotten to the stage where I mightn't have been able to make heads or tails of what he was saying, such was how his voice had deteriorated. But it was also the day that the executives from the growers association - the one that employed the labourers - came with a small mob from Los Angeles. I watched Angelo take to the porch to say that he and his people were protected by law and that the union leaders would have something to say about all this. But, goddamn it, the executives had brought their own travelling judge with them.'

'I was worried you was gonna say that,' said a weary July.

'*He* said that any reassurances Angelo had from the union weren't worth a hill of beans while he was presiding over the case. The executives were now willing to employ more expensive white workers if it meant they wouldn't be unionising. Angelo wouldn't surrender but neither would he raise arms, so the executives bundled everyone from the Roost into the automobiles and drove them away. I never heard from them again.'

July fetched more cocktails; this time whiskey, lemon and grenadine. Sunrise contemplated aloud how helplessness felt. It was paralysing, she said, and numbing too, and shaming thereafter. It was the most palpable emotion that she had felt until and since that day at the Itch, and it was very much in the marrow of her bones now, infesting her waking movements and driving them in certain directions. It was why she was here, she said.

'Explain,' said July.

But the rest of her story was thus remembered by July in a series of conceptual ideas, more akin to comic strips than to the vivid, particularised world that Sunrise had previously painted with her spoken prose. July had seen *Vida y Milagros de Don Fausto* at a special screening in Laguna the year prior, and as he had been very overwhelmed and perhaps a little frightened by the comedy picture. He often now found the misremembered dregs of its style seeping into his drunken recollections. In short, July's hangovers would oftentimes be haunted by plump sitckmen in stovepipes and waistcoats as they enacted the events of July's previous evening. And this was vaguely how he recalled Sunrise's story.

A devastated Livingston family had used the trundling Model T to get to some cartoonish Panhandle town and got to working as farm hands. July imagined tumbleweed and paperwhite night skies littered with black stars. And the ranch belonged to Walter Hale, Sunrise's current travelling companion, that was right! And once he had had quite the loving brood to whom he had been very devoted. And the broods had broods of their own. Mr Sunrise had become distant, yes, even in July's comic book impressions the girl's father was morose and blurred and absent. Caused by guilt at his not stopping the labourers' kidnapping, yes. But there were hoedowns at the ranch with the hands and the Hale gang! They had a great time of it.

And then a velvety black screen enveloped the memory and July knew nothing other than that the scarlet fever came back from the railheads with one of the cowboys. Everyone taken including the Sunrise parents and the Hale broods and the Hale broods' broods. Walter himself left indisposed in bed with a novelty thermometer and a very bulbous face. Nursed back to health by Sunrise and a physician with one enormous stethoscope, blank clipboard and an ambulance without a floorboard (the doctor's feet propelled it forwards). Hale recovered thanks to a mixture of a sonofabitch stew and incremental lifestyle alterations. Decided that he was in hell. Had only Sunrise and vice versa.

7

That afternoon July went out on the range fixing up some of the Babe Vicks's bob-wire that had fallen in the wind. The cattle he passed were mostly docile and seemed a little restless without the boundary, so July had only a passably easy time with the help of some boarders from the Itch. He liked being out on the range because it gave him some time and space to think, and thinking was all he wanted to do after hearing Sunrise's story. But before he had contemplated it in acceptable depth he was interrupted by Luella from Room 3.

Luella was pretty and personable and had thick brown hair down to her bottom. She was an excellent rider and had worked on ranches before, which meant she was ideal for the work at hand. There had been not a second of hesitation before she accepted July's request for her help. The two had known one another for a long time now because Luella was now a commercial traveller and found excuses to conduct her business in town whenever she could despite that most folks around couldn't afford her products. Sometimes she just handed out bibles or Macy's catalogues if she was on the payroll. Other times she brought along insect repellent and encyclopaedias, though people this far out in the boondocks tended to have a need for only one of those things. But more often that not she brought along furniture samples in a chuck-wagon and then left two weeks later without offloading any of it.

Apparently she had a fondness for the Pig's Itch and for July - the latter in particular. Despite her unprofitable trips to town there was always some excuse or another for coming back and staying at the Itch.

July figured the true reason was so that she could get into bed with him again, but Luella feigned ignorance and acted like she hadn't expected for the two of them to end up tangled and dishevelled under the sheets. July often got cold during the night and welcomed some heat from time to time, but he knew he ought to resist her advances and pledged to do exactly that every time she left town with her chuckwagon full of ottomans and hammocks. And yet whenever Luella returned July found himself down the Two Crows begging Elias and Viktor to make him some of that mysterious aphrodisiac vanilla dish. They served it only on Fridays usually, but July owned the only gin mill in town and was thus given certain privileges in other establishments.

The two of them got along handsomely outside of the Room 3 too. July was particularly fond of Luella's relentless denial of any of her faults, which to July was confirmation that she was the most insecure person he had ever met. Never once was he able to laugh at Luella's wider-than-usual thumbs or her long earlobes without her trying to bite his head off. July found it tremendously endearing. She was the absolute antithesis of Mélanie: *im*perfect and *in*capable of making fun of herself. For this reason Luella was a welcome distraction for July and he rarely found himself imagining Mélanie when he bedded Luella, which could not be said for the girls he had been with at the cat house across town.

It also happened that Luella was the most audacious human being in the entire land, which July found entertaining to no end. There was never a time when she was not devising some devilish scheme or escapade and there was nothing that frightened her, not even July's obvious obsession with Mélanie and consequent depression. In fact Luella seemed to relish in that and was now firm friends with Mélanie, which July suspected was some cruel tease on Luella's part. Her boldness was clear as day in the bedroom too, where those wider-than-usual thumbs of hers often went on adventures all of their own, much to July's surprise.

He was out in tranquil nowhere when she loped up to him on the back of her appaloosa. There was a wind that day and so the two of them had been covered in dirt and sand like they had just ridden out of hicksville. So far about a mile of rope had been fixed up.

'Hidy-do,' said Luella.

'Hey,' said July, who had been thinking about Sunrise and Mr Hale.

'You wanna go for a ride?'

'Where to?'

Luella shrugged.

'That way,' she said, gesturing in the direction opposite to the way home. July hummed and mused and spat out some of the sand collecting on his tongue.

'I reckon we head back,' he said. 'What's that way but more desert?'

'Antics,' said Luella.

'There could be snakes,' said July.

'Are there not snakes in town?'

'Well, yes, but there are people to help us in the case that one of us gets bit. Willie Bridger is an expert on venom. And there is Dr Wagner of course.'

'Security is so often the enemy of adventure, July,' growled Luella, digging her spurs into the appaloosa and sending him galloping away. July hurried after them on the back of his mare, whom he had called June. They rode for a few hours until it became too hot and they figured the horses would need watering before too long. It was too risky carrying on and so July ultimately persuaded Luella that they needed to head back, much to Luella's chagrin.

'You're all bores in this town,' she said. 'I've up and left home more times than I can count. I'm always seeking pastures new, yet none of you people have ever lived anywhere else, with the exception of the mademoiselle. It's remarkable.'

'Don't be so sore just because you've never had a nice home.'

'I've had plenty of nice homes.'

'Doubtfully. Why would you leave any if they were nice?'

'Because you sometimes have to leave where you're happy, July. Otherwise you'll never get to be who you wanna be, unless what you wanna be is a cellmate in Folsom State for six months.'

'I've got it covered. Bitsy's father -'

'Yes, yes, Bitsy's father knows a feller in the Prohibition Unit, you've told me before, and it seems to me like you need to keep saying it. What happens when Bitsy leaves, huh? She won't have any reason to keep the law from raiding the Itch, will she?'

'Bitsy won't leave,' said July.

'Why not? She's an ambitious gal, ain't she? She's got brains and talent and she wants to go places. Why won't she leave?'

'Because it's nice here.'

'You're all insane!'

(ii)

Mr Slade followed a woman up to Room 3 that evening but stopped to speak to Doc on the way up. She had brought a stool from home and propped it up against the wall adjacent to the Room 2.

'What are you doing, Doc?' he asked.

'Looking at my arms,' said Doc.

Doc couldn't believe her luck at this job. All she had to do was sit on her stool and relax. Where before she had worried that she wouldn't be able to cope with the social pressures of working at the Itch, she was now only concerned with keeping entertained for the hours that she was paid to sit and do nothing. She even brought some cigarettes along.

'What's so special about your arms?' said the boarder who was with Mr Slade. Her name was Luella, Doc remembered.

'They're plumb crazy,' said Doc. 'Look at them, they never end.'

Luella challenged Doc to an arm wrestle and Doc reluctantly accepted the proposal. They got on their knees and put their elbows on the stool. Doc won with ease although she reckoned that Luella might have been going easy on her.

'God, I'd love to have arms like that,' said Luella, taking Mr Slade by the hand and leading him towards the stairs.

'You can do plenty with the ones you've got,' Mr Slade said warily. Doc didn't know what he meant by that but felt a rush of affection towards the two of them as they scooted into Room 3. But then Mr Slade thrust his head out and shouted down to her:

'Anything suspicious, kid?'

'No, sir!'

Then the door closed again and Doc giggled to herself. Not only had Sunrise got Doc out of having to do a dreaded interview but she had also inadvertently created a scenario in which Doc had the easiest, most pointless job that the world had ever seen. And yet Sunrise felt guilty that Doc had to sit around and do nothing and so came out and played checkers or pegity or bridge with her whenever she could. This pleased Doc. Generally Sunrise liked to take Mr Hale out to do whatever fun and exciting things were available to them, but often Mr Hale preferred to stay in bed and sleep. Then Sunrise would become a little deflated and so came out for a pick-me-up with Doc. They liked to swap stories and Sunrise told Doc all about her travels to the north country. What piqued Doc's interest was tell of a prep school in Seattle for smart kids; one that would do her well in eventually getting to the zoology college in Boston that she had her heart set on. She would need a reference and her grades and Sunrise reckoned that would be enough. But Doc was contented in town and anyway was loving her time with Sunrise.

'Hello, Madam Security,' Sunrise would say.

'Hidy-do,' Doc would reply. 'All clear!'

Sunrise was also in a predicament because she had lost Doc's favourite ballcap - the one that she had taken off Doc during her anxious experience. Sunrise had completely forgotten to return it until two days later, when she had been walking through town to the Bellingham place to drop it off. Before she knew it some pussyfooting kid had shouted '*Yoink!*' and had filched it from Sunrise's hand. She was down an alley and the kid was so nimble that she'd only seen the back of his head as he'd glided around the nearest corner.

'Fuhgeddaboudit,' Doc said for the hundredth time that evening, watching as Sunrise divvied out the cards between the two of them. They were going to play Egyptian rattlesnake and the cards were real ritzy and pristine. They got Doc wondering: 'Say, Sunrise, what is it you do for a living?'

'Nothing, currently. I worked as a hand and saddler for a while. That's been my only job, really. I might have been a seamstress but I never really got the chance.'

'Was it fun?'

'Was leather tanning and strap adjustment *fun*?'

'What does Mr Hale do?'

'Nothing also.'

'So how do you afford to move around?'

'Well, he was the big shot at a ranch down in Rockwell. Do you know where Rockwell is?'

'I think so,' said Doc.

'The ranch was in his family for years. They made a lot of money off it. That's where I worked in the saddlery. So while Walter heals from his sadness we are using that money to see places.'

'What kind of places?'

'Places like this.'

'What's special about this?'

'I heard that people who are born here tend to die here,' said Sunrise. 'I heard stories of that all the way back east. Your town's kind of famous for it, how about that? *Snap*! So I figure it must be one helluva place; just right for Walter. We've been to some other towns too. We even visited Utah.'

'Hell, I thought you were trying to make him feel better. *Snap*!' shouted Doc.

'I'm hoping this place is so hotsy-totsy that he can't help but improve,' said Sunrise.

'*Snap*!' shouted Doc.

'Goddamnit. It's done the business so far. He's been up and about more than I've seen him in months.'

'That's swell,' said Doc.

The sound of rhythmic creaking came from above, followed shortly by a woman's panting and moaning. Doc wondered if someone was getting hurt up there. Sunrise looked up nervously at the ceiling and seemed to gulp. It was Room 3.

'You reckon everything's all right?' asked Doc.

'Oh, I reckon so,' said Sunrise. 'You know, lots of people reckon I'm either Walter's daughter or some kid-belle of his. Takes a while for people to realise that I'm just a squeeze.'

'Just a squeeze, plain and simple?'

'Just a squeeze, Doc,' Sunrise said. '*Snap*!'

'He's lucky to have a squeeze like you,' said Doc.

'You'd make a good squeeze,' said Sunrise.

'What *is* a squeeze?' asked Doc.

'It's a modern word meaning companion.'

'Does it pay well?'

'I guess it doesn't pay at all.'

'What do you get out of it?'

'You get to help someone else. That's all I've ever wanted to do, really. My father was a very helpful man, you see. He helped where he could and was always very upset when he was too scared to do it. I liked that about him.'

'You've helped me,' said Doc.

'Getting out of the interview?'

'Sure. And I've never had a friend to play with before, not unless you count family members. It's nice to have a friend, weirdly enough.'

They played in quiet for a few minutes, interrupted only by the occasional snap or sandwich that the card pile provided. Doc later realised that it was the first time that she could remember being in the Itch without having picked up a spittoon on the way in.

(iii)

Once the deed was done July felt typically underwhelmed and unfulfilled. Luella had given him all the surprises that he could have hoped for and yet he still carried a feeling of indifference with him as he got into his clothes. Luella smoked naked on the bed and read from *Chéri*.

'Would you like to hear some?' she asked July.

'I ought to get downstairs.'

'Would you like to purchase a pew? I reckon I'm going to go to sleep presently, so make up your mind while I'm sharp.'

Their relationship was very transactional. July hurried up his dressing and then left the room, breathing sharply as the perfume left his lungs and was replaced by that familiar tang of damp wood that he was so accustomed to. Doc and Sunrise were where he had left them and he felt like joining them, so he wandered down and sat on the floorboards with his back up against the banister.

'Hidy-do, ladies,' he said. 'Mind if I sit?'

'Join us.'

There was a squeaking and a rattling from upstairs and then the sound of footsteps on the floorboards as someone walked across the ceiling. It echoed and quivered through the infrastructure and July rolled his eyes.

'Is that Room 3?' he asked.

Doc and Sunrise nodded at him sheepishly.

'It's very audible, ain't it,' said July. Then he caught the significance of such a revelation and kept schtum about it thereafter, sensing the palpable discomfort surrounding him. 'Has Miss Livingston explained to you her reasoning for coming all this way, Doc?'

'No?' said Doc.

'I think perhaps Doc can age a few years before she hears of such traumas,' said Sunrise.

'You told it so well, is all,' said July.

'My life has been vivid,' nodded Sunrise.

'Please tell it,' said Doc.

'I like you very much, Doc, and I would like to tell you how I came to be here. But I think that, Mr Slade, it's your turn to tell a story, seeing as I poured out my heart and soul to you first.'

'Must everything be bought and paid for?' July asked wistfully.

'In this world, yes,' Sunrise said. 'I don't believe I owe you anything anymore, do I?'

'No, I guess you don't.'

She beamed a honey smile and clasped her handsome hands together in a tight bind. There was no denying her charm and thus no denying her request. Doc, on the other hand, well, anyone would say no to her and they would move along quickly afterward, but there was something different about her today. She was smiling more and she was less restrained in her pose, as though the ropes had been cut from her and the ceiling lifted above. There was certainly less about her that was repelling. July was pleased.

'Right,' he said. 'Would you like to hear of my greatest achievement? The pride that cometh before the fall?'

'Leave out the fall at the end as I'm in no mood for tragedy,' said Sunrise.

'You'll find it out soon enough,' said Doc, 'everyone in town's had an earful about old July's broken heart.'

July's jaw dropped and he stared at Doc, who blushed like a rose and appeared to momentarily take on the form of a hangdog.

'I'm so sorry,' she whispered. 'That was awful mean of me.'

But July was delighted with her audacity.

'I ought to work on that,' he said, finding movement in his body again and feeling a smile touch his lips. 'But it's true, I have it in me to be absolutely insufferable, so let me be talk of a time when I was admirable, and perhaps Sunrise's impression of me won't be so tainted by the time she leaves town.'

'I reckon that's a smart idea,' said Sunrise. 'But is having a place like the Pig's Itch during a time like we are living in fill you with pride?'

'I break the law and I get people inebriated,' July shrugged. 'It's pretty good, I guess, but that is not my greatest achievement, oh no.'

'Come on, get to it.'

July began a story that kept the broken halves of his heart from losing one another. Often he told it to himself to help him remember that he was not entirely worthless, and in doing so he kept himself alive. The story was the essence of his positive existence; a small fraction of his spirit but the fraction that allowed him to constructively affect the world. Without it he was the wreck of a man that wandered behind the bar when Mélanie was in for drinks; the shell that kept always to the same side of his half-empty bed; the semblance of a human being who was often now impassive when listening to Chopin or Mozart. Without this story July was dead, but of course he did not caveat the tale with this detail because he didn't want to make Sunrise or Doc vomit or groan. So instead he pressed on.

It began with a lonely French flower called the Lune Solaire, the seeds of which July had procured from Mélanie's father Léo upon their arrival in town. He was a botanist and he told July that he would need the hundreds that he had provided because the flower was stubborn and pernickety and thus July would likely fail in growing it time and again. Not only this, but the flower was so greedy that success in growing one would render it impossible to grow another within a distance seen by the naked eye. It drew the rarest nutrients from the soil and it did so in scores. Once one had grown there it would be alone until the time that it came to die. But July had been a competent florist by this time despite his youth, so he scoffed at the botanist. He saw his forewarnings as a challenge; an affront to July's proficiency and hence a rallying call. July would grow a garden of Lune Solaire and rightly laugh in the face of Léo.

Léo also believed that Lune Solaire needed consistent moonlight as well as sunlight for the duration of its growth in order to survive, and so anything less than clear skies during the lunar phases of waxing gibbous, full moon and waning gibbous would destroy its chances. That was how it got its name, he said. He handed the seeds to July and away July went, protecting the seeds with his life as he crossed town back to his home. This was a time before July had acquired the Itch and so he had the freedom enough to focus on his gardening, which was convenient considering the task ahead. The Lune Solaire would require his utter devotion and he intended to give it, but July first wanted to corroborate Léo's caveats. From New York he ordered a range of encyclopaedias and even branched out into floriography and rare symbology when researching Lune Solaire, and what little he did find confirmed what Léo had said. In fact it seemed that the botanist had spared him the horrible truth of the matter: that the chances of growing such a flower at all were well-nigh impossible. It seemed to be the only living organism on earth that preferred not being alive.

But July was not deterred and he began his task with feverish excitement and a stubbornness all of his own. He vowed that he would not be beaten by the botanist or the books or the Lune Solaire itself and told of his intentions to everyone he spoke to, leading to his story reaching all the way up the west coast. He consulted with a number of meteorologists from Los Angeles as to when would be an ideal time to plant the Lune Solaire and a Tuesday afternoon in mid-summer was eventually decided upon. July and his team believed that the long dog days of summer would be followed by cloudless nights of bright moonlight. A pedologist from Portland heard tell of July's endeavour and travelled down with a Conestoga wagon filled with specialised soil that the lady had spent weeks preparing specifically for this purpose. With the day fast approaching July was finally prepared, and he was not a moment late with the planting of Léo's seeds.

For two weeks he waited and on the final day of the final phase of the recommended lunar cycle a stem appeared from the soil. It was like any other stem and its early leaves were like all other leaves, but to July it was verification of his coaxing the most stubborn of beings into doing his bidding. Many people in town celebrated with him and flattered him to no end. July felt his hubris rise and rise with every complimentary word or pat on the back. It was at this time that Mélanie - who had hidden herself in Léo's house while perfecting her English - made herself known to the town. July immediately set his sights on acquiring her affection, although he would wait until the Lune Solaire had bloomed before allowing distraction to take a hold of him. In no time at all that was exactly what happened, and a tumbling array of fragrant petals - snowy and velvety and blossomy and weeping - had appeared in the sepal. It was dazzling to behold and yet July felt a niggling headache growing at the back of his skull and it caused a fury in him.

It was that only one flower had grown that he was angry. Léo had not written off July's chances of growing a single Lune Solaire flower; only of growing a family of them together. It was a stubborn flower but more significantly it was a lonely flower. So while the folks around town were commending July's spirit, application and accomplishment, there was a darkness enclosing itself around July as his insecurities protruded from his surface of arrogance. It kept him awake at night that he could only grow one of these bewitching organisms, and it kept him from pursuing Mélanie despite that she seemed lonesome in town. He desperately wanted to talk to her but his desire for success in the realm of botany had infested itself in his essence and was dancing in his waking and sleeping thoughts.

Then July began to drink harder than ever. He was already drunk every night because of the War but now he was drunk before noon every day too. The slender boy he had once been was mostly incapable of absorbing the alcohol he consumed and he wished to consume all the alcohol in the world. His headaches he attested were a result of some malignant abscess, though the doctors couldn't figure out what it was and so gave him morphine, which quickly came to replace the alcohol. As the weeks drew on July expected to kill himself either accidentally or deliberately, but in his haze of intoxication and depression July missed the empty skies that came around in early September. They passed him by like birdsong. Hot afternoons filled with long shadows and dry adobe preceded boundless darks of stars and moon, but July only saw the four walls of his bedroom and sweated only because he was dying.

He was dragged out of bed by Willie Bridger because something wonderful had happened outside. A second Lune Solaire had arrived mere inches from the first. July wept and the town cheered once more, only they were not as excited as they had been the first time because the miracle had already occurred in their eyes, but not to old July. This was the true vindication of his efforts and the summit of his achievements.

The Lune Solaire was neither stubborn nor lonely anymore, and soon enough it offered up a second rainbow of petals and pistils to compliment the first.

'It was as though the sky had breached and a hand had come down to intervene with the world around me, only it was not God's hand. It was my hand. I had ignored the laws of nature and they had bent to accommodate my wishes.'

Inside July's heart a clenching had unfurled and his shoulders had become loose. He noticed that his back straightened and his headaches went away. His days of milk and honey were finally upon him and he felt a desire to stand in the sun with his flowers and protect them. Community spirit led to a volunteer guard rotation to watch over them while July had to work. He slept in the flowerbed for weeks. Suddenly he was a different man and felt all the better for it. He approached Mélanie at the soirée and they eloped to Belle Rive.

'And then the fall?' asked Sunrise, but she likely knew the answer to that already.

'Do you believe in soul mates, July?' asked Doc.

'How could I not?'

'Hm.'

'Have you read *The Symposium*?' asked Sunrise.

'What do I look like to you?'

'Aristophanes suggests in it that the reason we crave the love of another is because we were originally born with four arms, four legs and two heads,' Sunrise explained. 'Some had two sets of male wibbly parts, some two sets of female wibbly parts and the others with one of each. We were mighty powerful and our bodies were round and we were threatening even to the gods, so much so that our pride got the better of us and we began climbing Olympus to put it to the test. Though Zeus considered killing us all he knew that this would mean no more tributes and so he decided to split us all down the middle, ensuring that we were no longer a threat and also that the gods would receive twice the tributes. And it is because of that act that we humans seek the love of another; that we seek to feel whole in the arms of our own true love. We are merely trying to reunite with that other half.'

'The Greeks sure sound crazy,' said Doc. 'Imagine if I had another set of arms. Oh, boy! I reckon I could do my pantry chores while playing the yoyo in the living room at exactly the same time.'

'But originally Zeus flipped our heads around which meant that our private parts on the back of us. Imagine that!' pressed Sunrise. 'All you boys would have had little tails! And when a person found their other half they were embrace them and hold them very tightly. It was all we could do to be united and it would lead us to die of starvation because we would never leave this union. And so Zeus had our wibbly parts put on the front of our bodies so that we could... you know... with one another.'

'What?' said Doc.

'It'll make sense one day.'

'If you're unlucky,' added July.

'And so this allowed us to be sufficiently fulfilled without having to hug forever.'

'Why, this is surely baloney!' said Doc. 'What proof have you got?'

'Aristophanes said the navel marks the footprint of the separation; the only place on the body that acts as a memoriam to our lost other. Of course it is all absolute nonsense but it is not without merit. Aristophanes was contented with and even admiring of fairies and lesbians. That cannot be said about Coolidge or any modern leader. And it could perhaps be a comfort to you, July. Should you continue to feel that Mélanie is the one for you then perhaps you should convince yourself that Aristophanes was right. In which case if Mélanie does not desire you then she is not that other part of you. She cannot be your one.'

'So that is to say that love is reflective and not complimentary?' asked July after a minute of intense concentration.

'I suppose that would be the argument,' admitted Sunrise. 'But to lose half of yourself would not necessarily be to lose a half that is identical in all ways to the one that you keep. Perhaps the other half is very different and so the love shared between the two can still be complimentary. In fact that half might be entirely opposite to your own. That could be why opposites sometimes attract and why sometimes they don't.'

'And what if you never find that other half?' asked July.

Sunrise seemed to sour and deflate.

'I don't know,' she admitted.

'Perhaps some of us were not born with another half,' suggested Doc. 'Perhaps we just see everyone else searching for their other half and then we think that we ought to do the same.'

'I guess it all just means that love is depravity,' said Sunrise.

'You two really know how to cheer up a sucker,' said July.

8

What made Hampstead particularly pleased with himself today was that he had figured out how to make it up to Doc Bellingham without the help of that useless dud Bitsy. She had weaselled that horrible obscenity out of him and given him a bit of food for his troubles. He was sick and tired of people thinking that he needed food. He was independent enough to feed himself. Hell, Hampstead was responsible enough to feed all of his friends thrice a day if he could keep track of their movements a little better. His best friend Tuna was particularly tricky in that respect; always on the move and always up to some fiendish scheme or another. These days he was investigating an establishment on the outskirts of town called the Rag Doll. Always there were strangely-dressed women in and around it and there was a constant cycle of suspicious-looking fellers coming in and out, sometimes doing their best to keep their faces covered.

The investigation really appealed to Hampstead, who very much doubted that the Rag Doll was a covenstead as Tuna hypothesised. It seemed that Hampstead was more grown-up than Tuna because Tuna still believed in witches and ghouls and the like. But Hampstead had pressing matters to attend to. He had procured Doc's trusty ballcap and he intended to return it to her as soon as he could - although he decided against doing it at the schoolhouse because his friends might see him do it and barrage him with irritating interrogatives. So he went to find Mr Bellingham in the hope that he could direct the boy in the right direction, though Hampstead was uneasy about going near the planetarium.

He would go to wherever Doc was, put the cap on the doorknob, knock on the door real loud and then run like hell. As long as she saw him from afar then all was well - he just didn't fancy talking to her.

On his stroll that late afternoon he nearly soiled himself. It was not that he was full from the meatloaf and muffins luncheon he'd stolen from the cafeteria, but that he was given such a horrible surprise that he momentarily lost control of all motor functions. How he stayed on his feet he never figured out. A small crowd had gathered around the federal bank and were murmuring up a storm amongst themselves. Hampstead pushed his way through and saw the most terrible, terrible thing that he could have imagined. A word - a bad, bad word - had been painted onto one of the columns, stretched only halfway around it so Hampstead didn't have to crane his neck to see the full thing. He knew immediately what had happened and for a moment time stood still and he left his body altogether. Somehow he seemed to maintain a number of vantage points simultaneously, each with a good view of Hampstead's body, which was pasty and motionless among the horrified crowd.

When he returned into his physical form Hampstead pulled the ballcap low over his face and walked, jogged and then all-out sprinted from the scene. What was Bitsy playing at? Why had she done that to him? It had torn old Hampstead apart to spell out that profanity and now it was being paraded around without his consent. Hampstead worried that Bitsy might have signed the obscenity off with his name. Perhaps he had been in such shock that he had failed to notice it. But what would Bitsy get out of that? Even though it seemed like nothing Hampstead was still frightened to death. It seemed that the old she-devil was doing everything in her power to make his reconciliation with Doc a struggle.

After what seemed an age and a century to boot Hampstead finally arrived at the dome site. He was so flustered by his earlier ordeal that he didn't even get the heebie-jeebies from being there. The first thing that occurred to him was that he was no architect; the planetarium building was nearly complete after all. How the hell buildings got made he would never understand.

'Stay back, kid,' said a friendly voice. Mary Harper, Doc's auntie, approached from the site with a hammer in hand. She was sweaty and gruesome but Hampstead was glad to see a warm face. She called out for Charlie and Charlie trudged over in his overalls, an axe wielded mightily over his shoulder.

'Hidy-do, Hampstead,' he said.

'Hidy-do, Mr Bellingham, Mrs Harper,' said Hampstead.

'Ain't that my daughter's cap?'

'Why, yes. I was hoping that you could direct me to her location so that I could return it to her.'

'Why do you have her cap?' A wry smile had appeared on Charlie's face.

'I stole it off some dame - not sure who. She was carrying it around near the derrick, so I cornered her and nabbed it. Now I would like to return it.'

'Tell you what, why don't you give the cap to me, and I'll return it to her. It was stolen from someone who was returning it to her, so it's probably best that she never finds out who did the stealing. Now, I'll give you the benefit of the doubt and assume that you did steal it for the reasons that you're explaining to me, but I can't guarantee that she'll do the same. Doc's more like her mother: a worrier. Sometimes she can't see the best in people because she always figures that they're up to something malevolent. Me, well, I reckon you mean well.'

'That I do, sir!'

'I'm glad to hear it, kid.'

But Hampstead felt the need to prove it. There was something about old Mr Bellingham's face that needed assuring of Hampstead's moral nature.

'Now, I can tell you're a good man, Mr Bellingham,' Hampstead said. 'I don't know you so well, but I can tell. There's something about you. So let me recommend you don't go anywhere near the bank today. It might cause you great distress if you do. Please keep away from it, and if you see Doc then please tell her that ought to do the same. It's a bad day for the chivalrous and the courteous.'

'O.K., I'll remember.'

'I just want to be neighbourly.'

'You're certainly that, Hampstead.'

'Far out. I guess I'll be on my way then. Nice seeing you, Mr Bellingham, Mrs Harper.'

'Kid, Doc told me that a coloured feller from the schoolhouse got his bellybutton out from atop a flagpole not so long ago. D'you know anything about that?'

'I sure as hell don't!'

'Well, I'm glad to hear it, because a feller that wants to charm a lady should know better than to show his bellybutton to her from atop a flagpole, right?'

'He sure should,' said Hampstead. He stood thoughtfully for a moment, then said quietly: 'What would you tell him would be a better method, Mr Bellingham?'

'He should talk to her,' said Mr Bellingham.

'I doubt he'd be brave enough to do that,' said Hampstead. 'Anyway, I'll be seeing you, Mr Bellingham. Nice job with the planetarium.'

'See you, kid.'

(ii)

There was time left in the day to fill and so Hampstead decided he would pick a bone with the hellcat. He guessed she'd be at the municipal hall but he was so riled up that even if she wasn't he'd walk around town all day and night to find her and give her a good old-fashioned dressing-down. When he arrived at the hall Mélanie lifted him off his feet and gave him the tightest squeeze he'd got since his father died. He'd never seen her so happy and he momentarily forgot about his blind rage at Bitsy, but Bitsy was smiling too and also gave him a hug, though not with quite the same ferocity. Hampstead was all disorientated, as was becoming a fixture of today.

'Something truly terrible has happened,' said Mélanie, her voice thick with exhilaration and Frenchness. 'I'm so happy!'

'It's perfect,' said Bitsy.

'What? What the hell are you screwballs talking about?' asked Hampstead.

'Somebody wrote something truly offensive on the sundry store,' said Mélanie. 'Also at the bank and also on the false front of the hardware place. The same abhorrent word in three different places.'

Bitsy had a smug grin on her face.

'What's so good about that?' asked Hampstead, focussing on her.

'It means we have something to fight for,' said Mélanie. 'Something has gone wrong in town and we can fix it. We can crack down on vandalism. There's still a need for our Bitsy, Hampstead!'

'You're a dang-near perfect-looking lady, you wackadoodle. Everyone loves a foreign beauty. Even I was taken the first time I saw you and I've got high standards. I ain't ever even kissed a girl for my high standards. So don't tell me that you got no purpose, because you do!'

Then he glared at Bitsy.

'What the hell's gotten into you?' asked Mélanie.

Hampstead's daggers softened and he breathed out through his nose. A proper gentleman doesn't hold a grudge, he reminded himself.

'I'm just feeling sore today,' he mumbled.

'Would some sewing cheer you up?'

'No.'

'Would you do it anyway? We'll take you for supper afterwards, Hampstead. That's fair, isn't it, Bitsy?'

'Yes. I'll buy us all food, and maybe you can ask Mélanie about that thing that you were asking me about recently?' suggested Bitsy.

'I've already it figured it out.'

'Something else?'

'Let's just get rid of that horrible word,' said Hampstead, then quickly adding: 'whatever it is.'

'Sure.'

For a few minutes they sat uninterrupted. Bitsy came to and from the piano while Mélanie listened and swooned. Hampstead worked the threads diligently and found comfort in being able to concentrate on a single thing, although the stitching of the 'U' in 'FOUR' proved disinclined to withdraw from the canvas, at least for a time. When he was done he unveiled the banner to the team.

VOTE FO R BITSY. SHE WILL STOP BAD LANGUAGE ON PUBLIC PROPERTY.

'*Voilà*! I fixed my mistake,' he said to Mélanie, who made no effort to thwart herself from smiling. The three of them collected a ladder from the utility room and set about fixing the banner to the pillars on the arcade outside the hall. It draped across it perfectly and for a while afterwards they simply stood and marvelled at their finished work. Bitsy gave Hampstead a pat on the head and a quiet congratulations, leaving Hampstead with no choice but to be absolutely forgiving of all that she had put him through.

'How are we actually going to stop this vandalism nonsense?' asked Mélanie.

'Is there something to be said for us perhaps letting it run wild for a time?' said Bitsy. 'Only if the town is desperate will they truly appreciate what we do.'

'Seems a bit hypocritical, no?'

Bitsy shrugged.

'We should acknowledge it. The banner is a start, but we need the town to know that we're on it. We'll speak to people over the coming days; tell them that they ought to remain vigilant and let us know if they see anything suspicious or outright incriminating. That way people know who to look to for help in spite of the fact that the problem is ongoing.'

Hampstead wandered over to the schoolhouse and jimmied the window to his homeroom with a crowbar he had once procured illegally from the carpentry store. This trespassing he did regularly in order to steal arts and crafts and the like because with them he could build small trebuchets and slingshots and, once, a shoestring violin. Inside he grabbed for the nearest chair and tossed it out onto the drive outside, followed by the two next closest. He slotted them one on top of the other and then dragged them all the way back to the hall and offered one to Mélanie and one to Bitsy. Turned out that they had been worried sick when he had just ambled off without letting them know.

'You don't have to worry about me; I'm the most independent boy I know,' Hampstead reassured them.

Bitsy smoked and Mélanie drank something from her canteen. Hampstead ate an Abba Zabba and practiced his belching. It quickly became apparent that there would need to be further alterations to the banner when passing folks kept asking them what democratic process they ought to be voting in. Some hadn't even heard of the Nineteenth Amendment, which made Hampstead laugh, but he stopped laughing when Bitsy ordered him back inside and he had to spend another twenty minutes removing more thread from his magnum opus of sewing. Truly it had been desecrated now.

BITSY. WILL STOP BAD LANGUAGE ON PUBLIC PROPERTY.

'Bitsy will stop bad language on public property,' Mélanie read aloud.

'Remind me what the point of all this is again,' said Hampstead, shaking his head and stewing over the cut he'd given himself on his fingertip. He was right keen to rat Bitsy out to Mélanie but thought better of it considering what he'd been feeling the past few days. But still it made no sense to him that Bitsy herself would create a problem that she planned to solve. Hampstead believed that a person should only make problems if they're keen on the consequences.

(iii)

When Bitsy was a kid she loved to cause trouble just like Hampstead, only Hampstead was calculated whereas Bitsy had been delusional. Hampstead didn't crave the love of anyone in particular - that Bitsy had noted - but Bitsy had always wanted to impress and dazzle. Yet for many years of her adolescence she had persistently mistaken attention with adoration. For Bitsy there was no distinguishing between a reprimanding and an acclamation because both were given to her and that meant that she was not ignored. When she was eight she had gone to the photography emporium and asked them to take a picture of her genitals because she knew that it would cause a scene. When she was nine she had meticulously poured hot coffee all over the couch in an attempt at artistic expression. At eleven she had booted a chicken so hard that for a moment or two she believed it had overcome its flightlessness. Often she still had nightmares about that incident.

The boy Hampstead knew that if he caused trouble he would get trouble and that trouble was no good thing. How he had learned it so early on Bitsy had no idea. Sometimes Hampstead helped others out and other times he made life a living hell simply because he felt like it; it never had anything to do with how others perceived him. In that sense he truly was very independent. Bitsy was a bit green about it but wanted to keep him around so that she could learn from him. There were better sewers in town but Hampstead was unique. She had never seen him embarrassed before. In fact this trouble he was having - the trouble that Bitsy declined to help with at the beanery - was the first time she had ever seen the boy socially dishevelled. Perhaps that was partly why she hadn't wanted to embrace it: it threatened to ruin her perception of Hampstead.

For most of her teenage years she had lived in the spare room above the stenograph office downtown. Her father was a senator and her mother a travelling sales representative, and both of them been quite content to leave Bitsy to her own devices for weeks at a time prior to Bitsy defenestrating herself from the top floor of their house. She had intended to land with a combat roll, just as her father had taught her, but it went a little awry and she broke both wrists and a vertebra. The rehabilitation took months and the marshal decided that Bitsy ought to live with a more present group of people, so he picked the journalists at the local paper. It didn't exist anymore but at the time it was perfect for Bitsy, who had no money for rent but could earn her keep as a copyeditor. She spent a great deal of time shadowing the political correspondent Miller Forbes, who first fanned the flame for Bitsy to follow in that line of work. Even being born into a political family hadn't done that.

The new life benefitted everyone because it meant that Bitsy's parents no longer had any real responsibility back in town and so made plenty more money away from it. Her father met every prospective lobbyist in the country and her mother sold to every consumer. Bitsy didn't complain because she figured her parents just weren't meant to be parents. The newspaper was an excellent place to learn that all press is not necessarily good press, and so she started fixing up her act. She liked impressing the writers and the editors and grew to realise that pissing them off would do little tangible good for her. Whereas before she would create havoc and her parents would have to come back home and watch over her, now she would be put in isolation and often denied her supper. Only in positive action would she be rewarded at the stenograph office.

When Bitsy returned from college in Michigan she expected that she would revolutionise town and turn it into an Eden. She had spent three years contemplating its inequalities and its injustices and she knew how she could fix them, even without federal restructuring. But when she discussed the wage gap and Jim Crow and disenfranchisement she was met with tutting and scoffing. Without a collective movement there was no real way for change and Bitsy came to feel quite inadequate, eventually taking up residence above the stenograph office again, where she quickly became a junior editor. Yes, she helped Charlie Bellingham and the Bridger twins drive the heat out of town, but that was much more them than her. Bitsy had once had designs on becoming a beloved insurrectionary but had fallen way, way short, and now the thought was far less tantalising.

The Volstead Act passed a few months after Bitsy started as junior editor. She suddenly saw an opportunity to better things for the people in town, so contacted her father in Washington D.C. and asked him for help. Bitsy had learned from some of the reporters at the paper that many agents in the IRS were unhappy with their wages and were inclined to accept bribes in exchange for turning the other cheek. Many were imbibing what they confiscated. Bitsy wrote some more letters and sent some telegrams and eventually town was assured of its immunity by her father, much to the delight of July Slade and his little band of bootleggers. In fact there was no shortage of celebration in the months that followed and Bitsy was heralded as something of a hero.

A few years later and there was a local county crackdown on speak-easies and Bitsy this time had to travel to D.C. in order to retain protection for the Itch. One of the agents joined Bitsy on the journey back home and filled an entire chuckwagon with July's moonshine, but July was more than happy to provide, considering the circumstances. It was then that the town gathered together to celebrate Bitsy's contribution to both business and morale, leading to the unanimous decision that Willie Bridger ought to contact his acquaintance Edwin Hubble, requesting that a star be named after their very own Bitsy.

After Hampstead told Bitsy the cuss word Bitsy got a new lease of life. Suddenly she was able to indulge in the reckless tomfoolery that she once got herself into when she was little, whilst also being able to gain appreciation from the rest of town. When she first wrote the word she went and devoured a rare steak and gravy, then a second helping. When she wrote it a second time she had to go for a long walk afterwards. After the third time Bitsy simply collapsed into bed and slept a good ten hours without dreaming of anything. But what felt especially good was not vandalising the property of others - but removing the vandalism that she had done.

Mélanie persuaded Bitsy that they ought to stamp their authority with vehemence rather than wait it out. They filled up their buckets with water and rags and dragged them to the bank. There was no one coming near it, but Bitsy could see the faces of the clerks in the window light up when they saw the approaching saviours and it gave her an adrenaline like she had not experienced in a long time. They got to work and within twenty minutes the paint was cleaned off the property and the job was done. The clerks and the guards came out and cheered and by the evening the place was busy again. Bitsy desperately wanted to tell Mélanie what the truth of it was but Mélanie seemed jovial enough as it was - what was the point in upsetting her?

Once all three exhibitions had been cleansed Mélanie accompanied Bitsy for a drink at the Pig's Itch and they celebrated merrily, only Mélanie drank quicker and harder than Bitsy and Bitsy felt comparatively inept. She accused Mélanie of cheating through her being French but Mélanie only answered by requesting more chartreuse from Mr Cricket. Bitsy found one of the boarder-cum-barmen who was very attractive. And Bitsy felt her heart quicken as he approached with a sheepish smile plastered on his face. He had a wide and chiselled jawline, stained yellow hair and the widest pupils that Bitsy had ever seen. Everything about him looked rather good at that moment.

'What is your name?' Mélanie asked him.

'Cosmo,' said the waiter.

'Cosmos?'

'Cosmo,' said Cosmo.

'A shame,' said Mélanie, 'this one here is a star.'

'You are Mademoiselle Celestine?' he asked.

'Mrs Monroe, *oui*,' said Mélanie.

'Mr Slade's fiancée?'

'Once, *oui*. Now of another.'

'*That* is a shame,' Cosmo smiled delicately at Mélanie, though Bitsy was feeling the moonshine a little too firmly to be sure of his intentions. He poured them some more drink and then waltzed away, careful to turn back every so often from either behind the bar or indeed when he went out to serve customers.

'You are lucky,' said Bitsy. 'He's got one helluva face. Why is it that you are married and can still receive such attention and yet I, a bachelorette, cannot draw an eye for more than a moment?'

'Ha! I did not think you were interested, Bitsy.'

'I am interested in having someone interested in me. But you don't seem interested in anyone at all! Your husband is away most weeks of the year and yet you are not even a little intrigued by the attention of a dapper gentleman. You could have your way with any of the men here. Sure, some aren't too delectable, but why won't you even acknowledge it? Is it a burden?'

'Firstly, this is July's place, no? I am not here to insult him; I am here to patronise his establishment.'

'Secondly?'

Mélanie shrugged.

'Like you said: I'm not interested.'

'And thirdly you do not want to betray your husband?' Bitsy raised her eyebrows.

'Sure, why not.'

A girl of mixed race appeared at the table looking gracefully awkward. She was so tall and slender that she seemed to be swaying despite that they were indoors, and she had a nasty bruise on her face.

'Doc!' cried Mélanie.

'Oh boy, Mademoiselle Celestine, it's good to see you, but right about now July is up a creek without a paddle,' said Doc. 'The poor man misses you so and I just don't know how to deal with it. He's had a lot to drink today, you see. He, Sunrise and I were playing ping-pong and the only way we could persuade Mr Hale to join was through busting out the drinks, and let me tell you, I've never felt quite like this before. We were playing doubles but honestly it became more like quadruples. I've never felt *anything* like this before.'

Mélanie was lost for words.

'Go on,' said Bitsy.

'Hey, Miss Bitsy. Still no word on your star but I'll be visiting the telegraph station tomorrow, on my honour. So, Mademoiselle Celestine, poor old July, he saw you come in with Miss Bitsy just now and it cut him up worse than I ever seen anyone. He keeps talking about how tough it's been since you left. He says: "I spent all my years waiting for her and then waiting for her to come back", or something to that effect. He remembers the sound of your heartbeat. I said to him, "Mr Slade, every heartbeat sounds the same. It could be someone else's heartbeat for all you know", but he seems to think that it really is yours that he can hear in his head. He keeps on calling out for his "Eurydice".'

'That all sounds a little insufferable to me,' said Bitsy, following a few moments of stunned silence.

'Dang right he's insufferable, and not just a little, Miss Bitsy. But he's a good man, I reckon,' said Doc. 'Just cut up to hell and back.'

'I will talk with him,' said Mélanie.

'Are you sure?' asked Bitsy. 'It don't sound like a conversation I'd be too enthused to partake in.'

'He is a good man, as Doc says,' said Mélanie. She got up and thanked Doc for looking after July. 'If not my Orpheus.'

9

Doc's whuppings had finally relented in the days leading up to the annual soirée, so her bruises were about healed. It was Doc's suspicion that her father had done the legwork in persuading Momma to ease off, and had been so efficient that Momma was even willing to let Doc collect Pop-pop from the hill that afternoon. Pop-pop was grouchy and rigid because it was hours before nightfall but he gave Doc a customary hug and a squeeze of her cheek. When she asked him if he was excited he couldn't resist a smile because he, like most others, had fond memories of the soirée. He wanted to know all about Doc's new job.

'I'm working security details mostly,' said Doc.

'Huh?'

'Yeah. The new boarders upstairs got robbed - well, they didn't really; they only pretended to. But Mr Slade asked me to keep an eye out upstairs for any unbecoming or dubious behaviour, so that's what I've been mostly up to. It's real easy, I'll say.'

'So, you just sit around silently and watch the door? You don't do any talking or anything of the type... with people?'

'I guess that's what's in the job description,' said Doc, 'but mostly I just hang around with the new girl Sunrise. We play games and what not. She really is the cat's pyjamas, Pop-pop. We bump gums and usually Sunrise has a hankering for story-swapping or card-playing. Sometimes she gives me a little drink too.'

'She gives you drink?'

'Just an ickle, Pop-pop,' said Doc.

'So you *are* making friends?'

'Hell yeah I am. I'm even making friends with July, and he might be the loneliest man in the whole wide world. He might be even lonelier than I am, Pop-pop. He might be the loneliest man to ever live.'

'Oh, you never met my father. Or his father. Or my mother,' said Pop-pop with a wry smile. 'Loneliness has no consideration for time, Doc. It exists in spite of it. Maybe July should take comfort in that.'

'What kind of crazy comfort would that be, Pop-pop?'

Papa and Momma arrived separately to one another, each with a daughter respectively. Because the glad-rags that Doc had left at the haberdashery had never been found by Papa, Elsie looked a real freak-show, although at least the t-straps fitted her feet better than they had her sister's. Further up her body she had been garbed in an old shawl, prairie skirt and stupid stockings, but Doc knew better than to tease her. Not only would she be chewed out to no end by her mother but she would possibly get licks from her two sisters: an unholy triumvirate capable of inflicting limitless damage. So instead Doc smiled at her little sister and apologised once again. Momma nodded appreciatively.

Inside the hall a crude stage had been set up at the end where one might have expected a fireplace to be. Tapestries and carpets adorned the walls, and kerosene lamps gave the place a dull glow. Lots of people were there and everyone looked something special, including old Hampstead, who was donning a slim-fit jazz suit. The jacket was beige and the tie was striped, and on top of his grinning, stupid head there was a ridiculous homburg made of red felt, far too big for the boy and completely juxtaposing the rest of his outfit. Doc couldn't help but smile. In fact she smiled so much that her cheeks began to hurt. Hampstead caught her eye for a second and then looked away, perhaps blushing.

'Ooh, heck, there's Miss Livingston and Mr Hale,' said Doc, pointing Pop-pop in the right direction. Sunrise was wearing a gingham house dress and Mr Hale a pair of silly knickerbockers that Sunrise must have raided for him from July's lost-and-found. He looked ready for golf, not a dance, but Doc would have introduced them to Pop-pop if they were in the nude. She dragged the old man over and she noticed him limping a little on his left leg, which Pop-pop assured her was as a result of cramp.

'That is one fine handshake,' Sunrise told him. 'Nearly crushed my fingers, you did!'

'He doesn't know his own strength,' said Doc.

'It's an honour,' said Sunrise, shaking her hand better and grinning. 'I've heard a lot about you. You're the father of the west, apparently.'

'I'm not sure that I like that so much,' said Pop-pop.

'No?'

'Walter Hale,' said Mr Hale.

'William Bridger,' said Pop-pop.

'Heard you're building a planetarium. I've never been to a planetarium. I'd never heard of one.'

'I saw one in New York - that's what inspired me. It was the most incredible experience I'd ever had,' said Pop-pop.

'Even better than being under a clear sky?' asked Sunrise.

'There's something about a planetarium. It's as though you can reach out and touch the sky. You can't, of course, but you might feel closer than any hill will make you feel.'

'Perhaps one day you will actually be able to get out among them.'

'That would be swell, wouldn't it, Pop-pop?' said Doc.

'It sure would. Hell, I've thought about building an automobile or a freighter or such like for just that; "The Iron Horse for the Stars" I'd call it. But I'll be a dead man long before I can do that, long before. Yes, sadly I think that I will be in the ground sooner than I will be in the sky. A curse of being born too early, I suppose. One of many.'

The annual soirée was held at the ancestral home of Dwight Edgars, the grandson of a Tennessean slaveholder who came west during the Rush. The grandfather, whose name was Malachi, drove a buckboard all the way from Knoxville to the Sierra Nevada, carrying a dozen of his slaves in the back. This upset the many wayfaring frontiersmen already in California who had no free labour of their own. And because Malachi found such fortune in the mines the other 49ers colluded to have him murdered and his money taken from him to be distributed among themselves.

But Malachi was made privy to the conspiracy thanks to a tip-off from an antiabolitionist cotton farm owner from Louisiana called Gayle. Malachi moved south, built a grand manor house and continued trading slaves within the state borders long after the Compromise, never telling any of them that their subjugation was no longer permitted within the boundaries of state law. Malachi employed numerous small-time prospectors to sweat it out in the Sierra Nevada, all the while sitting on an ever-increasing fortune that he didn't have the smarts to spend on anything. And soon enough one of his prospectors got careless and let slip to an old-timey miner in Sutter Creek that he was working for Malachi.

Because the 49ers were still sore about the advantage the slaveholders had obtained in the gold fields they reignited their interest in having Malachi murdered. Knowing that his property was manned by a regiment of well-paid and highly-skilled mercenaries from Mexico and South America, the 49ers were forced to appeal to the law for the help. They did this by truthfully claiming that Malachi was still keeping slaves, and thus a posse of prospectors, marshals, sheriffs, deputies, generals and rangers was formed and the Edgars residence stormed. The mercenaries surrendered immediately and Malachi was strung up on a ponderosa half a mile south from the property. Long after his death the 49ers maintained vehemently that Malachi's killing was justice for his illegal and barbaric slaveholding, but on the placard roped over his shoulders they had written:

Here hangs Malachi, who had no regard for independent entrepreneurial spirit.

But though the prospectors managed to find much of Malachi's accrued wealth during the attack, there was nothing to be done about the almost invaluable property itself, which was then inherited by his only child, a daughter called Marguerite. This was after a long time before a state tribunal and then a failed appeal by the prospectors. And Marguerite was the child of one of Malachi's dairy workers - the slave girl Ida whom he had raped. So now the house was in the hands of a mixed girl raised as a slave and whose mother was a slave. And Marguerite thought the house was where the devil was, so she and her mother sought help from abolitionist attorneys and found a way to survive the no man's land of emancipation.

It later transpired that Malachi had a white son named Frederick back in Tennessee. But Frederick, though keen to buy the estate from Marguerite, had no intention of continuing his father's wicked legacy and demonstrated this by not making his relationship known to the law. He said that he was desperate to purchase the property and would do so for a price way beyond what Marguerite would ever hope for from an external buyer. There was also a willingness to pay remittances for as long Frederick owned it - alongside the weighty fee he would pay up front. And these remittances were paid still today by the late Frederick's son Dwight, who organised the soirée as a way of reaching out a hand to the descendants of his grandfather's slaves. It was an attempt to show that Malachi's legacy was destroyed. Or perhaps it was just to make himself feel more virtuous. Marguerite and the others did not know that the money Frederick paid them with was stolen from the cotton fields in the east. Perhaps if they had they would never have sold it to him and the property would never have been returned to the Edgars family. Malachi's final victory was that he had kept his slaves in the dark for so long that they struggled once brought into the light.

'If Dwight Edgars had any real backbone or moral resolve then he would turn this place into a negro school,' Pa was telling Doc. 'Instead it is up to the Negroes among us to make a Negro school, and this will take time and blood because we are the minority and we are unsupported. Dwight Edgars is content enough to see that we Blacks are given only industrial training because this will keep us in the dark. He told me so. I put my ideas to him and appealed to whatever nature he has. He cited Booker T. Washington but Booker T. Washington was naive. Not a third of Blacks your age are attending school on the regular, Doc, think on that. Not one of our race has ever been to Princeton. Never has there been an attainable ideal before the eyes of our children; one that they can be risen to by a curriculum particular to each soul. On a foundation of education they can rise, but I need more support from these people.'

And all of this Pa had said with great earnestness and a with a restless desperation. And all the while Doc wasn't really listening. She was watching Mademoiselle Celestine as she slowdanced with one dreamer after another, appearing unenthused and lonesome despite that there was not a one person in this room that was likely to refuse her hand.

'You know what I reckon, Pa?'

'What's that, Doc?'

'If every single person in the whole wide world thinks that you're extraordinary, I'll bet that feeling gets real ordinary after a time.'

Pa sighed having been at least half-hoping for engagement. But he would not fight with Doc tonight. He would keep dancing with her and Doc was relieved.

'I'll bet,' he said.

'You wish you were ordinary,' said Elsie, overhearing as she waltzed by with Hattie. The two looked thoroughly detestable and there was no doubt that she was feeling a real sourpuss about her appearance, and Doc was to blame.

'Say that again, I'll give you three licks and a boot to boot,' said Doc.

'Saw you dancing in front of the mirror this morning. You're a little strange creature. I reckon I saw you kiss yourself in the mirror once too.'

'Hey, that's a lie!' shouted Doc.

'Mwah! Mwah! Mwah! I'm Doc Bellingham and I like to kiss my reflection and also frogs!' teased Elsie, and Doc felt her father's hands cunningly tighten around her long arms so as to stop her from flying at the little sow-girl.

'Elsie, go,' said Pa.

'Mwah!'

'*It's amphibians in general!*' Doc snarled.

But the two sisters faded into the ballroom, leaving Doc seething and yet numb.

'Does Elsie not dance before the mirror?' she asked quietly.

'Perhaps, perhaps not,' said Pa. 'And if not then it must get very tiresome caring about what everybody thinks when nobody is watching, huh?'

'I guess.'

(ii)

Hampstead had done his absolute best to catch Doc's attention in the hall. He had put on his finest hat and got the craziest dining jacket he could possibly hope to find from the haberdashery. It was a little gift from Mélanie. Everything about him screamed whacky miscreant, and that was exactly what he wanted. Would Doc thing he was a bad boy? So far he'd shown her his bellybutton and appeared at the dance looking as dapper and spruce as any kid ever had. If she didn't think that he was independent enough to afford such clothing then she would have to assume he was bold enough to steal it. Either worked for Hampstead.

The two of them caught eyes and Hampstead sniggered to himself beneath the cap, but then did a double-take just as Doc looked away, for the grandiose figure beside her. It was only Mr Bellingham, but he looked the crispest, snazziest sheik to ever walk the land. Hampstead's jaw dropped and he almost cartwheeled his way over to the fine gentleman, who was owning the Ivy League look that Hampstead thought only college kids were capable of. He had never thought it possible for a man of Mr Bellingham's age to look so distinguished in such a conservative zoot suit. Yet here he was, a miracle of fashion.

'Hidy-do, Mr Bellingham,' said Hampstead.

'Hey, feller,' said Charlie.

'What's new?' asked Hampstead.

'The planetarium's coming along well, I suppose,' said Charlie.

'It's a mighty fine accomplishment, although I won't much fancy staying around past my welcome.'

'I think you're welcome anytime, Hampstead, once it's done.'

'I get a distinctly different impression, Mr Bellingham.'

'From who?'

'Mr and Mrs Screaming-Meemie,' said Hampstead, feeling the goosebumps on his arms and resisting the urge to shudder. 'They don't want me there, I swear.'

Mr Bellingham planted a big shovelly hand on Hampstead's head and rustled his tight knots of hair. Hampstead assumed it didn't feel too good against Mr Bellingham's hands, but then again Mr Bellingham's hands were likely made of maraging steel and spider silk, so who cared.

'Say, Mr Bellingham, how far do you reckon you can throw a softball? I know it's a little personal but I imagine you've got one helluva range on you, ain't that right?'

'Pretty far, I suppose,' said Mr Bellingham. 'Though I know someone who can throw a ball further than I can, believe it or not: Doc. Look at her arms and tell me she ain't built like a trebuchet. She'd make a great pitcher, I'd say.'

'She certainly is a trebuchet,' said Hampstead, but, unwilling to have his attention diverted, blustered on: 'but if you were to measure your range, what would you reckon you would get, say, in feet and inches?'

'Oh, kid, I've no idea.'

'I reckon I can do about thirty feet,' said Hampstead. 'But if you don't rightly believe me then you can come round whenever you like and you can make an assessment of your own. Hey, I know that face.'

'What face?'

'That face you're pulling, Mr Bellingham.'

'And what face am I pulling?'

'It's a "how *old* is this kid?" kind of face. I've seen them around plenty.'

'Yeah, I'll bet you have.'

'Ain't you gonna dance tonight, sir?'

'Perhaps with my Doc again, unless someone gets her first.'

'What about Mrs Bellingham?'

'We've got no chemistry do myself and Mrs Bellingham. It ain't much of a charming sight, us dancing.'

'She's dancing real well with the feller Mr Grant. What makes you suppose that you couldn't do as good as he is?'

Mr Bellingham said nothing but looked a little forlorn.

'Well, perhaps you oughta ask Doc then. I'd watch out that you don't trip over her wrists though,' said Hampstead.

'It's a very brave thing, to ask a lady to dance with you. It's a very *adult* thing,' said Mr Bellingham. 'Only the most prestigious of gentlemen ask for a lady's hand.'

'That's news to me,' said Hampstead, scrunching up his eyebrows. 'I always just assumed that the gentlemanly thing to do was to let the lady do the asking.'

'If only it were so easy,' said Mr Bellingham.

'I suppose I'd better be off. Maybe to mingle. Maybe to dance. Who knows,' said Hampstead, insisting on a handshake and then wandering off. For a while he paced the dancefloor and studied the made-up faces and mirrorball glimmers that reflected off their eyes. With each step he realised he was walking further and further away from Doc but he didn't care. It was much more advisable to keep his arm free. Desirability was pretty important if you were to look mature, and it was difficult to look desirable if you were taken. He found the back wall and put the sole of his foot against it by bending his knee. The back of his head gently pressed against it and he pursed his lips and wished he could smoke a cigarette, but his mother would likely freak. What a drag.

Doc was dancing with Willie and the guy playing the fiddle seemed to have orchestrated the whole piece around the dance rather than the other way around. He had never seen dance partners look so natural, which was strange because there was no way in hell that Doc should be able to dance with a body like that. More likely her arms and legs would make an acceptable set of monkey bars. Good for her, thought Hampstead. She was certainly beautiful in an unconventional kind of way, but he could not moon her in here because her father was watching, and because Hampstead felt pretty bad still about the whole bellybutton ordeal, even if he had come out of it a rowdy scallywag. What freaked him out about it was that he couldn't keep a check on his impulses. Although it was fun being so spontaneous it was also dangerous, and Hampstead had hoped for better from his inhibitions.

Willie Bridger and Doc eventually disentangled clumsily and the former clambered up on to the stage, receiving a rousing applause as he did so. Then everyone went quiet.

'I'm glad to be here,' he said, limping gingerly into position. 'Did anyone hear from Alma? Has she come? No? Not to worry.'

He gathered himself, clicked his neck and then yadda-yadda-yadda'd about Bitsy and the work she was doing about town to come down hard on vandalism. Hampstead was fuming, especially when the crowd erupted into chants about no more cussing and such like. Then Willie confirmed that the planetarium was coming along nicely and that he was very grateful to his family for helping to build it, but the crowd insisted that the mastermind ought not be modest. He accepted their pleas a little uncomfortably. But without the saucepan hands and tree trunk arms of Charlie Bellingham, Hampstead knew there would never be a planetarium.

(iii)

In knowing that Lester Monroe was still voyaging in the Pacific, July had felt a little ease in coming to the soirée tonight because he would not have to watch Lester and Mélanie fondle each other on the ballroom floor through the night. But what was infinitely worse than that hypothetical scenario was the actuality of Mélanie being fondled by every *vaquero* who could get her for a dance. She never once looked happy.

'Does she look sorrowful?' July asked Doc, tempting her to the parlour room with a cigarette. 'Or is that my wishful thinking, you reckon? I can't tell if I'm imagining it. I don't want her to look happy in the arms of so many men, so perhaps I'm tricking myself into thinking that she's gloomy?'

'July, it is rare to see someone look so sad,' admitted Doc. 'Believe me.'

'Yessum,' said July.

'Do you have a broken heart?'

'A what?'

'A broken heart,' Doc repeated.

'Gotta have a heart for it to break.'

'You're so blue. Is that what a broken heart is?'

'I don't know, Doc.'

This line of conversation did not fill July with optimism. He was suddenly edging for his cigarette to burn through as though he had thirty pairs of lungs.

'I might have a broken heart,' said Doc.

'Doc, you don't have a broken heart.'

'How do you know, July?'

'Well, what have you got to be broken-hearted over?'

'The boy Hampstead.'

'Did he give you the icy mitt?' asked July.

'Naw.'

'Then what?'

'I reckon he might like me and I reckon I might like him. But I don't reckon either of us knows what to do about it. It's such a troubling situation, July.'

'You're confused, clearly. You're probably just in love,' said July, finishing his cigarette and stubbing it out on the bureau's ashtray.

'But it hurts.'

'Yes, it does.'

'So how is that any different from having a broken heart?'

'Doc! Just forget about it, all right?' July cried. 'Gimme that.'

He snatched her cigarette and he finished it off in one drag and nearly threw up.

'Was it worth it?' Doc asked after a few moments of July's spluttering and choking.

'Yes,' wheezed July. 'Catch you later.'

Back in the reception hall there was an announcement being made by Dwight Edgars: it was about time for the Hourglass Dance. This was a tradition of the soirée and involved an unrestricted, unruly dance to a live band which came to perform *Der Ring des Nibelungen* in its ethereal majesty, though reduced from the fourteen hour standard to one that was a little over sixty minutes. And in that sixty minutes the guests of the soirée would dance in pairs. They would dance however they wished and were told to go for as long as they could. The last couple standing got their wages covered for two weeks by the estate and told to make use of that time as they pleaded. Most people just stuck around in town and enjoyed some time off work. No one had ever got to the end of *Der Ring*. Once big Johnny Poplar had a heart attack around the half hour mark, so for two years thereafter the Hourglass Dance had not featured at the soirée. But popular demand had reinstated it and it was arguably the staple of the event nowadays.

Everyone sought the arms of another. Barefoot Doc found Willie, Bitsy found Charlie Bellingham, Maggie Bellingham found Davey Grant, Hampstead found Mr Cricket, Sunrise found Mr Hale, Sidney was found by his mother. And Mélanie... Mélanie had seen July and was making her way towards him. July wanted to slip into the crack in the wall and hide there in perpetuity. No angel had ever struck such fear into a heart before. No creature floating so elegantly and delicately through the droves had ever silently forewarned such a doom as this. But July had nowhere to hide and no movement in his legs to boot. He watched dumbly as Mélanie arrived at his person and held out her handsome hand, which he stared at blankly.

'Let's dance, July,' she said, and July nodded. He took her hand and let her lead him through the myriad shadows and essences that apparently existed too. For that time he was floating with her because there was a cloud beneath his feet. He could see his legs moving, step after step, and yet there was a cloud beneath them and they weren't moving at all. Then Mélanie stopped and turned to him and fixed them both up into a closed hold. She didn't meet his eyes but merely straightened up, while July felt her fragrance hit his nose and choke him up. Into him went notes of honeyed tobacco and pearls of jasmine, spring blossom, French grass and soft leather. If July had been blind the smell alone would have conjured an almost entirely accurate picture of her in his head, only she would have been assuming a graceful arabesque on an empty stage before a sold-out theatre, and she would have been wearing a leotard and tutu and fitted canvas shoes that had a whispered shade of magenta.

The band began to play and so the dance commenced. July was sweating heavily and couldn't keep his head still. He could feel curious eyes on him. He wanted to look everywhere, until a glance from left to right saw his eyes catch Mélanie, who was now finally looking at him. And then July settled and he breathed again because it was those eyes that he could get lost in.

'But now we are in trouble,' he said. 'We have to dance awhile.'

'I want to,' said Mélanie.

'Why?'

'Because I want to. We have not danced in a long time.'

'Because you left me, Mélanie.'

'Yes.'

'This is cruel,' said July. 'If you care then you will tell me to go and sit down and will keep out of my sight for the rest of time.'

'I'm not stopping you,' said Mélanie, and July was reminded of how gentle her grip was and yet how powerless he was to refuse it. Her presence was his bondage; her touch his restraints.

'I can't,' he mumbled. 'But I can't keep going either.'

'Why not? Why not for me?'

'For you?'

'Yes, July. I want to dance. I want this moment. And I want it to mean nothing except for that it gives me the chance to get what I want.'

'Mélanie...'

'It is my choice and I want you to respect that and to humour me for this dance.'

'But the *Hourglass Dance*, Mélanie? Christ!'

'Someone else would have intercepted me and there is no one in this room that I would rather dance for such a stupidly long time with.'

'Don't say those things!'

'It doesn't mean anything, July. Do you think that is a declaration of my doubt - to say that I'd rather dance with you than some lecherous drunk that has already rubbed himself all over me tonight? Do you think that is an implication that I regret my leaving you? Don't be silly, July. You flatter yourself.'

'You're the love of my life. Is it not obvious how this will hurt me?'

'I don't care in this moment, July. For this moment I want to indulge myself and take what I want and I don't care of the consequences. I am always so restrained and contented. And my heart is broken for you always. But not right now. This is my moment to do as I please, and I please to dance with my friend.'

'Hear me, Mélanie. You are the love of my life. Have a heart!'

'Perhaps I am the love of this chapter of your life, July.'

'The love of my *life*,' July said.

'Perhaps you don't even love, July. Perhaps you only grieve.'

'They're the same thing!'

'You are such a wet blanket, it beggars belief!'

July scowled and Mélanie sensed victory:

'And you need not grieve anymore, you old fool,' she said. 'Think of all the things that you are living without now that I am gone. You don't have to eat Chicken á la Reine twice a week anymore. You don't need to worry about your weight. You don't need to worry about sleepless nights sharing that tiny bed. You don't need to brush your teeth as often. You don't need to hold in your gases. You don't need to care about what my father would think if he were still here. You don't need to quit smoking. You don't need to plan for the future. You are free.'

'I'll do you some better,' said July. 'Those improvements are merely tangible. What about how I no longer have my ego crippled by self-doubt and impotence? I no longer awake in a sweat because I have dreamed of letting you down. I no longer battle the unrelenting anxiety of losing you to another. I no longer circle thoughts of how best to please you, day-in and day-out, all the while knowing at the end of the day I can never do enough. I no longer fear the mornings in knowledge that I might wake up without you.'

Mélanie stared at July and her jaw hung a little.

'Then why the moping?' she asked.

'Because I would forsake all of these liberties and mercies for you to come back to me for a time. Hell, Mélanie, I would take the pain of losing you again if I could first hold you awhile.'

'You are holding me now.'

'And it is the happiest and the saddest that I have ever felt.'

July breathed and realised that they were still dancing. What moves they were performing he would never remember. Perhaps they were dancing in a way that was reminiscent of their talking, for that was all that had consumed July's mind and was thus surely how he was moving his body.

'The devil has known this dance,' he muttered.

'Then stop,' said Mélanie.

But July could not despite that he had no desire to win two weeks of freedom from the Pig's Itch. His face fell and he understood his defeat and it became painted on his face. If he had tears to cry then he would have cried them, but all his eyes would do now was look away from Mélanie's, whose gaze was nearing traumatic. When this parting of looks occurred Mélanie slowly released his hand and July knew that she had caught herself. For a moment they were the only pair separated in the entire town, but then Mélanie embraced him once more and it was to comfort him rather to satisfy herself, and July wanted to cry and cry until the Mojave needed rain no more.

10

Mélanie Celestine always had a hankering for food despite that her figure would suggest that she abstained from eating almost entirely. But what was greater than her hankering for food was her desire to watch and listen to others eating food. Something about it just gave her a tingle; a kick. Throughout their time together July had barely eaten a morsel because of his anxiety, so she had had to make a traditions out of it, such as Chicken á la Reine on Tuesdays and Thursdays. If he hadn't been anxious Mélanie suspected that he would probably have succumbed to obesity by the end of her relationship, such was her desire to watch him make short work of every edible item in the house. He had been on the end of all of her strings apart from that one - the only one she *desperately* wanted to pull.

Often Mélanie felt great shame about this fetish. She often invited friends out for meals at the Itch or the Two Crows or the Pie House and this was problematic for a number of reasons. It meant that sometimes she had to see July time and again and July could easily mistake that for a suggestive signal; intent to rekindle what they once had, when in actuality it was because the speakeasy's cook made notoriously crunchy and chewy foodstuffs. The fetish also made Mélanie dishonest. She would often bring her friends to restaurants on the pretence of comradery, only in truth to do it on the basis that she needed a fix.

Her husband Lester liked to inhale his meals and that was about all he was good for. Mostly he was away on some voyage or another and that suited Mélanie down to the ground. It was not that she was repulsed by him, in fact it was far from it; she thought him quite handsome and he had the most chiselled clavicles that she had ever seen. And also she knew that he had no desire to have sex with her, which was also ideal. Lester liked his boat friends a lot more than he liked Mélanie and Mélanie had known this from the moment she had first conversed with him and he had mentioned their illicit interpersonal activities with such vehement disgust that it could only have been out of shame.

In fact Lester had been the nonpareil choice of spouse. No longer was Mélanie courted by every cocky *garçon* in town, or at least for the most part. At functions and soirées the dreamers would try their hands, but that was the extent of it nowadays. The ring was a shield in that respect, so she wore it proudly and loudly and drew attention to it whenever she was approached by men made of eyes. And Lester was away for months at a time. And Lester didn't bed Mélanie when he was home which was wonderful because Mélanie didn't much feel like letting another man inside her ever again. So in a way the ring acted twofold as a guard: one from unwanted conversation and one of chastity. And of course Lester loved to eat meat like it was the rapture's eve, which was simply delightful for Mélanie, who had begun dreaming about the sight of the man at mealtimes.

If he ever fattened up then it would be collateral damage rather than a desired outcome. Mélanie had no wanting to see Lester - or anyone for that matter - become broad in the beam. She just wanted to see and listen to everyone eat, and that was her only acknowledged vice. She loved to hear others play musical instruments but that was harmless. She loved to dance and that was harmless. She loved to help Bitsy and that was harmless - mostly. She loved to chew the fat with the little one Hampstead and that was harmless. She loved to see town made better by its people and that was harmless. But the creeping desire to be around the hungry scared her a little.

So Mélanie practiced abstention. She took others for meals only if she had done a good deed and considered herself worthy of such a treat. She rationed her own food and kept herself in shape. It was easy enough because there was plenty that Mélanie wanted that she had gone without through her life. Most of the things she had been roped into had been against her will, even if she had not voiced this. It wasn't too difficult to do but every now and again she felt the tension rising to the surface and threatening to spill. It made her angry and then it made her despair. And often someone else suffered as a result, and at the soirée it had been July who had been dealt the bad hand.

It was difficult for Mélanie to explain why her itching for satisfaction had led her to demanding a dance off of poor July but she was sure it was that. All her life she had avoided and abandoned and abstained from what she wanted and maybe her love of eating was nothing to do with eating at all; maybe it was simply all that denial culminating in emotional savagery. She wanted to take advantage of someone in their moment of weakness because she was tired of restraint. When a lion escapes from the menagerie it tears its keeper apart, Mélanie imagined; hoped. That was the best explanation that she could summon and yet it did not help her to sleep easier in her big, empty bed.

So four days after the soirée Mélanie went to seek help for her affliction. She wanted to better herself, plain and simple.

'I have a thrill that is potentially problematic,' she explained to Doctor Wagner, the wiry son of a Scot with little patience for Europeans, least of all the English and French. But Mélanie suspected a softer interior to the gaunt man.

'And I am well-practiced in keeping it down,' she continued, 'but then the control I use to keep it down is no longer there to quash my selfish traits. I become cruel and unempathetic whereas usually I am kind and empathetic.'

'Yes, I've heard people talk of you as though you are one of God's angels, Mademoiselle,' said the doctor. 'You and this new lass whose name is Sunrise. She keeps pestering me. A good kid, no doubt, but incessant on watching me work and learning. Some are just born to be physicians, or so she thinks.'

'Nonsense; I am no angel,' said Mélanie. 'What can I do? How can I keep my impurities balanced? Why must it be one or the other and not neither?'

'Practice your breathing and do not waste my time again. I am a doctor and I am not a friend to ponder man's nature with over a beer. Nor am I God. Perhaps you ought to pray some, or repent in some way.'

Mélanie lowered her head and sighed audibly.

'You should know too,' the doctor said after a few moments, 'that you're entitled to your vices for as long as you do everything in your power to maintain your virtues. Understand?'

(ii)

To make money Mélanie used to moonlight at the bordello three towns over. She had chosen this particular drum because it was far enough from home to avoid familiar clientele and because there was a restaurant next door where she could invite her patrons for meals. At the bordello she had been the belle of the ball and the madam's cherished protégé, with only July initially knowing the truth behind her night-time escapades. Eventually July's insecurities got the better of him and he began making arrangements to get Mélanie away from the place, but Mélanie refused to work at the Pig's Itch for a number of reasons. Firstly there was the fact that she did not want to work for July. Secondly was the bizarre notion that selling a service to drunk men by being attractive and implicitly flirtatious was any better than prostitution. Thirdly was that she was Madam Blake's confidante at the bordello, and that meant she had someone she could depend on. She had never had a relationship like that before and she certainly did not have one comparable with July.

Eventually July and the Bridger twins got her out of the house and had fixed her up as a knocker-up about town. Mélanie was used to getting little sleep from her time at the bordello and so it suited her being an alarm call. The work didn't earn her much but neither did prostituting herself. It put the cherries and the biscuits and the cheese on the table while the remittances - thereafter translated into wages - that Bitsy received from her senator father put the bread and milk. Madam Blake died of some venereal disease not long after Mélanie quit, which was no surprise to Mélanie because, to her, Blake had always been dying along with half of the girls there. Not long after leaving Mélanie realised that she had probably been right to do so. But Lord was July insufferable about the whole ordeal. He wrote and read aloud his poems to Mélanie about her so-called reformation and rediscovered integrity, much to Mélanie's chagrin. She knew that he meant well but she wanted to stab him in the throat.

Many men and many fiancés might well have blackmailed Mélanie with the secrets of her past but July was above that moral depravity and Mélanie doubted it ever even occurred to him, even when she left him. What low standards she had that meant that she felt indebted to him! Only he and the Bridger twins knew the truth of what struggles she had undertaken prior to being a knocker-up. Perhaps the newsie on Municipal Road had his suspicions because Mélanie always requested the papers from the town where she had once worked, albeit only to look at the obituaries. Steadily the sight of more and more of her old friends' names appeared and soon enough Mélanie figured there weren't any left. They'd all died of the fever or been murdered. When entirely unfamiliar names started showing up she realised the entire clergy had been replaced. Then she stopped reading the paper and felt an unrelenting sadness.

And she explained to July why she was so blue and July decided to write some more poems. He began to play the troubadour and Mélanie's grief became his purpose, which Mélanie found to be somewhat strange. If he ever became some big city's poet laureate - as Mélanie truly believed was his desire - then perhaps they would be souvenirs of a time when she was close to notoriety. Though, on reflection, his poems were unmetered and uninspired. Mélanie had deliberately left *Poèmes Saturniens* and *Le Bateau Ivre* and *Les Fleurs du Mal* in places July would have been sure to find, then related to him the Parnassian politics that she found so intriguing. When she conceded that that particular line of education was to no avail in the quest to improving July's verse, Mélanie resorted to a pulpy retelling of Rimbaud's life and affair with Verlaine, but only at the point where the latter twice shot the former did July pay much attention. There was a sea of Symbolist and Decadent and Parnassian poetry stowed away in Mélanie's head and yet July pressed on without much care for any of it. Only Verlaine's *Marco* did he like. Mélanie recalled one of July's more hapless attempts at indulging his own hubris:

Here is my ivory girl.
For me there is no other
And for her I shiver and tremble because
so in love with her I am.
Beauty unknown since Eve saw Adam.

Since fair Saracens and Jewesses
Christians and godless angels
Since spirit and flesh and the grass in Provence,
and the tusks were cut and the milk pasteurised,
the nets of the veil transforming white sunlight on white skin.

The manna of her affection, lucky men oft find,
of the distant lands to which my heart sometimes follows,
is twined through the melodies
of a nightingale on a bough.
Here is a garden where flowers of lack grow in numbers.

In a jewel I rejoice and in her I lose my tongue.
Dumbly stutter and froth and teeter
on the brink, look down to the chasm,
sink.
And it is my ivory girl whose arms I find.

Of course July had never quite managed to get Mélanie under a white veil. Yet still he would ask insufferable questions such as: 'Have men historically loved as I have?' and 'Is this love my own? Or is it a love that transcends time and individuals and is shared, like a great cosmic web that we are all engulfed in?' and 'Could you tell my heartbeat from another's?'

After she left July Mélanie heard that the poor man hadn't picked up a pen for reasons other than to fill out inventory lists or invoices. She pitied him terribly at times because there was a connection still between them. Many millions had had their hearts broken throughout humanity's time on earth - a good number of them by Mélanie - but July she hurt with. But fortunately he was very pathetic and often wretched and this helped Mélanie from succumbing to her guilt and sadness. Never once did July really consider what Mélanie wanted and never once did he ask her if she was happy after they parted. Come to think of it, perhaps he had never even asked about it when they were together. He just basked in his adoration, took her to the pictures and didn't have sex with her, though the latter two of those things Mélanie did not complain about.

And then there was dear Bitsy who Mélanie longed to tell everything to. Bitsy was like no other; she did not court Mélanie and she did not understand why people did. To her all relationships were entirely practical and engaged with through the shared desire of self-betterment, in which sense she was very conservative as opposed to how she was politically - maybe. It was still difficult to tell what Bitsy actually believed in, but she had read *The State and Revolution* last year and wouldn't shut up about it for a while. But her mechanical thinking and feeling was so attractive to Mélanie that at times she couldn't quite believe that this person existed before her. To Bitsy the symmetry on Mélanie's face and the curvature of her breasts and the delicacy of her fingers were of no importance, and nor did they even exist in the first place. Mélanie was just a person to Bitsy; a vessel to carry her over the tides of self-repression and failure.

But Bitsy would never want to hear of Mélanie's past because that would make Mélanie a very real entity and Bitsy's view of her would be skewered. It was easier that she thought of her as how she saw her: a helping hand. And Mélanie liked that, despite that she often dreamed of a time where she could tell Bitsy where she had come from and where she was going to. July she could talk to but what good would that do anyone? Sure it might temporarily relieve Mélanie of her frustrations but they would only return later to her and all the while July would think that it meant something more than melancholia. Alma Bridger would understand but she never left her attic anymore. Willie Bridger kept to his hill and to the stars. There was no one who knew the truth of her past that she could discuss it with. No one in town was more coveted and yet more lonesome than Mélanie Celestine.

(iii)

Monday morning came with a choking dust and dry air. Through the streets Mélanie walked with her baton in one hand and a bamboo stick in the other. Once she had got Hampstead to fashion her a pea-shooter but the bullet had gone straight through the first window and shattered it, for which Hampstead felt very guilty. But Mélanie commended him on how well-designed it had been and told him truthfully that she was very sad to have to retire it so soon. She kept it under her bed because one day she would wreak havoc with it on all the men who opened their windows and doors to her while proudly revealing their tent poles underneath underwear.

Usually Willie Bridger would be on a pre-sleep run at this time of the day. He liked to do his best to keep fit and was always very polite to Mélanie when they inevitably ran into one another on their respective adventures. But today Willie was no where to be seen and Mélanie had a typically sullen time of it. No one likes being woken up for work in the morning, even at the call of an angel. Perhaps that was a good slogan for Bitsy's campaign. After all she would eventually get caught painting bad words on buildings, so it was probably right that she quit while she was ahead. Mélanie knew that she would eventually have to concede to Bitsy that she saw straight through her lies and reveal that she had known all along that it was Bitsy herself who was the serial vandal about town. One thing about never getting close to anyone is that it makes it difficult for you to know how close they are to you.

Mélanie knew what Bitsy was thinking but Bitsy was in a blissful world of walls and barriers and ignorance and had no idea.

On her patrols Mélanie liked to peer into kitchen windows and watch people eat their breakfast - though there were few that were awake and busy before the crack of dawn - but the morning was so arid today that she couldn't bear to hang around. She whistled through town in an hour and didn't wait to see anyone after providing the alarm. Then she was at the foot of Willie's hill and looked up. The collapsible chair was there but there was no sleeping Willie Bridger sat in it. It had not rained through the night so it would not be that Willie was holed up in the Itch after a merry few hours of twilight drinking. Mélanie followed the promenade and then circled around the base of the hill to where the trail upwards began, and there was Willie Bridger. He was collapsed and his bright red skin was glistening with sweat, his shirt torn open by his own hands and the bare chest beneath rising and falling frantically. There was consciousness in him and he saw Mélanie, but he said with slurred words that Mélanie was Doc, then not long after that she was his sister Alma. Mélanie quickly checked his pulse and felt that it was rapid and then Willie slapped her hand away from his throat.

'Get up,' Mélanie said, reaching underneath his arm and pulling, but Willie snarled and once again tried to bat her away.

'Doc,' he said.

'*Mademoiselle Celestine*.'

'Doc.'

Eventually the old man relented when Mélanie threatened to murder him. She hoisted his arm mover her shoulder and stumbled under his bones on the way back to the surgery. When there she handed him over to Doctor Wagner as though he were a package.

'Should I tell his family?' she asked the doctor.

'You want to tell anyone that Willie Bridger is in this state?'

Mélanie went quiet and waited in the lobby as Wagner took Willie into the office. Ten minutes later the former emerged alone.

'Exertional heatstroke,' he said.

'Why?'

'He pushed himself far too hard.'

'Why?'

'Folly.'

'Is he all right?'

'He'll be fine. He's watered and cooling, but fetch another pail, will you?'

'*Oui.*'

Mélanie jogged to the borehole but kept up a face that did not show concern because she did not want to draw attention to herself. There were a few pitchers sat one on top of the other and she filled up two of them, which she reckoned was all she would carry. Then again she stumbled back to the surgery and dragged the pails along the floorboards so as to not get heatstroke herself. Then the doctor left her to help Willie with his cups. He was all fingers and thumbs and so Mélanie had to hold the rim to his mouth as he sipped and swallowed. The lips he eased open were dry and cracked and his skin was peeling on the ridge of his nose. There was a terrific vacancy in his eyes and his shoulders were slouched to the point that they almost blended into his collar.

It was funny because Mélanie couldn't remember ever seeing the old man like this. There was no halo of rising sun bending around his head as there was on the average morning, even to be seen from below his peak. There was no protective aura in the way he held himself. There was nothing perennial about his face. There was only deflation and resignation. Perhaps it was always like that, Mélanie thought. Perhaps that was part of why he never showed his face during the day. Perhaps it was to hide it. In the dim light of a kerosene lamp at the Pig's Itch he could still get away with it if no one was looking too closely.

'I want to tell your Maggie or Mary,' said Mélanie. 'I want to tell them that you're a total idiot, Willie.'

'What good will that do, Mademoiselle Celestine?'

'They ought to know.'

'It will frighten them.'

'Perhaps it will be good for people to see that you are not impervious, even if it should frighten them.'

'I'm still here, ain't I? What's the point?'

'They would be upset with me if they knew I hadn't told them.'

'Then let us keep that hypothetical scenario hypothetical, yes?'

The old man knew a great many dark things about Mélanie and had never breathed a word of any of them to anyone; not even to Mélanie herself.

'Fine,' she eventually said. 'But you are not well.'

'I am well enough, but I am overdoing it is what it is.'

'You are fighting the tide of age?'

'Fighting the tide of age would be like fighting the tide.'

'But you are doing it, no? I don't know that your body can handle it, Willie. Look at you. You're a state.'

'I am fine and I am grateful that you helped me, and I know I can trust you to keep this between us.'

'Of course.'

'Old age is a lonely time, Mélanie. We do what we can to fight against it, even if it is the tide.'

'Youth is lonely also.'

'Then perhaps it is ageing itself that is lonely; perhaps time. My father was a lonely man. My daughter Maggie is lonely. My granddaughter Doc is lonely. Loneliness seems to transcend generations.'

'You are sounding like my old fiancé.'

'Why does July stay in town when he is clearly so lonesome? If the sight of your face itself gives his stomach a thousand punches then what is he doing staying here? Is he a masochist?'

'I believe he feels both joy and sadness simultaneously when he sees or thinks of me. It hurts him but it heals him.'

'How can that be possible? How can it be possible to feel two contradictory things at one time?' asked Willie.

'It's peculiar, but not unique,' said Mélanie.

'I know. I have felt it many times in my life as I'm sure most have. I don't anymore because I am too old and it's too tiring. Do you feel both?'

'I do not feel the extremities, but yes, I feel them both.'

'And you do not grieve for anyone? Your father?'

'I miss him but it was his time.'

'He doesn't tether you to this place?'

'*Non.*'

'You, Mélanie,' Willie pushed himself up. 'You are different. You can get out of here. I worry a lot that my sway in town is fading and that the mirage will shatter soon. I can feel it coming. But if I have any influence left then let me use it to get you out of here. Find somewhere better.'

'Why would anywhere else be any different? This place is home. I have something to stay for.'

'What?'

'Bitsy.'

'Bitsy doesn't look at you twice, Mélanie.'

Exactly.

'You're an angel locked out of Eden,' Willie said quietly. 'You are a frowning angel.'

And with that Mélanie felt a nearly unquenchable thirst to sock Willie Bridger in the jaw. The Willie of old would not have spoken to her like that, so perhaps he was right. Maybe he was more his shadow than his form now and one would assume in this case that his reign of security was indeed coming to an end. Old Willie would not have thought of her as everyone else did. Her reflection was the same in the eyes of almost everyone she spoke to, but never Willie's, not until now. But in Bitsy's eyes there was a unique reflection, and Mélanie wanted to go and find it, so she walked out of the surgery without saying another word, her fist clenched to the point of whitening.

11

The two places that Hampstead trusted least of all in this world were the Presbyterian church on Oakley Way and the telegraph office across town. Both he claimed were filled with liars and crooks. Of the church's misgivings he had proof: in the last election Hampstead had been tasked by the session with rooting out any fraudulent voting. Hampstead spotted handwriting belonging to the same people on multiple respective ballots but was told to keep schtum by the elders. He suspected that the rigging was the work of them and their wives and he wondered why in the hell they had made use of his scrupulous qualities if only to shoo-shoo his discoveries. Probably it was a favour to his mother to keep him busy. Ever since then he had walked quickly past the church and had skipped services on Sundays, much to the chagrin of his mother, but Hampstead reminded her that he didn't need a pulpit to remember to worship *under* the authority of the word of God; Hampstead was a small kid and God was supposedly infinite. He was always about.

As for the telegraph station, well, Hampstead found their lies less sinister but still refused outright to believe that one could simply send electrical signals from one place to another, where they are then translated into word-messages. It was either false or witchcraft and Hampstead preferred lies to witches. Now there was a zitty kid that worked there and his name was Sidney. He was the beau of a lady-friend called Miss Grimes out in San Manassas who had moved there for college, leaving poor Sidney in town without a diploma from either high school or college. It was safe to say that Sidney was somewhat lacking in intelligence when compared to his belle, and this made him real anxious and insecure about the relationship. To combat this Sidney had begged and begged on bended knee that Miss Grimes apply for employment at the San Manassas telegraph station. That way they could send and receive replies to and from one another without delay. Sure they might draw the heat from their bosses from time to time but what did it matter so long as it wasn't the Politburo on the other end of the line. Or Al Capone.

But Sidney was so hung up on the girl that his exploits at the station were now the town's worst-kept secret. He moaned to every pair of ears that came within thirty feet of his kisser and no one could shut him up. Even the crotchety Civil War general that ran the station knew about it. But today there would be a visitor who really did want to listen to Sidney's problems.

'Hello, *hombre*,' said Hampstead.

'Got a message to send or receive?' asked Sidney.

'Just want a jibber-jabber.'

'We don't sell those.'

'Naw, I mean that I want to chew the rag with you about something.'

'Me?'

'Hell yeah.'

'Why? Do I know you?'

'Sure, you used to go to my school,' said Hampstead.

'Everyone used to go to your school; it's the only school in town.'

'You're about seven grades my senior. I'm going into the fourth in September.'

'I dropped out of high school.'

'For love?'

'No, for my sins.'

'Hell, if it ain't for you then it ain't for you,' said Hampstead contemplatively. 'But I reckon you got a lot of know-how in ventures outside of basic academia.'

'Oh, you do?'

'Well, you've got a lady and you've made it work despite that you're miles apart.'

'Saying that it works is rather optimistic, kid.'

'She still you girlfriend?'

'She hasn't told me otherwise.'

'Well, until the attorneys turn up at your doorstep with a notice of relational foreclosure then I'd say you're doing O.K. What's your secret?'

'Hell if I know. Say, you're a kid. Kids are honest. Why do you reckon she won't respond to my telegrams? Sometimes we'll be sending telegrams like *zip-zip-zip*! Back and forth like a sailboat. Then all of a sudden she leaves me waiting. No explanation. When she eventually replies hours or maybe even days later she won't even acknowledge it. What gives?'

'Maybe she's busy,' said Hampstead. 'San Manassas is a big town, so I heard. There must be plenty of people wanting her services.'

'Yeah, I'll bet there are,' muttered Sidney. 'Sometimes I think that my conversation ain't intellectually stimulating enough for her and so I send her poetry. I don't understand any of it, in fact I think all poets are daisies, but Miss Grimes really likes Walt Whitman and Emily Dickinson and the like. Sometimes I even try and write my own.'

'Hell, I write some stuff myself,' said Hampstead.

'That right? Has it got you anywhere with the ladies?'

'Well, I don't show it around so much, Sidney. I figure that being the idiot that I am it's a safer bet to keep it to myself than to flaunt it like it's a bellybutton on a summer's day.'

'You write poetry?'

'Novels. I love books, you see.'

'Like what?'

'Are you sure you want me to tell you? You may be severely repulsed by the sight of me.'

'I'm already repulsed by most people, especially young'uns. Go on,' said Sidney.

'I got this one about a feller named Albert who works down the mines during the Rush. He's married to a broad called Nina and they have a daughter called Albertina.'

'I like it,' said Sidney.

'The problem with Albert's family is that they're all very dependent on him. He's the one that makes them the money down the mines. He's the one that collects the lodes. He's the one that discovered a fortune on a sailing trip to Cape Horn. He's the one that traps for them in the spring when the mines flood. He's the one that fixes up the snake oil that Nina needs.'

'Right.'

'Now, Albert loves Nina and Albertina very much, perhaps more than he can understand. Whatever that means. He would do anything for them and that's exactly what he's gonna keep doing. He's gonna break his back day-in and day-out until it breaks so hard it can't be unbroken. He'd rather see his back get awful crumpled than he would see Nina and Albertina go hungry. And as the Rush fades out so does the money for the family, so Albert has to ration his share of the money and thus the food. He turns thinner and thinner until one day he climbs up the ladder from the mine, takes in a deep breath of the desert air, then dies. Just like that.'

'He dies?'

'He dies so quietly that the vultures get to him before his people do. By the time Nina arrives there's nothing left of him but a bit of carrion that the birds ain't yet chewed at.'

'How old are you?'

'So naturally Nina and Albertina ain't feeling so good. They've found themselves in real hardscrabble times and without anyone to provide for them. Nina's kind of a dullard and Albertina's sort of a kid still, so it ain't looking too promising for the pair.'

'Then what?'

'Well, that's it. That's all I got so far. I can't think of an ending.'

'I ain't repulsed but I am very disappointed.'

'What I'm trying to tell you is that everything written by an idiot is unfinished,' said Hampstead. 'Now, I ain't calling you an idiot outright but you most certainly are when compared with the lovely Miss Grimes. So even if your poems have a conclusive beginning, middle and end, they ain't done until you get good at writing them. I figured that about my novel and so just decided I wouldn't kid myself. I won't allow myself to think of an ending until I've got smart.'

'How are you planning on getting smart?'

'Independent learning.'

'What does that entail?'

'Lived experiences.'

'Then why are you asking me for advice? That's not very independent.'

Hampstead felt a little forlorn all of a sudden.

'It's not worked out as well as I'd hoped,' he said. 'I'm a little peeved because I've come in here seeking advice and all I've seemed to do is dish out my own. What the hell?'

'Then quickly ask me something and be on your way. I'm sickantired of this kind of baloney.'

'How the hell do you know if you're in love with a girl or maybe it's her daddy that you're in love with?'

'Get the hell out of here,' said Sidney. 'Goddamn bozo.'

It was funny because Hampstead had been getting a real kick out of the conversation until then. He had even been thinking forward to telling Sidney about the song he was writing, called *What's This Bug That's Got Me All Shook Up?*, the tune of which had been inspired largely by Bessie Smith's *Cake Walkin' Babies* and was probably quite derivative. It even came accompanied by a dance which involved a lot of clicking and thigh-slapping. Hampstead had choreographed the whole thing. What a drag!

(ii)

When the school bell rang that afternoon Hampstead and his two buddies went to the Outpost. It was a temporary facility made of adobe stolen from the planetarium building site and sticks and branches from

Mrs Doe's orchard. The boys had constructed it about two hundred yards away from the mysterious covenstead that all the funny-looking ladies and shady-looking gentlemen frequented in the cover of darkness. Over the course of six months they had turned miscellaneous materials into a six-foot high platform fitted with a scrambling tunnel and an encircling protective trench filled with mud. The boys had wanted a proper moat but the water kept getting absorbed by the ground and so they settled for mud. Hampstead's friend Tuna had procured a pair of broken binoculars - military-standard - from the bottom of Willie's hill a couple of months ago, and now they were finally fixed and going to good use.

On all four sides of the Outpost were apotropaic marks sourced from history books at the library. Hampstead had also taken it upon himself to weave some initial 'M's and hang them in front of the entrance to the scrambling tunnel. No women or girls were allowed past the protective trench and the boys consistently reminded one another never to let a female get the last word in a conversation when in sight of the covenstead. None of them could be bothered keeping up with that in the comfort of their own home or at the schoolhouse. The final piece of the puzzle was the wooden crosses that Hampstead had stolen from the storehouse in the garden of the Presbyterian church. It might as well be the elders' penance for their previous duplicity, he told his buddies.

The tallest and most decorated of the three friends was Tuna. Tuna had the strongest thumbs that anyone had ever seen, had won the Suds War and was always getting sent home from school and yet never learning his lessons. There was no one more admirable in the entire town apart from maybe the Bridger twins. Tuna was the one who was leading the investigation into the covenstead and had brought a blueprint to Book Debate Club yesterday and had convened a meeting of the boys inside the old water closet. It had been cut short by a mistrustful janitor but Hampstead and their third amigo Hector had got the idea of the thing. *Surveillance, surveillance, infiltration.* The two former elements of the plan sat very comfortably with the boys, who liked spending their summer evenings out and about anyway. Spying on the covenstead gave them something more stimulating to do than chasing cats. The lattermost element of the plan, however, was a step into the deep, dark unknown, and it had caught Hampstead with his breeches down and his jaw hanging.

'It is Satan that pulls the strings of the Tuna marionette,' he said wearily.

'You want us to go *in*?' asked Hector, who was little and forlorn and had rickets. He had been a premature baby and, coupled with how black his skin was, was effectively prescribed the condition by the fates. Or so Wagner had told his mother. It wasn't too bad but he often complained about his back, and his knock knees were beginning to show. He was the sweetest boy in the whole wide world.

'Well, not you, Hector,' said Tuna. 'If you get seen you ain't exactly gonna be busting out of there with any great pace.'

'Thank God,' said Hector.

'So it's gotta be either me or Hampstead. Thoughts, Hampstead?'

'To what end are we breaking into a witches' lair?'

'To expose them. It's no good standing here at the Outpost with our hands on our hips and old Heck humming suspiciously. We have to start taking this seriously. There's some freaky shit going on at the place and I don't like it one bit. The sooner we get the word out the better.'

'It's only grown-ups that go in and out of there,' Hector reminded Tuna, 'so why should us telling the adults that there's something weird going on make them see sense?'

'Are they adults going in and out of there? Or are they demons?'

'Shuddup.'

'So,' said Hampstead, 'one of us goes in and comes out and tells the whole town that there's witches around. What good will that do? We might as well just go and tell them all that now and they can prove it for themselves. But they won't listen to us either way. If we actually go in or we just say we do, it makes no difference.'

'Now this is the part of the plan that we didn't get time to go over in the outhouse,' said Tuna. 'It's very daring.'

'Go on.'

'We will have to borrow a kodak from the emporium.'

'I ain't no shutterbug,' said Hampstead, 'and neither are you, Tuna. How do you reckon we can work one of those things under time constraints and a very real threat of being turned into soup or some such horrible broth? Also, how the hell do you reckon any of us can afford to loan a camera from the emporium? Do they even do that?'

'Well we ain't gonna do it with permission or money, genius. We're going to have steal it.'

'We're stealing *camera devices* now?!'

'We'll return it! Besides, if we prove to the whole down about the shady stuff that's happening at the cat house then they'll probably give us the camera as a reward.'

'That's a good point. But what about actually using the camera?'

'I will have to source that information from the owner as though I am considering making a purchase. I'll sweet talk him to high heaven. *Hello, dear fellow. I am mighty persuaded by the look of this bea-utiful-looking camera machine, but I am such a clutz. Would you explain to me how I would use such an item?* Yadda-yadda-yadda.'

'But then he'll figure out that you stole it,' said Hector.

'Not if I have an alibi,' said Tuna. 'I'll make sure he knows both exactly when the camera was stolen and where I am at that precise moment. That way I cannot be implicated.'

'Not necessarily. He might suspect a friend of yours stole it on your instruction. All he would need to do was find out from the schoolhouse who your pals are, then get a location on us at the time of the robbery.'

Tuna glared at Hector but he understood that the kid was right.

'We need someone we aren't involved with to steal it then,' he muttered.

'No,' said Hampstead. 'Who's gonna do that? Even if we were willing to pay, we haven't fifty cents between us. Who's gonna commit a crime for a few dimes?'

'I've an idea!' said Hector. 'Don't pay them to steal the camera but instead pay them to ask the kodak guy about how to use it: the job you were going to do, Tuna. That way they aren't committing the crime and we can steal - *borrow* - the camera without being suspected. We won't need alibis because why the hell would we steal a camera in the first place? None of us have ever shown an interest in that kind of horseplay. It would need to be someone with good memory and someone that no one would ever expect us to be involved with.'

'Someone trustworthy,' agreed Tuna.

'Someone unsuspecting,' thirded Hampstead.

'Someone who famously has no friends,' said Hector.

They all arrived at the same answer at the exact same moment but only Tuna and Hector were happy about it. Hampstead felt a little bit cold inside. Would he ever shirk this bizarre, unrelenting connection to Doc?

'Hector, your job can be persuading Doc Bellingham to do this for us. Your rickets won't be a hindrance there,' Tuna said.

'Glad to be of service,' said Hector.

'But what if they suspect that she stole the camera?' asked Hampstead.

'Well, she's always getting into trouble anyway,' said Tuna. 'A couple more lashings from her momma won't hurt her too bad.'

But Hampstead felt mightily uneasy about the prospect of throwing Doc under the bus again. Come hell or high water he would not be responsible for her misfortunate again, at least for a few weeks. Still he had pangs in his stomach as a result of his guilt. Still he didn't know how to look at her too well. Still he couldn't read his own mind.

'And we will be doing her a favour as it will give her a chance to speak to someone other than her own reflection,' said Tuna. 'Everybody wins, right?'

'I'd say so. Why, let's see how much we can give her and I'll head to her house now,' said Hector.

Everyone pulled out their coins and they cobbled together fifty-six cents on the dirt in between them.

'Dang, I was wrong,' Hampstead acknowledged.

'Don't take that and show us a clean pair of heels,' Tuna warned

Hector. 'I don't want to have to chase after you at a leisurely walking pace. You know you won't get far if I do.'

'I'll stay honest, I swear!'

'I believe you, but you'll catch licks from us both otherwise. Catch you soon, Heck.'

'See you, Heck.'

'See you, fellers.'

Once Hector was out of the scrambling hole and into the middle distance Tuna patted Hampstead on the shoulder and indicated that he had something serious on his mind.

'Hey, Hampstead, can I ask you something?' asked Tuna.

'Sure thing, Tuna.'

'Sometimes I feel like I'm the big cheese around here.'

'You saying you're the boss of me and Hector?'

'Naw, just that it feels like it sometimes. Ever since I won the Suds War, you know. It feels like me making Hector sick from soap really stamped my authority on the group. If we worked for Chrysler I feel like you and Heck would be on the assembly line and I'd have an office upstairs. Hector would have a chair to sit on, naturally. It's not that I'm better qualified or more intelligent than you fellers, it's just that's how people perceive me. Perception is everything, right?'

'It's a lot of things,' Hampstead shrugged. 'Are you upset about this?'

'I just wouldn't want you to dislike me if I came to embody the role more than I already am,' said old Tuna.

'I wouldn't dislike you. I don't believe that a friendship is worth existing unless it's more-or-less unconditional. Obviously I wouldn't keep you around if you bit me or kicked me straight in the neck or something. That wouldn't be so hunky-dory-sunshine. But if you think you're the guy then you should embrace it. In truth I quite like having someone look after me.'

'You do?'

'I guess.'

(iii)

On his walk home Hampstead rued his words. He also rued his acquaintance with the hellcat Bitsy. The obscenity had sprung up a half-dozen more times around town, Hampstead realised. Trying to avoid it was like playing cuss-word-peekaboo. And why had he said he didn't mind being bossed around by Tuna? Maybe it was the honest truth, whatever, but why had he said it? That didn't make him look maverick. It made him look like a bootlicker. *Perception is everything.* Hampstead would likely never live this down now.

Hampstead's dog Goose was asleep in the front yard, as was his favourite summer pastime. Always he stretched out to cover as many inches of his body in sunlight as was physically possible for the son of a bitch. Often this created a tripping hazard for Hampstead's partially-blind grandmother Mabel, who didn't come round much since Goose had his growth spurt. He also liked the front yard because it allowed him to be the first to see Hampstead get home from school on an afternoon, but today Hampstead was late because he had gone to the Outpost, so Goose hadn't made it. He lolled and snoozed and a couple of flies hovered around his tongue, and Hampstead was in no rush to deliver him from his slumber, so tiptoed the final few yards of the street before creeping over the dog.

Of course Goose was no heavy sleeper. On the rare occasion that Hampstead was in the house the kid would inevitably be up to no good, crashing and hurtling around the place on his various projects and endeavours. For many years there had been a battle between curiosity and lethargy in Goose's soul and his canine inquisitivity had triumphed. Whereas before he would attempt to nap whenever possible he knew now that he could only afford to do so when Hampstead was out, for otherwise he would simply miss too much. Even after lights out and into the witching hour there was always the possibility that Hampstead would have to pee. If he had to pee then he would have to go to the bathroom. If he had to go to the bathroom then he could get distracted by a bug or a photograph or a loose nail en route. If he got distracted by a bug or a photograph or a loose nail en route then he would not go back to bed. If he did not go back to bed then he was up for the day and activities would resume.

Now that Hampstead was out more Goose was generally better rested. When he was better rested he was less cranky and got more positive attention from both neighbours and Momma. He became less inquisitive about foreign affairs and less inclined to hunt the neighbourhood cats, of which there were many. Hampstead and his pals had them covered anyhow. Generally Goose lived a life of luxury but his happiness soared on weekday afternoons more than did at any other time. Goose lived for Hampstead's return because without Hampstead his life was pleasant but unexciting. If Goose could sacrifice his many naps for a life spent at Hampstead's side then he would before kicking dirt over them with his hind legs.

It was the boy's odour that caused Goose to wake up that evening.

'Sorry, feller,' said Hampstead, embracing Goose. Hampstead had some energy and a little bit of rage pent up and so invited the dog to play fetch with him. Goose duly obliged but infuriated Hampstead very quickly with his lethargy and lack of cooperation. It was hot out in truth but it was still maddening for Hampstead to watch the bastard chase after the ball and then lie down with it still in his chops. So Hampstead resorted to playing catch rather than fetch; throwing the ball directly at Goose in the hope that he would then have the energy to return it for another round, but again Goose seemed more interested in lolling around and basking in the sun with Hampstead.

From the porch table Hampstead retrieved his baseball glove, ran back to Goose and pulled the ball from his sloppy mouth.

'If you're not gonna fetch or catch then you can dang well throw it to me!' he said. 'Up!'

But Goose only rolled over.

'Up, Goose!'

Goose panted excitedly on his back with his tongue dragging along the grass as he sprawled around. His tail was wagging like fury but this only got Hampstead more riled up.

'Play with me!'

Goose threw himself onto his feet and then back off them again as if to tease his master. Hampstead wiped the sweat from his forehead.

'Goose!' he spat. '*Goose!*'

Hampstead clapped his naked hand against the gloved hand over and over again but the dog would not budge. The boy considered giving him a swift boot to power him up, but he wanted to give him a chance and kept breathing as deeply as he could to stop himself from seeing red. Again he wiped sweat from his brow and he stamped his foot. Goose continued to pant.

'You can either catch, fetch or throw, you goddamned mutt.'

Then there was a sense of finality in the way that Goose slumped onto his side and gave up looking at Hampstead altogether. He would likely loaf around like that for a few hours, Hampstead knew, and he felt an aching in his chest and a throbbing in his temple. He walked over to the dog and kicked him in his back. Goose shrieked and bolted into the house, leaving Hampstead crying in the dregs of early evening sunshine.

'Play with me next time!'

12

Someone had spotted that the collapsible chair on Willie's hill was empty despite that it was the middle of the day. Word had spread rather quickly and a search had ensued through town. Every establishment was checked and its respective proprietor interrogated. Twice. The bank clerk Lucille said she hadn't ever seen Willie Bridger in the bank. Doctor Wagner said he thought Willie Bridger was fit as a fiddle and didn't expect to see him for many years to come. Even the priest declared the Willie Bridger had nothing to repent for and was not a priority for religious intervention. Everyone became so lost in the search that they failed to notice when the collapsible chair once again found its occupant.

July and Luella were working again on the Snake Run Cattle Outfit Ranch boundary bobwire. Still not one head of the herd had escaped and by now the boundary was nearly up and standing as it once was, although this time special effort had been made to drive the posts deep down to the bedrock. Luella was a fast and strapping worker, often hammering longer and harder than July could, although July didn't mind. He found her laboriousness impressive. With only a few dozen yards left to replace they had found themselves at the end of the boundary closest to town, where the hill was visible to the naked eye.

Charlie, Maggie, Elsie, Hattie and the barefooted Doc Bellingham ran across at the sound of the hammering and interrogated July and Luella for any information on Willie, but July needed only to look at the hill to see that the old man was sat up there and to wonder what in the hell had gotten into these fellers. The fury in Maggie's eyes was nonetheless of intrigue enough for July and Luella to follow the family to Willie. They collected the outfit's Babe Vicks, Sunrise, Bitsy, Sidney from the telegraph station and the curious Itch boarder Mr Hoyt on their way, plus a few other stragglers. The crowd pulled up the hill together to confront the old man, who humbly grinned and nodded in greeting as they approached.

'What's given y'all the screaming-meemies?' he asked.

'Where the hell have you been?' said Maggie. 'We've been worried!'

'No one's seen my sister thrice or more in the last couple years and yet you all accept that readily. I'm missing in action for a few hours and suddenly there's a lynch mob here to tell me what for?'

'We know where she is! We know she's safe!'

'Do you not trust that I can look after myself?'

'No one can look after themselves indefinitely,' said Sunrise, to Maggie's surprise and fortune.

'Exactly,' Maggie said. 'But what we trust less than that, Pa, is your ability to ask for help, you stubborn bastard. Hell, you're out of breath still and that's just from climbing up this dang hill of yours. Won't you start taking it easy?'

'Take it easy?' laughed Willie. 'My girl, I sit and I sleep and I drink and I eat. And I watch above. That's all I do.'

'But it's taking its toll on you, Pa.'

'Let it try.'

'Where did you go?'

'To stretch my legs.'

'You're insufferable.'

Maggie turned and strode down the hill. Her husband Charlie looked helplessly from her to Willie, then followed her down. Doc put her arms around Willie and asked if she could stick around for some stargazing once night fell, to which Willie replied that she could as it was a Friday night. It occurred to July how tired he was and how much his fingers were hurting from the prongs of the devil's rope that he and Luella had been fixing, so he hoisted her and then himself back onto the saddle of June, and they trotted down the hill together.

At the bottom was Mélanie, sat smoking on the bench outside the telegraph station and watching proceedings with an air of disinterest fixed on her. She caught eyes with July as he trotted by on the horse and for a few seconds they maintained that contact, July's stomach swirling and twirling as it always did on such occasions. Then he nearly rode into a tie rail and so had to pull on the reins at Luella's impatient behest, and then Mélanie was out of sight. July contemplated the encounter all the way back, during the dismount, as they walked onto the veranda, into the house and up the stairs to the bedroom.

When they got inside he pulled Luella in close to him and let her know how he was feeling with the one heavy hand on the small of her back and the other clasping the fat of her buttock.

'I thought you wanted a siesta?' asked Luella, putting up no resistance as July threw her clothes aside and kissed her all over.

'I did,' he said.

'What changed?'

'I don't know.'

Luella flattened up for a moment as though she were deep in thought, then continued reciprocating July's advances.

'You'll be tired,' she whispered.

'This will help me sleep.'

They proceeded to make whoopee repeatedly throughout the night and into the next day, not once stopping to talk or sleep or hydrate or breathe. Eventually July found himself too sore to continue and had to collect some ointment from the cabinet downstairs, but that only made him sting more. It was then that he had to call it a day and he thanked Luella somewhat dispassionately. But before he could leave she sat up naked in the bed and called for him.

'You have to get out of here,' she said.

'Hell, that's what I'm doing,' said July, gesturing to the door handle that he was about to turn.

'You gotta get out of this town,' said Luella.

'You're full of it,' said July.

'What are you so scared of?'

'I ain't scared of anything, Luella.'

'Yes, you are. If you weren't scared then you would have gone long ago. There's nothing here for you except sadness. All your choices are made for a woman who left you. I just had perhaps the greatest night of my life but I can't help but thinking that you will think of another when you remember it.'

'So it's inconvenient for you, is what you're saying?'

'Gee, you are something. Here.'

Luella threw back the sheets and reached across to the bedstand, pulled open the drawer and removed from it a delicate, beautiful Steyr. It glittered like oil on water and yet it was only a deep black.

'I bought this off an Austrian,' she said. 'He was given it for the War but fled here before it started. He said it reminded him of how cowardly he was. I said that I would take it off his hands because he oughtn't feel cowardly about himself. I think you should have it, July.'

'I think you're full of it,' July repeated.

'Take it with you when you leave town,' Luella said. 'It's self-loading; the first of its kind.'

'I've guns downstairs.'

'July, I doubt you'll be able to use this properly without weeks of practice. The double-barrels you've got in the showcase are a different question altogether; I doubt you've got the proficiency for holding one steady.'

'I'm long past feeling emasculated,' July said. 'Don't think you can use that tactic on me. I was a man once and then I paid for it. But be glad I'm not drunk right now because otherwise I'd be giving you licks.'

Of course July did not tell anyone without prompting that he had shot and killed men before. Thrice in the War and once since during some poor bastard's robbing the Itch. The first time he had killed a man in Flanders the pain had weighed heavy on him and he had suffered nightmares and vomiting and weeping and desolation. Then the second time he was cleansed of the pain and it just felt like nothing. And then the same for kill three and kill four. If he were to take the Steyr and shoot a bad man in the chest now he imagined it would also feel like nothing. July thought of the Lune Solaire twin flowers that he had grown. He could picture them so vividly it was as though they were the looming beasts of a nightmare come to torment him in his waking hours. They were at once so beautiful and yet so frightening in the context of his downfall. How can two contrary things exist simultaneously?

'I have no need for it,' said Luella. 'So I will leave it here and you can take it or you can ignore it. It's a ticket out of here, July.'

'Are you leaving me?'

'Leaving you?' laughed Luella. 'How can I leave you if you don't even see me in the first place?'

July felt morose and left without apologising. It was late afternoon and he wandered out of Luella's room expecting to find Doc and Sunrise in the depths of a card game or story swap. But neither of them were outside despite that Doc's chair was there. July knocked on the door of Sunrise and Mr Hale's room and waited a couple moments before the latter of the two opened it.

'Hello, Mr Hale,' said July. The old man had a disturbed look about him that was noticeable even above his typically forlorn aspect.

'Hello,' he said.

'Does either yourself or Sunrise know where Doc is? She's meant to be sat right out here watching the door.'

'Not seen her,' said Mr Hale.

'All right, well, I'm sorry about her professionalism or lack thereof. I'll go find her and get her back here real quick, you can count on that.'

'Don't trouble yourself.'

Down the stairs went July and he found Mr Cricket smoking behind the cash register. *Linger Awhile* was playing on the phonograph. A couple of customers were drinking at tables and the guarded Mr Hoyt was further down the bar.

'Have you seen Doc Bellingham?'

'Hell naw.'

'Damn it.'

July stoked out of the building and heard Mr Cricket sardonically call after him about having to fulfil more obligations than was initially agreed upon when he first arrived at the Itch. July went onto the veranda where he squinted in the sunset. The sound of gentle crying filled his ears and he sought the source out in the alley behind the Itch, where he found Sunrise doing her best to fix up her face and clothes, readying to come back inside.

'Hidy-do,' July said gingerly.

'Oh, jeepers creepers,' said Sunrise. 'Hey, July.'

Even in the state that she was in she was no bug-eyed betty, though perhaps that was because her features were obscured by the shadows of the alley.

'I'll be swell, don't worry about me. You head back into the drum now.'

'I ain't seen you cry before. What's eating you?' asked July.

'Oh, I'm just a dumb dora.'

'Oh, bushwa! You ain't no such thing. Are you hurt?'

'I'm really O.K., July.'

'You want some rotgut?'

'I could go for some.'

'All right, well, would you rather stay out here where the clientele can't see your tears?'

'Please.'

Briskly July made his way into the Itch, finished a short argument with Mr Cricket about whether the proprietor ought to pay for his own stock, carried a glass bottle of giggle juice back out onto the porch and handed it over to Sunrise.

'There you are.'

'I didn't see you on the bar when I came down.'

'I was just playing hooky for a nookie,' July said.

'Hell, not even the deaf-mutes could miss the sound of the bed creaking when you and Luella are at it.'

July blushed and apologised.

'I often feel like crying but I don't want the fellers in there to think me a daisy, you know, so I do it in hiding too,' he said. 'I done so much crying in my time because, to be honest, melancholy is a voyage I'd be eager to take these days. I'm on a freight train straight to Woe Town, Sorrow County most days. It ain't easy to get off, neither.'

'I know about all that, July.'

'Hell, of course you do,' July laughed. 'But what I mean to tell you is that you can tell me what's eating you and you can know with absolute certainty that it won't sound trivial to me.'

'Sometimes the world can just catch up with you,' said Sunrise. 'And there ain't much that you can do about it.'

'Did Walter hurt you?' asked July.

'I'm really all right, July. We got some creases in our friendship is all.'

In July's peripheral vision the unmistakeable figure of one of his employees dragged across the end of the alley. July turned as Doc did a doubletake all of her own, then stood awkwardly with her long arms wrapped around a large terrarium. It normally would have required two men to carry but old Doc had the limb span to support it with her wrists and underarms while her fingers remained free to carry a lit cigarette.

'Doc!' said July.

The girl was motionless but she turned her eyes slowly to behold the sight before her. In her eyes it was clear that she was a little affrighted by it but she crept over nonetheless and took a tentative seat on one of the gin barrels.

'Hidy-do,' she said.

'Hidy-do,' said Sunrise.

'Where in the hell have you been? You're late.'

'I got to collect Mrs Batty's frogs. She said it would be a good way of keeping me in class because I can't get food for them anywhere other than the school cupboard. So if I don't go to school then the frogs die.'

'Mrs Batty is risking the lives of her frogs for your attendance?' asked July.

'She knows how much I love them; I couldn't bear to let them die,

I swear. I got my suspicions she got them in the first place just for this purpose. I've spent a lot of time trying to find where to get some of my own and had no luck. She must have travelled a hundred miles at least. Say, have you been crying, Sunrise? Aw, gee, you didn't get robbed for real did you?'

'What do you mean, "for real"?' asked July.

Doc stopped and stared at him.

'As in, someone stole a helluva lot of her things rather than just a couple bits and pieces, Mr Slade,' she eventually said.

'Naw, it ain't that,' said Sunrise. 'Say, this panther piss is mighty strong, July.'

'And how!' said July, taking the bottle that Sunrise was offering over and having a few sips of it himself. He then turned to Doc who was still holding the terrarium in her arms. 'How many you got in there?'

'Three.'

'They poisonous?'

'Naw, these are Red-eyed Tree Frogs.'

'Are they gonna be a problem?'

'Hell no.'

'Do you smoke?'

'Hell yeah I do.'

'That ain't well-rolled. Here.'

July pulled out some makins and got to fixing up a proper cigarette for Doc, who watched attentively as he went about it. Then he took Doc's from her mouth and stubbed it out. He put the new one in between her lips and lit it using his box of Bryant & May's. Doc coughed and spluttered but found a rhythm within a few puffs.

'That's way better,' she said.

Then July rolled one for Sunrise and one for himself and continually distributed further cigarettes as the afternoon wore on. The moonshine made its way around the circle and even Doc found herself getting involved. They sat quietly awhile until Sunrise decided that a story would do her the world of good.

'I really think a good story is just the cat's pyjamas,' she said.

'That's why I love the movies so much,' said Doc.

'You know, I've never been to the movies,' said Sunrise.

July and Doc found their jaws on the ground.

'There ain't no picture houses in Rockwell,' shrugged Sunrise.

'We ought to go, I suppose,' said July. 'There's one in Laguna. You go there plenty, right, Doc?'

'Hell yeah.'

'We'll head there tomorrow.'

'Oh, bully!' said Sunrise. 'Now, who's got a story?'

No one said anything. The drink was sipped by July and Doc kept on with her cigarette. The frogs clucked gently from within the terrarium.

'Won't you tell one, Sunrise?' asked Doc.

Sunrise hummed.

'I told July a few days ago that I had a friend once upon a time and he loved the Greek myths,' she said. 'He used to tell them to me all the time. He lived and died by them.'

'I heard they have some real humdingers,' said July.

'Too right,' said Sunrise. 'There's one that's always stuck with me for some reason although it's been a while since I last heard it. Would you like to hear it?'

'Is it one of woe and despair?' asked July.

'Yes,' said Sunrise.

'Then yes, please.'

Sunrise dragged her palms down her cheeks and breathed in loudly. July and Doc sat to attention. The evening was coming in around them, but it was warm and pleasant and drowsing.

'So, Apollo was the god of light, music, poetry, archery and knowledge - probably some other things too - and was a great hero revered by all,' said Sunrise. 'He led the sun through the sky in his chariot and he killed the terrible python with a thousand arrows. The python had terrorised the people for centuries and its death meant that people in Greece could celebrate and praise Apollo, who became a bit arrogant because of it. He was so arrogant in fact that he ridiculed Eros for his wielding of a bow and arrow, mocking the fact that he could hardly use them compared to Apollo. Eros was furious and so stood on the peak of Mount Parnassus and accurately fired a golden arrow into the heart of Apollo. And with a lead arrow he pierced the heart of the river nymph Daphne. Thus in Apollo's heart grew a great love for and infatuation with Daphne, but in Daphne's there grew resentment and disgust at Apollo. Daphne was a virgin who practiced chastity unwaveringly anyway, so I'm not entirely sure what the point of the lead arrow was, but I guess it just really drove home the idea that Apollo wasn't getting anywhere near her.

'Eros - a crafty bastard - offered to help Apollo, who was able to chase Daphne to the ends of the earth, constantly having his advances and his pleas spurned by the resistant lady. All the while Eros motivated Apollo to persist, though Apollo would have done so anyway, such was the desire in him. Again and again he told Daphne that he would love her forever, just as other men had done before. Leucippus, for example, was a handsome man who disguised himself as a young girl in order that he might be accepted among Daphne's company and simply be in her presence, but he had been killed by the nymphs who figured his devilry.

'But this devotion from Apollo was so durable that Daphne began considering her options, right. She eventually turned to her father Peneus the river god. She begged for an escape from Apollo's merciless harassment. She begged and she begged and she offered to undertake a harsh existence so long as it freed her from her bane and protected her virginity. "Open the earth to enclose me or change my form!" she pleaded of her father, who did not hesitate to help her. He opened up the earth as she asked but he pulled Apollo rather than Daphne down into hades. Peneus did not want his daughter to suffer for Apollo's hubris, believing that a time spent in hell would be the perfect way to cleanse Apollo of his love and lust. Having been told of his punishment Apollo asked to take something of Daphne's with him into the underworld so that he never lose the memory of her entirely; so that his love would linger without vanishing, but that his obsession would end. When the horrors of hades commenced that is exactly what happened.'

'What of Daphne's does he take?' asked July.

'Something that is truly unmistakable; something that no one else can have: her voice,' said Sunrise. 'She said "goodbye" to him. That's all he wanted and all he needed to cope with hades. And during his millennia in the underworld Apollo began looking for Daphne, knowing that her time on earth would have come to an end after a while despite that nymphs had tremendous lifespans. But he could not find her - hades is large - and when his sentence was complete he was free to leave. By this time Daphne was indeed long dead. Apollo kept his despair and his loneliness but his obsession was gone, so he could come to terms with Daphne's passing and he mourned her properly. He went to her resting place and he turned her bones into the seeds from which a laurel tree would grow. With his powers of youth and immortality he rendered it evergreen so that she would never grow cold. He weaved the threads of the leaves into his breastplate so that he might keep her close to his heart during battle. He carved a lyre from the bark so that she would be in his music. He kept to its shade in the summer so that he was protected by her.'

They sat in a drunken quiet for awhile longer, the sound of the chirping Red-eyes breaking the silence intermittently.

13

Nosferatu was July's favourite picture. He got such a kick out of it that he had spent an entire week's wages on repeated viewings when it came to the picture house a couple of years ago. When it had its run in Laguna July had rented a room above the Hello Girls office at Mercury Communications so that he was only a couple of blocks away whenever there was a showing. For a week he saw no sunlight but for a creeping of dawn at the time of the daily first showing, but his back was always turned to it as he made his way through the lobby of the picture house. *Nosferatu* had such a profound effect on him and he simply could not understand why.

Everyone these days talked about talkies. Talkies this, talkies that. But not a one of those shorts could lay a glove on *Nosferatu*. From the moment Erdmann's ominous horns and clarinets kicked in before the titles you knew you were in for a wild ride. That score would stand the test of time and July wouldn't hear otherwise. The crazy thing about the obsession was that July had little time for the *Dracula* novel. He read it once when he was a freshman and found it middling at best; patronising at worst. When the picture was released he initially had to be persuaded by Mélanie to go and see it because she had been able to see *Der Knabe In Blau* when she had still been living in France. She claimed that *Nosferatu* didn't live up to her expectations, but July was thoroughly delighted.

Your wife has such a beautiful neck...

What a kick July got! When he was in front of that screen he forgot everything else. It was as though he was transported to a world of unimaginable horrors but one that was endlessly preferable to the tiring dramas that existed outside the double doors. Perhaps when he first saw it the appeal was born of novelty and perhaps now the appeal had evolved with July's own psyche. Maybe the appeal now lied within escapism. Either way he loved that goddamn picture and he really knew his onions about it. He used to give Mélanie the jitters when he talked about it; he was so hard to stop. That and chess were the only fields in which he was more knowledgeable and accomplished than her and he wanted to make the most of it.

But there was something entirely more frightening than F. W. Murnau's masterpiece or indeed the memory of lost love. It was sat on the roof of the mom-and-pop grocery store, leaning on the false front as it fiddled with a cloche hat and chewed on a beaded purse. It was almost two feet long and had a very shaggy tail, a cap of crown hair and a cream ring around its neck. It was smacking its lips at July, who froze on the boardwalk and raised his eyebrows. It was the missing greyhound jockey that July had heard tell of; the one that had escaped from Babe Vicks's collection at the Snake Run Cattle Outfit. And it seemed now to July that Sunrise's burglar had finally been found. He was surrounded by jewellery and powder to boot.

But ought July turn the monkey in? That would render Doc redundant and he would have to either fire her or reassign her to the bar. He wanted to do neither of those things because he very much enjoyed his triumvirate of storytellers and players. July resolved to ignore the monkey. It seemed pretty contented even though it was by itself, but then again July didn't know how sociable monkeys were. At the photography emporium he had once seen a picture of an orangutan but had initially assumed it was a wiry fellow in a costume. It was only when the photographer corroborated the authenticity of the image with one from an encyclopaedia that July believed it. Then he went and read *On the Origin of Species.*

So July nodded at the jockey and walked on by. If he were indeed to let the monkey continue roaming free - and he intended to - then he needed to ensure that it would not wreak havoc if it got theft on its mind again; in the event that the monkey went back for more of Sunrise's things it would be good to know that Doc would not be torn to pieces by it. So July made his way to the library and pottered into the non-fiction section. He browsed the wildlife works and eventually found a short paperback about primates. After perusing through with wide eyes awhile he found a little critter not too dissimilar to the missing jockey and decided that this - the 'capuchin' - was the one. In the temperament section it said that capuchin monkeys can become aggressive when bored or enclosed and have been known to bite when threatened. Because of their short stature July surmised that they posed little threat to human beings, but even so he worried that Doc could still be in the firing line of a nasty nibble if the capuchin came back for more of Sunrise's things.

So July decided he had to do the right thing and that was to monkey-proof the Pig's Itch and give Doc a new job, but he worried that Doc would not take well to a more hospitable working role. He would have to bribe her, and it just so happened that the initial shock of seeing the capuchin had reminded him of the shock of seeing *Nosferatu* the first time, and now he was hankering for a trip to the pictures again, so he made his way to the Bellingham household and collected old Doc. Doc was seeming mighty guilty about being late to her shift yesterday. but July, now knowing that it probably made little difference whether or not Doc was there outside Sunrise's room, told her it was all swell.

In a soft voice July explained the situation but said to Doc he would compensate her with fortnightly trips to the theatre. Doc was convinced that she was being removed from her position for yesterday's tardiness so July took her to see the capuchin, who had made himself real comfortable atop the mom-and-pop store. Doc couldn't quite believe what she was seeing but was at least convinced that she had not been downgraded. July explained that he had been reminiscing about *Nosferatu* and was consequently itching for a trip to Laguna, which Doc was delighted by. Even more hotsy-totsy to her was being reminded that they would be going every weekend, and *further* hotsy-totsy was July's conceding that he would have to invite Sunrise along for the ride.

When they arrived in Laguna Doc's calves were cramped because of their length and the lack of legroom at the back of the bus, so they had to take a slow walk to the picture house to give her time to recover. When they arrived they stood and looked at the marquee which said:

RAOUL WALSH'S... WHAT PRICE GLORY?

And the lady in the lobby booth told them to wait an hour until the next showing, so the three of them stopped by a candy shop. Doc got some Haribo gummies and Sunrise got some Dubble Bubble Bubble Gum. July bought himself two Baby Ruth chocolate bars and they proceeded to melt all over his hand as soon as they left the store. He cursed his luck while Sunrise and Doc laughed their asses off at him for being such a goof. But they weren't laughing when July pulled out two canteens and got the girls to smell the inside. They were filled to the brim with rotgut and July warned them that they ought to stop laughing at him if they wanted any.

When the three of them drunkenly exited the picture house late that afternoon they squinted into the sun and collectively agreed that the real world was an absolute bust. Doc rolled herself a cigarette and this time did a much better job, even with a clear anxiety in her eyes as July watched on. It was smokable at least, and she seemed real proud of herself when it started burning. Even July said well done. They then got on the last bus and got back to town with the pleasant exhaustion than one experiences after a feast, mixed with gentle intoxication.

On the bus Doc sat at the back while July and Sunrise awkwardly found themselves on the second row. There was a lady with a baby nearby and the baby kept looking at Sunrise and giggling in between hiccups. The mother, a sunkissed brunette with a flowery bonnet and riding boots, was initially sceptical of how intrigued her kid seemed, before she got a good look at Sunrise and asked if she wanted to hold it. She said the kid was called Eve.

'What do you talk to a baby about?' July asked Sunrise, watching over her shoulder as Sunrise cradled the thing.

'July, you slay me,' laughed Sunrise. 'You just gotta make goo-goo noises and all that schtick. It ain't difficult.'

'Might as well give birth to a cooing slab of adobe,' said July.

'Why don't you sing to her?'

'Why don't *you*?'

'I don't know any songs, July.'

'Not a one?'

'Not a one.'

'Too bad,' said July.

'You know some. You're a musician, ain't you?'

'I know how to play the G chord and the F chord on the piano. Maybe an A Minor. And I once accidentally played one of the pentatonic scales, whatever that means.'

'Liar. Sing to her.'

'I ain't a musician.'

'Just one.'

'I'm drunk.'

'Dutch courage.'

July looked puzzledly at Sunrise and wondered why he was tempted. With the baby's long white linens now draping over the young lady's breast and lap it was as though they were meshed in one article. It was difficult to refuse such a sight. For a moment July looked to Doc sat at the back and she smiled affirmatively. It appeared that she could hear them from back there.

'I learned this song from a British kid at Flanders,' July explained to the baby. 'It's a ballad from across the pond, going way back.'

'You don't need to explain it to the baby,' cried Doc from behind.

'I'm nervous!' said July.

July began quietly and intended to stay quiet. It was called *Scarborough*

Fair. Sunrise smiled and the baby continued to coo and gurgle as July sang, and then afterwards there was quiet for a moment but for the rattling of wheels and the zipping country that they passed.

'I hope you don't mind me saying that you are the wettest blanket I ever knew, Mr Slade.'

July jumped out of his skin and caught a little whiplash turning to see who the source of the insult was. Doc had crept up on him and was now sat in the seat behind, leaning forward and grinning out of her ears.

'Back!' shouted the driver, and Doc duly did as instructed, patting July with a hand on the end of her stupid arm.

'She's full of phonus balonus,' Sunrise laughed. 'I thought that was lovely.'

'It's the song I know the best,' July said defensively.

The baby Eve had looked little more than indifferent since the song began. July supposed that if she were three or more years older she would have told him to shut up long before he did. Perhaps babies were not as bad as he thought.

(ii)

They got back to town and Sunrise reckoned she had the flu and was sneezing like a kitten. Despite that Doc was ready to go to bed she was more inclined to go to the hill. She wanted to tell Pop-pop all about the picture. It was dark out and July was sceptical about her going by herself.

'I do everything by myself,' Doc reminded him.

July though was desperate to go to bed and be done with the day. He said that he had met his social quota and that he was beat and Doc didn't have any idea what that meant. But Sunrise said she was more than happy to bump gums with the town patriarch despite her ailment and so agreed to escort Doc to him, though Sunrise was maybe a half foot shorter than Doc. Folks - save for Hampstead - generally let Doc be, but it was nonetheless unfamiliarly agreeable for Doc to have someone to link arms with on her walk. They bid goodnight to July and made their way up the hill, following the thrum of the Aeolian harp in the darkness.

Pop-pop was pleased to see Doc and surprised to see Sunrise.

'Ain't you due to go back to your parents one day soon?' he asked of Doc.

'Momma thinks I was at work,' said Doc.

'You'll catch her wrath and know that you'll have rightly earned it,' Pop-pop said.

'Yadda-yadda-yadda.'

'Hidy-do, Mister,' said Sunrise.

'Why, hello, Sunrise,' said Pop-pop. 'Another angel for this town's heavenly host, you are.'

'I don't know about that,' said Sunrise, sneezing. 'Doc's the true angel of the two of us.'

'I am not,' said Doc. 'Do I look like an angel to you?'

'What does an angel look like?' asked Sunrise.

'Well, they don't have arms like this, that's for certain. And they dress in long white vestments and have blonde hair and beautiful pale skin.'

'Have either of you seen a real angel?' asked Pop-pop.

'No,' laughed Sunrise.

'Guess what we did today, Pop-pop,' said Doc.

'Saw a picture?'

'Hell yeah!'

'Any good?' asked Pop-pop.

'Hell yeah!'

'Was it a talkie?'

'Naw.'

'What's it about?'

'Two squabbling men with a long-standing rivalry find camaraderie with one another.'

'Impossible. Men are too stubborn to find camaraderie with one another after a long-standing rivalry,' said Pop-pop.

'Hell, that's why it was in a picture and not in real life, Pop-pop.'

'Will you fetch the cartograph, Doc?' asked Pop-pop, trying once to stand but feeling the weight of his body on his brittle ankles.

'Sure.'

Doc moseyed over to the hamper and rifled through it. It was too dark to see so she scratched a match on its box and held it down to illuminate the container. To her surprise she saw first a small tub of Princess Pat's face powder and a chamois to boot. Then close to them was a rouge cream. Doc wondered what in the hell Pop-pop was doing with these things. Not even Momma wore rouge, so it was unlikely that it was a gift for her.

'The cartograph, Doc?' asked Pop-pop.

'Oh,' said Doc, blowing out the flame and discarding the match. She dug around at the bottom of the hamper and pulled out the map which was folded neatly thrice over. Pop-pop winced as he leaned forward to take it from her.

'Are you smoking these days?' he asked her, smelling the smoke from the match on her clothes.

'Hell yes,' Doc said.

'Ease up,' said Pop-pop. 'One day you're smoking tobaccy and the next you're packing heat. You'll be a cowboy before you know.'

'Aw, Pop-pop, I wouldn't know anything about guns.'

'Growing up so fast you are.'

'I notice very few carry guns around town,' said Sunrise. 'Why's that?'

'No need,' said Doc. 'Not when Pop-pop's here. Tell her about the flivver trader, Pop-pop. You'll see, Sunrise, we ain't never had the need for a lynch mob or a hanging or a shootout here or nothing. Anyone with bad intentions comes into town, they have Pop-pop and - way back when - old Great-Auntie Alma to reckon with. It's a frightening sight.'

'The flivver trader?' said Pop-pop.

'Sure, you remember those fellers that you sussed out? They were real dewdropper types; lazy bastards who only wanted to make money by taking it off others but with no fuss. Hell, Pop-pop gave them fuss. Ain't that right, Pop-pop?'

'I reckon I remember,' mused Pop-pop. 'The ones who played with old Fitzroy?'

'Yeah!'

Pop-pop chuckled and nodded.

'Sunrise, let me caveat this story with this: these confidence men were dressed real dapper. Dapper like you wouldn't believe. Dapper like if you got all the stock from all the haberdasheries in the state and put it all in one big warehouse and sent the two of them to live there for three years with nothing to do but browse the garments, and then pulled them out again. That's how they looked. Savvy?'

'Savvy,' said Sunrise.

'Hell, before I start and before I forget, would you find me the Northern Cross, Doc?' asked Pop-pop, pointing at the cartograph.

'Why, can't you find that yourself, Pop-pop?' asked Doc.

'I must be tired.'

Doc hoisted herself out of the dirt seat and pointed at the constellation. Pop-pop squinted at it before looking up into the clear sky of stars above and finding the same group.

'Is one of those to be named after Bitsy?' said Sunrise.

'Naw, this one's named already. Cygnus is the Greek name.'

'His brother lost control of the sun chariot and had to be shot down by Zeus,' added Doc. 'Cygnus spent weeks collecting his brother's bones and the gods were so moved by the sight of it that they transformed him into a celestial swan. That's him now.'

Doc pointed at the constellation and Sunrise nodded.

'Doc remembers these things better than I do nowadays,' said Pop-pop. 'But on with the story. Dapper gentlemen, yes. Very dapper. But these lone star belvideres were no charmers, oh no. They decided to work a scheme on the late mechanic in town, Jacob Fitzroy. Jacob had a modest little repair shop which did real well when the Model T first started selling. He got his diploma just in time for the launch even though he was in his seventies at the time. But everyone in town cobbled their savings together and got a flivver and they were always in need of some repair or another, so it seemed that the old man had made the right choice. The whole place was coughing on the fumes and rattling with the wheels. Fitzroy made a handsome penny, but it was not long before folks around town realised that they had no need for these automobiles and that they were really just a nuisance. They were loud and smelly and no one much liked to leave town on long journeys, save for old Doc here on her trips to the picture house. It happened overnight. Cars that were in the shop for repairs were never collected. Others were ditched out in the desert. Some people sold theirs and others had no luck. Mostly folks just wanted rid of them.

'So Fitzroy falls on hardscrabble times and it gets around that he needs a bit of charity here and there, and everyone chips in to help him out with his mortgage because he was so good when we were all driving around like idiots. In fact Fitzroy was one of the kindliest fellers you could ever hope to meet; he never did anyone dirty. However, too many people get wind that Fitzroy is struggling and someone also hears that he has one old Model T left which was sent in for repairs and never collected. So one of these dapper gentlemen I was telling you about arrives from out of town all charming and wheedling. He offers Fitzroy a hundred dollars for the automobile, which, considering that the going rate was about three hundred, seemed pretty good to the desperate Fitzroy. Only the dapper gentleman doesn't have the full sum on him - he only has fifty. But he gives Fitzroy the fifty and promises that he'll be back in a week to collect the car and pay the rest.

'So Fitzroy takes the money and says that he looks forward to seeing this dashing gentleman in a week's time. All good so far. But then two days later *another* dapper gentleman appears at the repair shop and asks to purchase the Model T, but he offers Fitzroy two hundred dollars. Fitzroy, the poor old bastard, can't believe his luck. But he's an honest man and he wants to stay true to the agreement he made with the first gentleman, which is exactly what he does... *initially*. The second gentlemen ain't afraid of negotiating, you see, and eventually bumps up his offer to three-hundred-and-fifty bucks. I swear to god, if someone had told me that Fitz's head had exploded on the top of his neck at that moment I'd believe them. He must have thought it was his lucky week; it's an offer he can't refuse and the old man has bills to pay.

'So he resolves to compensating the first gentlemen when he returns in a few days' time. Said gentleman returns and is visibly distraught that he will no longer be able to buy this Model T, which tugs on old Fitz's heartstrings to the point that he decides to up the compensation he will give to this first man. Along with returning the original fifty he now adds in *another* fifty on top as an expression of regret. The gentleman is sad but he accepts the gesture and departs, leaving Fitzroy to turn his attention to the impending return of the second gentleman with his three-hundred-and-fifty dollars, which I suppose is more like three hundred if you factor in the extra fifty in compensation that Fitzroy gave to the first feller, but still a helluva lot for the old bastard. Only the second gentleman never shows up, leaving Fitzroy fifty down and still unable to shake this last flivver.

'But Fitzroy and the rest of us presume that there is no evil at play here. We assume that the second gentleman was caught in a terrible accident or some such thing and we go on about our lives, still helping out poor Fitzroy when we can. However, come the week after and a fine-looking dame shows up at Maud's livery stable and enquires about the prized paint horse of the remuda. It's this thoroughbred called Nancy; a black-and-chestnut mare with one helluvan engine. You don't stop Nancy once she gets going. So the same thing happens again only with different prices - I don't remember the specifics, although I imagine it weren't far off the price of the flivver, such was Nancy's desirability. This broad who claimed to want her was a real choice bit of calico, all dressed in glad rags and such like. She would have given even old Mélanie a run for her money.

'And, lo, three days later another good-looking dame shows up and the same thing happens all over again. Maud is a little suspicious, don't get me wrong, but no one in town is certain that this is a scheme yet and so she gives the ladies the benefit of the doubt and agrees to sell

Nancy to the second of them. She doesn't show up after Maud compensates the first lady and so the whole town convenes in the town hall to decide what the hell is going on. We got no cops around here no more you see, so we gotta deal with these things democratically and as one unit, which is exactly what we do.'

'It's exactly what we tried to do,' corrected Doc. 'Everyone was real mad and was thinking on forming a posse. What that posse would do once it got hold of its targets remained to be seen. But Pop-pop cooled them and said he would sort it. Two days later he comes back with the four schemers locked inside a wagon-cage. They were two couples, you see, all working together across the county, doing the same old scheme here, there and everywhere. They'd made a fortune. Pop-pop made them pay up double to Maud and Fitzroy and had a sketch artist brought in from Los Angeles to draw their faces for the paper. Their punishment was that they could never come back to town or any town in the county because people would know what they looked like.'

'Jeepers creepers,' said Sunrise. 'They didn't stand a chance.'

'Pop-pop gave them their just desserts and he stopped a posse from what was maybe gonna be a lynching,' Doc affirmed. 'What would we do without him, huh?'

'I ain't sharp enough for that kind of baloney anymore, kid,' said Pop-pop. 'I just ain't got the eye nor the stomach for it. I'm getting old. Why don't you take my place? You're getting your experience on security at the Itch, ain't you?'

'Not anymore, Pop-pop,' said Doc.

'No?'

'Naw, July thinks it was a monkey that stole Sunrise's things, so he's moving me downstairs because he reckons it's too dangerous me having to fight off the critter. I reckon I'll try to persuade him against it.'

'*Did* the monkey steal Sunrise's things?'

'No one stole my things,' said Sunrise. 'It was a bit that we did on the day we met, ain't that right, Doc?'

'Hell yeah it is. But we ain't going to tell July that we lied to him.

And if we were to then I would have even less of a chance of staying on as security because he would know there was no robbery anyway.'

'Even still,' said Pop-pop, clearly reluctant to indulge in this ridiculous line of conversation, 'I ain't up to it these days. I'm too forgetful and I'm too clumsy and I'm too old.'

'You talk like you need a cigarette,' said Doc.

'I'll smoke *you*,' said Pop-pop, pulling his thumb and index finger from his pocket to imitate a pistol.

'How long till the planetarium is done, Willie?' asked Sunrise.

Suddenly Pop-pop fell solemn. His whole figure slumped in his collapsible chair and the light in his eyes was no longer from within, but rather reflective of the moonlight as they glistened with tears. He gulped.

'I ain't sure I'm going ahead with it,' he said.

'*What*?' said Doc.

'You heard me, kid. I got such a bad feeling about it.'

'Sunrise, tell him!'

Sunrise looked uneasy.

'Seems to me like anything you do makes this town feel better,' she said.

'So if I do nothing they'll feel better?' Pop-pop said.

'Doing nothing ain't doing something.'

'What if it's a bust?'

'Why would it be a bust? Seems to me you know your onions about your line of work, Mr Bridger.'

'I'm losing the eye for it.'

Doc decided to threaten Pop-pop with the cold shoulder in the event that he cancelled the planetarium's opening, but that did little to make him budge. But Sunrise had a dastardly trick up her sleeve.

'Show them all one last time that you've still got it,' she said. 'Leave them all in no doubt, huh? Show them that you're still the man that chased the cops out of town; who caught the schemers; who's pals with *Edwin Hubble*.'

Pop-pop looked down at his knees and a smile flickered from one corner of his mouth to the other.

'Your father told me that there's someone else who don't much like the thought of the planetarium,' he said to Doc.

'He did? Who?'

'Hampstead.'

'Then you know it's nonsense!' laughed Doc. 'That kid thinks he's a real drugstore cowboy and that's proof enough of how delusional he is, ain't it?'

'Dang right,' said Sunrise.

'His buddy Hector got me to go and speak to the feller in the photography emporium the other day. It was real strange.'

'Why'd he do that?' asked Pop-pop.

'I ain't sure. All I had to do was ask the feller how to use one of the kodaks. He paid me fifty-six cents to do it and explain it to him. I ain't sure why he couldn't do it himself but he told me not to ask questions I didn't wanna know the answers to.'

'You reckon it had something to do with Hampstead?'

'Oh, most certainly. Anyway, I've met my *social quota* for the day and now I'm beat. I'm glad you could see sense, Pop-pop,' said Doc, putting a long arm around him as she hugged him goodnight and promised to see him in the not-long.

'Damn the both of you for putting me straight,' said Pop-pop, holding her tightly.

14

Over the course of many sultry days the sun draped the whole town in an ochre wash and the chalky ground underfoot was too hot to walk on, even for those who chose to wear shoes. It was simply too sweltering to do anything outdoors. Even Willie's hill looked ready to melt away as though volcanic. And the Pig's Itch was quiet and the three *amigos* gathered regularly outside Room 3 with the initial intention of further story-swapping, only this soon devolved into an observed quiet from July and Doc while Sunrise read or related the stories she had been told by her beloved Nathaniel back in Rockwell. Doc had challenged July's mercurial temperament and in doing so persuaded him that she and she alone could resist the advances of a sybarite capuchin.

All of the stories concerned the Greeks; some mythology, others philosophy. The Apollo and Daphne story had wandered about July's mind day and night for what seemed like an eternity. And Apollo's student Orpheus, who was taught to play the lyre by Apollo, had a story of his own that July had been trying to dissect although to little success. And some of these fellers that were talked about in this dialogue written by the ancient man Plato, though the players in this piece were pretentious but for the comedian Aristophanes. He, according to Sunrise, had come up with the story about humans once being of two sets of arms and legs, two faces, two sets of privates and of big, round torsos.

The cloudburst finally arrived and the adobe walls that marked the separation of property in town were muddied and slopped. July, who had been in a daze of heat and mistiness for several days now, suddenly felt a burgeoning desire to discuss. All he had been able to do during the heat was listen and acknowledge. But no longer would he be restrained to such idleness. In a matter of hours from the rain's first drive he was full of thoughts and questions. So he left Mr Cricket to tend to re-emerging patronage downstairs and found Doc on post outside Room 3.

'No Sunrise?' he asked.

'I heard her arguing with Mr Hale,' Doc said, gesturing to the door. 'I reckon they got a few things to iron out before we see her.'

'Arguing about what?'

'Hell if I should tell someone another's business.'

'Dern it,' said July, offering Doc some chartreuse and receiving a lit Gold Flake in return.

'I'm still here though, July.'

'I have questions that only Sunrise can answer.'

'What about?'

'The stories she's been telling us.'

'At least let me help. I'm awful bored.'

July mused awhile and sipped on his liquor and puffed on the cigarette. He knew that he had nothing better - or more interesting, at least - to do.

'Well, my first thought was about this Orpheus feller,' he said, taking a seat on the floorboards with his back against the banister. 'He played the lyre so well that even the Sirens' songs were drowned, so he plans to musically... seduce... everyone in the afterlife into letting him through so that he might rescue his beloved Eurydice.'

'Yes,' said Doc, 'the bud plucked before the flower bloomed.'

'Must have been quite a journey, and all only to lose her again on the way out. I wonder if any other man had ever made it there before him? I get the feeling he loved more than most.'

'I disagree,' said Doc, 'because he ought to have simply killed himself in order to join her. If not before he ventured into hell then at least after he lost her again. Instead he wandered around feeling sorry for himself. How can that be true love? Don't get me wrong, I probably ain't experienced it myself, but I'm sure as hell that a feller ought to do anything he can to be united with his beloved, and Orpheus did not. He just played his dang lyre and moped around.'

'Gee, Doc,' said July.

'And he was stupid too,' continued Doc. 'Why did he look back at her when he was told that doing so would keep her in hades?'

'Because he loved her.'

'No, because he had lust. He wanted to look at her face because he was so attracted to her body. Love I think would be joy in knowing that she was there behind him. It would be patience and bravery in the face of his fear. He was cowardly again - that's three times now - and how can real, true love make a person cowardly? Again, I ain't got experience to go off, but if love doesn't sure up a man then it sounds pretty dang worthless.'

'Then is love only existent in the action that is the most brave?'

'I guess so,' said Doc.

'But Orpheus went into hades to bring her back. How can that be cowardly?' pressed July.

'Perhaps it is not cowardly, but it was the more cowardly of his two options. Clearly he was too afraid to commit suicide, and so he went for the easier option. Once he got out of hades without Eurydice he only had one option if he wished to return for her, and that was to die. But again he did not do this of his own accord.'

'You are reducing one of the greatest romances ever told into a joke,' sulked July.

'Sure, he turns back to look at her, blah-blah-blah. Oh, what a hero; what a poet! Perhaps he was a poet and was acting all poetic-like in turning to look upon her, but what the hell! Just hold your dang horses, Orpheus.'

'At least they reunited in hades when Orpheus finally did die,' said July, defeated.

'I hope for her sake that they didn't. She could do better, even among the dead,' said Doc. 'So what was the thought that you had about this story, anyway? You never said.'

'I was just going to say that I reckoned Orpheus was the bravest man to ever live,' sighed July, and Doc burst into an ugly and yet infection belly-laugh. 'So all those fellers at this symposium; those philosophers and academics and writers and teachers, they were all wrong. But a twelve-year-old frog-lover was right?' July went on.

'Amphibians! And I don't know that word. What are you talking about?' said Doc.

'The symposium,' repeated July. 'Sunrise talked about it. Don't you remember?'

'Perhaps I was asleep. Explain it?'

'So there's a bunch of these Greek squares at some kind of a hoedown right, probably a long while ago. And they get a bit drunk and they decide to take turns explaining what they think love is all about. One of them talks a blue streak about how love is in medicine and in the harmony between good and bad. Another talks about love necessarily creates virtue. Another - Aristophanes - talks about all that conjoined people schtick, remember?'

'I remember that part.'

'Another of the fellers says that Love is a god. In fact maybe they all say that, but he's really keen on the notion. And the last feller talks about how Love is no god at all but is actually some kind of a force that exists between us. You can see its work in the birth of men and in the creation of art.'

'Any ladies at this hoedown?'

'Nome,' said July. 'I think one of the fellers talks about a conversation he once had with a lady, though.'

'Hardly fair, is it?'

'Men feel love differently to women,' said July.

'And how would you know that? You would either have to be a woman or ask a woman how she felt in order to know that for certain, and as far as I am aware you have never done either of those things.'

'Gee, it's just a feeling I've got,' said July, suckling on his canteen with aggression. 'Besides, if men and women don't experience love in different ways then it wouldn't matter if it were only men at the hoedown.'

'But my point is that you don't know and so you can't assume that.'

'Fuhgeddaboudit,' said July, acceptant.

'So anyway. I want to hear some of these details.'

'I can't remember all too well; that's part of why I came here. I wanted to hear it all again.'

'Think hard, July.'

'Well, going back to your silly little tirade about Orpheus's lust, I suppose I can compliment your feelings on it, for my sins.'

'You can?' smiled Doc.

'Sunrise remembered some words from the *Symposium* and I done written them down.'

July fetched a small and scrappy piece of parchment from his shirt pocket and proceeded to read aloud:

Evil is the vulgar lover who loves the body rather than the soul, inasmuch
as he is not stable because he loves that which in itself is unstable.
Therefore when the bloom of youth which he was desiring is over,
he takes wing and flies away in spite of his words and promises.
Whereas the love of the noble disposition is lifelong, for it
becomes one with the everlasting.

'Who said that?' asked Doc.

'One of the Greek fellers.'

'I don't understand it.'

'I guess it just means that lust is pointless.'

'So you agree about Orpheus then?'

'Whatever,' said July. 'Until ten minutes ago I loved this paper real and true, and now it is an epitaph to my defeat to a child.'

'Well, bully!' said Doc. 'So do you agree that love must be the utmost courage too?'

'Not always,' said July.

'Ugh!'

'For example, when Orpheus first goes to collect Eurydice he is intelligent. I do not think he is a coward in that instance, even if he chooses to take the more cowardly option. He knows that he is capable of getting to hades and he knows that he has the skill to escape it with Eurydice in hand. So why would he not do this? Why would he kill himself? To prove that he can do the brave thing? What would be the point? How can there be nobility in stupidity? Sure he ends up messing the whole thing up, but he wasn't to know that he would. He wasn't to know that Hades would put such a condition on his saving Eurydice. Perhaps he was naïve, maybe, but I think one can still love truly and not do the boldest thing. It is not a necessary condition. We could amend what you said to this: a man is in love if he chooses the bravest option when there are no smarter options available to him.'

'This is getting a bit silly now,' said Doc.

'Yes, but we ought to talk about these things because otherwise the only people who do are the squares who lived a gajillion years ago and never looked outside their poems and thought that everything was a god or a spirit or something and -'

'- never spoke to women about it,' interrupted Doc.

'Yes, yes. All of these things.'

'So the rest of us idiots ought to contemplate on these things because we might find answers that the smartest people in history couldn't?'

'I'm just saying that I doubt these people are actually real anyway. If you lived that long ago you might as well not be real. And if they thought it wasn't worth the common person discussing it then they can go to hades. We just take it that Orpheus was a coward because they say it in the *Symposium*? That's crazy!'

'They say it in the *Symposium*? Why didn't you tell me that?!'

'Because it shouldn't matter what any of them said! People lived then and people lived now. People felt things then and they feel things now. None of that will change. There will always be more Greek schmucks and there will always be Yankee schmucks too. Because they're old it doesn't mean that they're right, and they're especially not necessarily right in this case because they're all privileged whiners at some swanky hoedown!'

'They do sound it,' said Doc. 'It still feels good that they agreed with me about Orpheus though. Did they really think he was a coward too?'

'One of them did,' muttered July. 'Although he didn't say that Orpheus was a coward three times like you did. He had a little mercy.'

Doc took some more chartreuse and sighed.

'I'm sorry for making this into an argument. I reckon you wanted romantic answers and I just gave you damning ones. I ain't much for people-pleasing, as you know.'

'That's all right. You know, such is how ludicrous love is, I think that it's probably useful to hear it from the point of view of someone who hasn't been tainted by it, after all.'

'Bully for me, I guess.'

From underneath the door of Room 3 came sliding a set of yellowed pages with crinkles and creases and scribblings. On the front cover was the title and nothing else, and it was the *Symposium*. July took it awkwardly and opened it up.

'Thank you,' Doc whispered through the gap.

'And actually there are one or two things that we might agree on in here,' said July.

'That so?' said Doc.

'Sure.'

Though July couldn't remember exactly where the quote was he was not rushed by Doc, who sat serenely in quiet as the man flicked through.

'I would like to know your thoughts on this,' July finally said.

That a state or an army should be made up of lovers and their loves,
they would be the very best governors of their own city.
Abstaining from all dishonour, and emulating one another in honour.
And when fighting at each other's side, although a mere handful,
they would overcome the world.
For what lover would not choose rather to be seen by all mankind than

by his beloved?
He would readily die a thousand times rather than endure this.
Or who would desert his beloved or fail them in the hour of danger?
The verist coward would become an inspired hero, equal to the bravest,
At such a time love would inspire him.
That courage which, as Homer says, the god breathes into the souls of some heroes.
Love of his own nature infuses into the lover.

They sat almost plaintively for a few moments.

'I don't know that I have any thoughts on that,' Doc said eventually. 'But it sounds real pretty. What about you, July? Do you have any thoughts?'

'Yes.'

'Then tell me them and I won't interrupt.'

'I believe the speaker here - Phaedrus, I think - is saying that the world is better to be filled by those in love than it is by those not. Love teaches us shame and no person in love would rightly shame themselves in front of their beloved, and so the lovers act bravely. We might be laughed at and taunted by a thousand friends but that is nothing compared to the pain of being mocked by the beloved. The army that is full of lovers would never be defeated because not one of those soldiers would give up. But Doc, no matter how swell it all sounds, the world is better to have you - one who is not and has not been in love - as you are, rather than it would be to have you a different way, whether that be in love or otherwise. I really believe that.'

'Aw, gee, July. I'm gonna blush.'

'And what good has love done me?' July went on. 'I was a better man before than I was during or after. So I must disagree with Phaedrus, the idiot.'

'And I must agree with him,' said Doc. 'For it is the July who has *endured* love, not the one who was yet to find it, that is my friend.'

15

Doc had given Heck the instructions on how to use the kodak and Heck had told Hampstead. It was probably not going to work and anyway Hampstead was feeling all guilty and upside down in his tummy. Sure they'd paid Doc to do it but it didn't feel right implicating her in the boys' shenanigans, least of all when he still hadn't had the guts to speak to her. On the night of her favour to them Hampstead borrowed and read *Frankenstein* to keep his mind distracted from the somersaults and gurgling going on downstairs. He finished it in one sitting but it was a big mistake. When sleep came he had a terrible dream where Doc was lost in Geneva or Ingolstadt or Scotland or somewhere like that. Hampstead didn't know what any of those places looked like but his dream consciousness told him it was maybe one of them. All he knew was that it was cold wherever it was. Maybe it was just Alaska.

And Doc was there in the dream and she was lost and she was very cold. But still Hampstead was unable to talk to her or even make himself visible to her. She was stood in the dark street with her goddamn bare feet and stupid long arms going a strange colour that Hampstead didn't recognise. He was terrified for her and desperately wanted to wrap her up in a blanket or set one of the buildings on fire so that she might have somewhere warm to spend the night. Still he couldn't get close to her. When he woke up the next morning he himself was in a cold sweat and was frantic like he hadn't been in a long while. To combat this he resolved to never letting the Doc in reality suffer like the Doc in his dreams, lest he succumb to guilt so wild and powerful that it would likely kill him.

So that morning Hampstead asked his mother what she expected the weather would be like over the coming twelve hours.

'I reckon we're in for a doozy of a rainstorm,' she told him.

'I reckon you're right about that,' said Hampstead, 'I mean, just look at the clouds, huh? It's grey as heck up there. Hell, do you mind if I take a nickel with me to school so that I can get myself an umbrella?'

'The department store ain't on your way,' said Momma.

'I figure I'd make a mosey out of it.'

'Do you know how to use an umbrella?'

'Sure I do.'

'All right. Go and get my purse.'

But of course Hampstead had no intention of using an umbrella himself. He rather liked the rain and it usually cleared him of his guilt for not having washed in the bathtub. Also it became prime mud season whenever it rained and Hampstead simply couldn't get enough of mud. He was like a little piglet in that sense. Where's little piggy Hampstead been today? Why, can't you tell? For a swim in the donkey corral.

The umbrella that Hampstead purchased was too big for his arms but he reckoned it was ideal for Doc. He tried to pop it three times and only on the third did it finally open, and then a gust of wind nearly took him off his feet and so he frenetically fastened it back up. He wiped the sweat from his forehead and cursed the thing before hiding it in the thicket outside the schoolhouse. All the kids would be kept inside during recess if it did come down like he expected it to, so he could relax about getting the umbrella to Doc before the closing bell rang that afternoon.

Everything went as planned through the day and Hampstead snuck out of his final class early so that he wouldn't miss Doc. Marcus Brannigan, a well-upholstered teacher's pet with very thin hair, tried to intercept him, but Hampstead swerved around the outstretched leg without tripping and then darted through the doorway before he got grassed up. He headed into the thicket and touched base with the umbrella before making himself as comfortable as he could in that particularly uncomfortable hidey spot. For a moment he got distracted by a little colony of doodlebugs making the way across the sand. With the rain starting to come down heavy Hampstead worried that they wouldn't make it back to their commune, but there was no time to do anything about it. The kids began flooding out of the schoolhouse and sprinting like mad gazelles. Some had their books over their heads and pretty much everyone had their heads bowed to keep their faces dry. If Doc hadn't been such a weird-looking creature then Hampstead wouldn't have had any hope of spotting her.

When she eventually limbered into view Hampstead made a quick note of whether she was going home or to the Pig's Itch. It appeared the former which meant a long walk. Hampstead freed himself from the coppice, stuck out his tongue to catch some rain and then made a beeline for the fishmongers, outside which he left the umbrella. The fishmongers was on Doc's way home and was where he would leave the umbrella for her. The shortcuts around town were all known to him from his and Goose's time spent chasing cats down narrow alleys and crawlspaces. He stowed away underneath the boardwalk on the opposite side of the street and watched closely as Doc noticed and then ignored the umbrella, walking on by with an air of suspicion clouding around her. Hampstead swore loudly. He pulled himself out and collected the umbrella, climbed up onto the fishmongers and then began vaulting from one rooftop to the next. He was like a little ninja or something. He figured that if Doc found the exact same umbrella further along her route then she would realise that it was intended for her and quit being so difficult about the whole thing.

But when Hampstead left the umbrella poking through the floorboards of the veranda Doc still veered wide of it. He gave up on the day's endeavour.

'How's the umbrella?' asked Momma when Hampstead got home.

'Stupid,' said Hampstead, throwing it onto the floor and grunting up to his room. He had to figure out another way to be Doc's guardian angel from afar. If they were never to speak - and Hampstead had accepted that possibility, what with his being a coward and all - the two of them would have to get by with this strange quasi-relationship that existed on two sides of a wide breadth.

The next morning Hampstead felt fresh and got up early and quickly scrawled a note on a page in his math book, then tore it out and stuffed it in his pocket. After gathering the remnants of a ball of thread from Momma's sewing machine he and Goose made their way outside with some tinned sardines from the pantry and went looking for strays, one of which they found under a trashcan near the trolley line. It was a peaceable tabby who purred when Hampstead tickled behind his ears. Hampstead had to order Goose to keep clear and look the other way so as to not spook the cat off, but once Hampstead got it into his arms and happy with sardines Goose was unable to resist his curiosity. He bounced over and sniffed wildly underneath Hampstead's arms, so Hampstead had to shoo him away again. They walked a whole half mile to the Pig's Itch where Hampstead tied the math book note to the cat's midriff using Momma's thread. Then he rapped loudly on the door.

For the company of your staff. Especially the lonely ones.

Doc could do with a friend and most likely the cat could do with one too. Hampstead sneezed and sneezed again as he fled the scene with Goose, cursing his allergies but pleased to death with himself for his cunning work. And, what was more, Hampstead had another grand idea up his sleeve to help Doc out today. What anyone could tell about Doc was that she was one helluva wiseguy. She was probably the smartest kid at school and the whole curriculum was wasted on her unless it was about frogs and toads and the like. Sometimes when Hampstead left his own lessons to go the bathroom he would pass one of Doc's classes and see her staring out of the window like she would learn more from the mesquite than she would the blackboard. *Too right*, thought Hampstead. But boredom could get awful lonely sometimes and Hampstead had found that his periods of idleness were often coupled with anxious thoughts and restlessness. He did not want the same for Doc. Sure she was good at being a loner but hell if Hampstead was going to let her have the screaming-meemies while she was.

So when he got back home from the Pig's Itch he still had a good half hour before leaving - assuming that he would skip breakfast. He and Goose turned the bedroom over looking for a particular cardboard box that Hampstead had not gone near in a couple of years by now. It was the box of his old comic books. Ever since he started reading novels Hampstead had decided that comic books were a little beneath him and he often scorned old Hector for obsessing over them at his age. But Hampstead had never done away with the comics because he was privately very fond of them still and wouldn't do without them at least *being* there.

He found it at the back of the chiffonier and it was covered in dust and cobwebs. He blew it clean and opened it up and pulled out a select few of old favourites. There was *Winnie Winkle*, *Thimble Theatre*, *Little Orphan Annie*, *The Gumps* and *Gasoline Alley* among many others. Hampstead was furious because now he wanted to read them all but didn't have the time, so he angrily skimmed through a few and tore out some of the strips that he remembered real well. Then he took some drawing pins from Momma's stationery tub. Then he realised he had ten minutes and so ate some eggs before stuffing everything in his bag and waltzing to school with a cocky spring in his step.

Because Doc was always knocking things off the desk with her stupid arms she liked to keep them underneath it with the discarded bits of bubble gum. That was where Hampstead pinned the comic strips. They hung down so that she wouldn't miss them. Then he scarpered back to homeroom just in time for the bell. He had snuck in through the homeroom window before everyone had arrived and then made his way to Doc's homeroom where he had deposited the literature. If she would only take them with her when all the kids dispersed to their day's classes then she wouldn't find herself bored for the whole day. And Hampstead had so many comic books that he would unlikely ever run out of strips for her to read. He could make a routine out of it.

During fourth period Hampstead really needed a pee. Mr Portnoy was very distrusting of Hampstead but allowed him to go to the bathroom on this one occasion because Hampstead physically could not keep still, even when Mr Portnoy instructed the big class bully Jerome to get Hampstead in a wrestling hold. Though he was very grateful Hampstead did not have the time to hang around singing his teacher's praises and so fled from the scene and relieved himself at the nearest bathroom. Then he passed Doc's class. She was sat in the far corner at the back by the window but she wasn't looking out of it. Instead she was looking down at something on the desk that she was hiding with her arm. She was smiling. Hampstead smiled too.

(ii)

It was darker than usual that evening and the boys had been instructed by Tuna not to bring any sources of illumination to the Outpost out of fear they'd draw attention to themselves. So far everything had been a success and it would be pretty embarrassing if everything went to the dogs because of some dumb kerosene lamp, Hampstead agreed.

'Take those walking boots off,' said Tuna. 'You can't go *clunk-clunk-clunking* around in a covenstead. You've gotta be light on your feet.'

'All boots are walking boots,' Hampstead muttered. 'Whoever heard of sitting boots?'

Heck came up the scrambling hole with a big grin on his face.

'By god, am I excited,' he said. 'I got a real jog on my way here; that's how excited I am. Even with these crazy knees of mine.'

'Excited to see me get eaten by witches? Some friend you are,' said Hampstead.

'You'll be hunky-dory,' said Tuna. 'In, *snap-snap-snap*, out.'

'And they still haven't noticed the camera's gone missing?'

'Most places do inventory on Sundays,' said Tuna. 'So we've got at least thirty-six hours before he figures it out, meaning thirty-six hours to get these pictures out to the public.'

It was a very clear night and the lights from the covenstead were meshing with the stars on the horizon. Hampstead had a feeling of resolve and determination in his bones, but also one of dread. It did not help that Tuna had brought his father's copy of *Macbeth* and was reading from it as though it were an instruction manual.

'Double, double toil and trouble;
Fire burn and cauldron bubble.'

'What about it?' snapped Hampstead.

'If you hear that then you get the hell out of there, got it? And, for that matter, if you hear anything about eyes of newts, let's see, toes of frogs, tongues of dogs, blah-blah-blah, that sort of thing. If you hear any of that then you get the hell out. But try and get some photographs as you go about it.'

'What the hell is a newt?'

'Fuhgeddaboudit,' said Tuna. 'Just listen out for any spooky incantations and move real quick if you catch any.'

'Fine.'

'I can come with you, Hampstead,' said Hector.

'Sorry, you'll slow me down, Heck. Besides, I want to do this by myself.'

'You're a brave man,' said Tuna.

'Shuddup, Tuna.'

Hampstead slid down the scrambling hole and hurt the soles of his bare feet as he landed at the bottom. There were thistles here and there but he wasn't going to be distracted. Adrenaline would carry him across no man's land. Tuna had assigned him some homework which involved building a small trinket to be worn on a necklace and reading *The Wonderful Wizard of Oz*. Hampstead had never read it before but found it delightful, going a step further afterwards and borrowing *The Marvelous Land of Oz* and *Ozma of Oz* from the library. He read them in one sitting. But all he really needed to know was that a canteen full of water would probably do the trick if push came to shove. The trinket was meant to serve as magical protection and Tuna had blessed it with a passage from *Deuteronomy*.

At the bottom of the Outpost Hampstead stood and held out his arms for the kodak to be carefully lowered down by Tuna and Heck. There was no way in hell it was going down the scrambling hole; it was far safer to have a rope looped and tied around it a bajillion times and gently moved downwards from the battlements. It was an Autographic Brownie which took 120 film, Hector had said. It had been a nuisance because they had had to steal both a spool and film separately, which had been problematic for Tuna during his little caper as he disorientated real easy despite all he said about being a leader.

'God speed!' said Heck.

'Make sure you get good photographs!' said Tuna.

Off Hampstead went, feeling the pit in his stomach growing and growing and the numbness in his arms and legs increasing with every step. This is what Doc must feel like all the time, he thought, looking at his limbs. He was wearing a black sweater, black pants and a black hat to blend in with his surroundings.

The lair loomed large like a castle as he approached. He knew how he was going to get in and that was through an upstairs window that was periodically opened a crack throughout the night. When it and the curtains were open the boys could see that the room would be empty for a couple of minutes until two figures - usually a man and a woman - returned, and both were shut once more. Hampstead roped the kodak around his neck and hoisted himself up onto the awning, quiet as a mouse. The window was still closed and so he took a shadowy position further along the wall and waited it out, his pulse accelerating with every moment of stillness.

Then finally it opened and Hampstead took one helluva deep breath. Then he crept along the wall and prised it wide enough for him to slip through. The room was deserted of people and only dimly lit by candle and paraffin oil. Remaining was an array of strange things that roused Hampstead's anxiety. Plenty of red for starters. Velvet everywhere and jewellery out the wazoo. Police equipment like handcuffs and batons and rope. Leather boots. A strange, perfumed aroma that lingered and hung with bodily smells. Stains on the sheets. A plush footstool. Another pair of leather boots.

Time was of the essence and Hampstead knew the camera would be a fiddly bastard and so he thought hard about what Heck had told him that Doc had told him about how to take photographs. Hampstead took cover behind the standing mirror in the corner of the room and twisted the knob of the kodak until a little '1' appeared in the circular red window. Then he pulled the front lever and the bed clicked into position. *So far so good.* The lens pulled out and snapped into the slot. The thing was huge when opened out but at least it was manageable. He turned the little dial to the '8 ft' option and held it in position. He had never taken a photograph before but he was real happy with his progress thus far.

With it pressed against his midriff he could see through the viewfinder what he was about to capture. The room. Perfect. Then finally he set the shutter speed and the aperture and he was good to go. He peered around the mirror to make sure that no witch had entered unbeknownst to him while he was applauding himself. The room was still empty. He shuffled his hips and stuck his torso out to the left, keeping his head and legs concealed behind the mirror as though someone had hit him across the stomach with a baseball bat. It made it difficult for him to see through the viewfinder but he could crane his neck at an angle that just about did the trick. Then he pulled the shutter release lever. *Voila*, he thought. No proof of sorcery in here but he was comfortable with the device and that really eased his anxieties. He crept to the door and squeaked it open.

The hallway was empty and dimly lit and red like the bedroom. No cauldrons, no cats and no black hats. Unwilling to waste film Hampstead chose to save his next photograph for evidence that was truly damning. He tiptoed to the bottom of a rather grand staircase that spiralled up from the end of the hallway and faced a door that looked as though it might be to a lobby. There was a small, square window about five-and-a-half feet up; too high for Hampstead. There were animated shadows and lights cast through it and onto the staircase behind him, as well as voices; some distinct and others muffled:

'... was expecting a cabaret,' said a man.

'You don't know what it means when a girl tells you to meet her at the cabaret? Where you been, boy? Gee, you're innocent. It's kinda cute on you, if I can be candid,' said a lady.

'My first time,' said the man.

'I'll give you a discount.'

'Is that a ruse?'

'How you mean?'

'To lure me into trusting you so that you can steal all my cash?'

'Honey, this ain't that kind of town. We don't abide by tricksters here. Even if I wanted to I'd end up getting filled with daylight by Mr Bridger,' said the lady.

'Who?'

'He lives on the hill. But what I mean to say is that I ain't in the business of fraudulence. I want to give you a service and I want money for it, plain and simple. No hidden fees, no games, no funny business. Does that sit all right with you, honey?'

'I ain't turning back now.'

The two clear voices fed into the muffled din that they had been protruding over and a distant door opened and closed.

So that narrows it down, Hampstead thought. *This ain't no cabaret.*

And his curiosity got the better of him. He shuffled back to the bedroom and squeezed in through the door, balanced the kodak on the footstool and carefully carried the two of them back out and down the hall. At the door he put down the footstool and crept onto it, slowly pushing his head up so that he could see through the window.

There were two big eyes staring back at him. Blue and wonderful and terrifying and angry. Hampstead fell backwards from the shock and the kodak with him, both landing in a very noisy heap on the floor as the door swung open and the footstall skidded away to the wall. Hampstead's stomach was in his face and his lungs were no longer working. Breath failed him and his pulse began to sound like a faulty metronome that got ever louder and ever faster. The eyes of the stranger belonged to a big mute feller whom Hampstead knew from around town. His name was Bert and he used to be a fireman but now people hardly saw him. His jaw was wide and his cheeks gaunt. There were scars on his collar and neck from the fights he'd picked. His father cut out his tongue for his sass when he was a child and now he was always real mad; so mad in fact that Hampstead would have rather come up against a witch and her cauldron.

In the moments that Hampstead was very much detached from reality he managed to scamper onto the staircase and haul himself up. The thought of the kodak didn't even occur to him. Perhaps it was broken already. He whimpered but he was too scared to call for help. The big man Bert followed him with ominous, stomping footsteps, and such a lack of speed that Hampstead found it even more unnerving than if the mute had been running after him. Was there something waiting for him upstairs that Bert was privy to and hence his tempered chase? Whatever it would be would not be as bad as Bert.

There might have been another hallway with another set of doors at the top of the staircase but all Hampstead knew was that there was space to stumble through. It felt so nightmarish and yet he couldn't convince himself that it wasn't real. All he felt was dread and terror and numbness. The marching mute's footsteps followed him and Hampstead felt like they'd always been with him. They became the only real thing in the world and they were truly terrifying. He could not sprint; only look in the direction from which he had come and stagger backwards. Always he was tumbling. Always he would be tumbling.

In the moment that Bert arrived at the end of the hallway the door closest to him opened and out walked an older lady who was scantily clad to say the least. She had a brutish look to her too. There were long teeth and thin lips and skeletal fingers to boot. In the confusion she turned to Hampstead and looked unhinged. A witch?

'What the hell?' she said. 'Bert?'

'Oh, lord,' said Hampstead. He felt a little bit of pee trickle down his leg but it was a small price to pay if he was going to get out of here without being chopped into tiny little pieces and thrown in a vat.

'What the hell are you letting kids in here for?' the woman said to Bert.

Bert signed something at the woman and then shrugged.

'You broke in here, you little wretch?' she said, turning to Hampstead again.

'No, I swear!'

'Did you break into this house?'

'No!'

'Don't lie to me!'

'I'm not! Oh, god! I'm not!'

Then two arms flooded around Hampstead from behind and he was engulfed in the strength of a man far bigger than himself or most men that he had ever known. Even Bert was smaller than this man felt. Hampstead panicked briefly but saw the firm black hands that had clasped onto his opposite shoulders and comfort surged through him. He swung around and buried his head in the man's chest.

'Pa! Pa!' he cried, tears streaming down his face and a sobbing now forming in his throat. All of him could breathe again but he was deeply distressed.

'I've got you, I've got you,' said the man in a low, soft voice. 'What the hell are you doing here?'

But Hampstead wasn't speaking properly just yet. He didn't think that he would be for a while. He was shaking like a leaf and weeping like a babe.

'Come on now,' said the man, lifting Hampstead off his feet and holding him the way a groom does his bride on their way over the threshold. But Hampstead felt immediately exposed and so did his best to curl up tight, wrapping one arm around his knees and the other around the back of the man's neck. It was doubtlessly uncomfortable for the man to cradle a child in such a way but Hampstead was not leaving anything to chance. He was a ball.

'We're going,' the man told Bert and the woman.

'Charlie!' said the frightening woman. 'What have you got for Sandi? That's her room, ain't it?'

Bert nudged the woman and signed something to her. She understood and nodded her apology at Charlie, who carried Hampstead past them. Then Hampstead once again covered his face in Charlie's arms so as not to see anything else on their way out. Only when the night chill hit the back of his neck did he dare to look. Charlie Bellingham dropped Hampstead onto his feet and Hampstead swayed and sniffed and wiped his eyes as dry as they would go.

'Let's get you home.'

Though the thoughts of the Outpost and the kodak and Tuna and Heck all crossed Hampstead's mind there would be no convincing him to do anything other than follow Charlie. He had saved him and he was the only one who would keep him safe. He tried to hold his hand but Charlie said that they oughtn't, so Hampstead just kept on his heels and they walked quickly in the quiet of the night. A couple of times Charlie again asked Hampstead what he was doing in that place but Hampstead had nothing but a stammer and a lump in his throat. Charlie understood pretty quickly.

It was still not so late and they bumped into a few folks on the way back home but Hampstead kept to Charlie's shadow. He didn't much fancy speaking to anyone and Charlie himself seemed keen to hurry on without catching anyone's eye. On occasion he would have no choice to interact with someone but he would tip his hat and nod his head cordially and that would be that. Perhaps he would say hello or good evening. Hampstead wasn't concentrating. All he could think about was how afraid he had been in the covenstead and how he could never face any of his pals again. He was a coward; a wuss. He'd let everyone down and it had been his hubris at fault. Everything was no longer as it once seemed.

'Look, kid. Best not to mention to anyone that you were in there, all right? You don't want to get in trouble,' said Charlie, leading Hampstead onto the boy's doorstep.

‘I won’t, Mr Bellingham.’

‘Adda boy.’

Hampstead took a deep breath and looked at his feet, steadied himself.

‘Thank you for looking after me,’ he said.

‘That’s all right.’

For a moment Charlie just looked at Hampstead. Then he turned and walked to the end of the yard and out of sight. Hampstead was in no fit state to face his mother and so hoisted himself up onto the ledge above the parlour room and pushed the window open. Goose was there and he followed Hampstead onto the bed and lay down next to him. The smell of urine finally hit Hampstead and so he tore off his pants and threw them out the window. He cried quietly all night and a couple of times Goose howled with him to make him feel less lonesome. Momma knocked on the bedroom wall to make Goose shut up but that only made Goose bark like crazy, so Momma stopped doing that and just let the gentle, intermittent *awwoooos* continue.

16

And the nights that followed troubled Hampstead to no end. Often the terrible images of the covenstead came to him in the depths of the night but they were not as troubling as the dream that deftly wove its way in between these recurring pictures.

In this dream Hampstead was diving in deep water. It began amusingly because Hampstead had never swam before. In fact he didn't even trust bathtubs or basins. But in the dream he was moving effortlessly and gracefully as though dancing through the warmth of a spring afternoon. It was from the shallows that he had come and he knew this because as he trailed deeper and deeper he found that the sea floor receded away at first slowly and then rapidly. Eventually it opened out into a grand expanse and there would be nothing below him but the darkness if he were to swim past the cliff edge. Above and aside he could still see ribbons of sunlight cutting through the gulf; themselves spinning and pirouetting in the active water. Yet the water was devoid of anything but rock and light and Hampstead. He expected fish and flowers and perhaps shipwrecks to boot. Perhaps there he would find treasure. In Kentucky Lake he heard that divers found valuable pearls in the bellies of oysters. But there were no oysters here, though if there had been Hampstead wouldn't have recognised them because he didn't know what they looked like.

Each time Hampstead arrived at the cliff edge he peered over and looked down without hindrance. He could see perfectly clearly and yet these magical eyes of his were wasted on the baron void and he lamented that. Nothing was below him except a growing darkness and a high-to-low-pitched creaking sound, the origin of which he could not find. He would twirl around and tread water and breathe in it, silently taking in the surrounding nothingness and finding a troubled sensation in his chest that began to irritate him. Then he would call out and he would find that his voice too was perfectly clear. It would carry through into the deep and the pitch of it itself would become deeper and deeper as it went. What he called out he did not know, despite that with every revisit of the dream he sought desperately to discern it.

After one particularly troublesome stint in the ocean - which caused him to clutch his linens with such strength that his fingernails tore through them - Hampstead awoke and resolved to never do anything irresponsible again. Somehow that would save him. Awhile he contemplated his blunders and considered again getting into smoking. That would at least create the illusion of a man with his affairs in order, and perception was at least a strong springboard. But until he was paid in actual currency rather than Abba Zabbas there would be no purchasing tobacco products for Hampstead. Instead he would fix his mistakes and vow to avoid making any more. And this would begin with a trip to the photography emporium where he planned to own up to his crimes and seek clemency from its proprietor.

Upon hearing Hampstead's explanation Mr Ledger sat with his index finger pressed on his lower lip. He was a surly white man with big grey eyes, a growing bald patch on the crown of his head and a crooked neck from taking too many photographs of the ground. It was commonly presumed that Mr Ledger had a gentle disposition beneath the icy façade that accompanied him day in and day out, but very few people ever ventured so far as to put it to the test. Hampstead was doing exactly that. Either Mr Ledger would thank the boy for his honesty and wish him well on his endeavours, or he would pull a sawn-off from the showcase. Hampstead found it more likely that he would be shown two barrels than he would be forgiveness. But anyway he was keen to get over his nightmares and he had to try. If he was forgiven then he would stop having nightmares and if he was shot and killed then he would stop having nightmares.

Hampstead figured that Mr Ledger might himself have died, such was the motionlessness with which he sat and mused. But Hampstead wanted to let the old man deliberate uninterrupted because Hampstead knew that his interruptions were never popular at the best of times. Mostly people were impatient with his impatience but once or twice he had been on the receiving end of a swift backhand or boot to the boys when his agility had failed him. Eventually Mr Ledger sighed and looked down on the whimpering child beneath the counter.

'You dumbfound me, Hampstead,' he said.

'I'm quite sure I don't know what you're talking about, Mr Ledger,' said Hampstead.

'What are we gonna do then?'

'I'm gonna make amends.'

'Eleven bucks for the camera. Two bucks for the carrying case. Added together and that's thirteen bucks,' said Mr Ledger.

'I'd say that's about thirteen, yeah.'

'And for the inconvenience and panic you caused me while doing my inventory, well, what would you say is fair?'

'Hell, I don't think you can put a price on inconvenience,' said Hampstead.

'Let's.'

'Poot. All right, say, five bucks?'

'You got another five bucks to give me, boy?'

'Hell, I ain't even got the original thirteen that you mentioned.'

'Then what are we doing?'

'I was thinking I could work for you. I could work for you for free. What's the going pay?'

'I ain't got anyone on the payroll currently, but that *vaquero* Sergio was on fifty cent a week before he went back to Guadalajara. I reckon thirty-five for yourself.'

'Hours?' asked Hampstead. 'I'm in school still and I ain't no truant.'

'Two hours after school every day plus six hours Saturday. I'll feed you some pan de campo or skillet potatoes or some such if the six hours is a little much,' said Mr Ledger. 'But only on Saturdays. I ain't no cookie and my larder's only finite.'

'Hell, I won't complain!'

'Say, you want to work off eighteen bucks' worth. That means we have to divide eighteen by point thirty-five.'

'That's beyond me,' admitted Hampstead. 'I'm more of a words kind of feller, though I can't spell all too well.'

'And me,' admitted Mr Ledger. 'Aw, shucks, let's just call it fifty cent then.'

'Hot damn!'

'That means we just have to divide eighteen by a half.'

'Comes somewhere in the thirties is my guess,' said Hampstead.

'Ten, twenty, eight, sixteen, sixteen, twenty... thirty-six.'

'Thirty-six what?'

'Thirty-six weeks, boy.'

'And if I do well?'

''scuse me?'

'Hell, I ain't one to fly my own kite in a storm but I reckon I'm one helluva good photographer. I took some real good pictures with that kodak. Shame it done broke otherwise I could prove it, and a helluva lot of other things too. But if I'm of use to you then what would you say to keeping me on a permanent basis? I've had a hankering for employment that pays in money and not candy.'

'You don't like candy?'

'Psh. Of course I like candy. But it don't make the world go round, Mr Ledger.'

'Perhaps after a period of probation I'll consider taking you on a full-time basis. Probation with reduced wages, but wages nonetheless, yes. Men become lackadaisical once you start paying them for their services.'

'I ain't no man yet,' said Hampstead. 'Don't worry. How long for probation?'

'However many more weeks it takes to fill out a full fifty-two. You fancy working that one out?'

'Hell, we'll cross that bridge when we come to it,' said Hampstead.

(ii)

There weren't a great many things that Bitsy was unsure about but church was one of them. Peculiar was how she described her relationship with the Presbyterian place down Boot Street. It seemed to her that she was Jewish; her mother's family she had been told had lived in a piedmont valley in Judea for centuries before emigrating to America. Mother had had to conceal her identity from the public eye during father's campaigns but she never forgot who she was. Now Bitsy had no family left on her mother's side and had never been to Israel. Father was Lutheran.

In her youth her father had taken her to see the Grand Council of the Six Nations in the north country, presumably to mock them, but Bitsy had been taken by the assembly and had something that she later considered to be a numinous experience. In between the weeks spent in D.C. Bitsy spent a great deal of time talking to the sachems and learning about the confederacy. America, it seemed to Bitsy, had a derivative constitution that muddied that of the Iroquois. Where Uncle Sam waded backwards through the mire of the two houses, the Iroquois passed legislation efficiently through the League.

Bitsy believed that there was a god or that there were gods. And these gods had not been elected by her or any of her countrymen and so were illegitimate. Yet Bitsy did not claim that they were obsolete; far from it. Bitsy was as opposed to anarchism as the next guy and felt that the world was always better with a strong leader - elected or otherwise. But if she got to the pearly gates she would go through and have a word and point to the Iroquois. 'That's how you do it,' she would say. Then if no one paid her any mind she'd push for reform via protest and demonstrations. Perhaps Hampstead would still be sewing her banners in the hereafter. There had been female council members in the confederacy since long before the Europeans had arrived on these shores. There was no colossal wall of bureaucracy in the confederacy.

But really Bitsy didn't know what the hell she thought anymore. A preacher-type was on the street corner every Thursday morning now and he was always dressed in red. He looked quite raving and often seemed to be foaming at the mouth and yet seldom was he alone. There would always be a little gathering around him to listen to his talk about blue collars and bourgeoisies and a ladder made of socioeconomics or something crazy. It made Bitsy feel real insecure about her own intelligence hearing such a loose feller talk so articulately. But sometimes she listened in to see if his philosophies matched his vocabulary. It had been the same when Bitsy had read Lenin's book: it hadn't swayed her so much, but it had certainly piqued her interest. She didn't much like the sound of revolution but the notion of reform made her cock her head once or twice.

Sometimes it got all too much for Bitsy. She couldn't wrap her head around her own head, let alone the world outside it. For now she resolved to be contented with her mission: eradicate her own vandalism. And it had made her very favourable among the populous thus far. The Briggs family, made of a mother, father and seven children all under the age of ten, was so delighted at Bitsy's work that they had invited her to accompany them to Sunday worship. She went and got a standing ovation from the congregation upon her arrival despite that Bitsy was famously not Christian. She sat between two of the Briggs sisters, Saskia and Jane. Saskia was eight and Jane six. When Reverend Kingsley was reading a passage about a feller called Zacchaeus, Bitsy leaned over to Jane and asked her if she was as bored as she was.

'No,' said Jane, and that was that.

What did catch her attention was after the service had concluded. A spotty teenager from the telegraph office approached her with a furrowed brow and a chewed bottom lip.

'Miss Bitsy,' he said.

'Hidy-do, Sidney,' said Bitsy.

'I reckon I got some news for you.'

'You do?'

'Ain't there meant to be some kind of celestial object taking your name?'

'So I've been told.'

'Next week's paper.'

'Excuse me?'

'In the paper next week. Monday. *The New York Times*. I been told that there's gonna be some announcements in the astronomy section. You know that I got a telegraph line straight to Hubble's office?'

'Of course I do,' said Bitsy.

'That's how I know. They said, "big announcement incoming". I don't hear much from them these days - much to my chagrin - but if they're telling me that then I don't know what else it can mean,' said Sidney.

'All right. Thanks.'

'You're welcome.'

Then Sidney left. Bitsy felt a twinge of dread and a singe of guilt, so she turned to the accompanying Mrs Briggs and quietly asked her about confession. Mrs Briggs, who was quite deformed in her middle age and far too touchy for Bitsy's liking, gently led her fellow churchgoer to the side and looked calmly into her eyes. Mrs Briggs' were watery and yellow.

'A prayer of confession of the reality of sin in personal and common life does not need to be a communal affair,' she said. 'If not done independently then it is not untouched by the words of others; it is not imperfect. Pray alone and return for forgiveness in His name.'

'I need to pray, then I will be forgiven?'

'Always.'

'That's one mighty simple process. Have you got paper?'

Mrs Briggs did not and so Bitsy sourced some from the sacristy, along with a blunt pencil. On it she wrote:

Alma, Big day for me next week I guess. Will suggest sundown on Monday. Probably the Pig's Itch. Would love ['love' scribbled out] *be glad to see you there. Regards, Bitsy.*

There was no eraser. Then she left the church without saying thank you or goodbye to anyone. She walked out into the day and let the sun kiss her eyelids before holding up her hand to shade her face. Along the way to Alma's place she passed two examples of her own vandalism and kept her head down and her eyes firmly fixed to the wall as she went. She felt in her pocket and found that she had left some chalk in it, so she stormily threw it to the ground and stamped it into dust. Left was a sprinkling of red in an abyss of orange and beige. It looked good and she felt better. For a moment too she imagined that the shame ebbing through her at that moment was likely not dissimilar to what little Hampstead felt when he walked by the word. He had tried to tell her about that but she still didn't really care all too much, even now that she could empathise better.

At Alma's house Bitsy shoved the note through the letterbox and rapped loudly on the door. Then she ran away to the municipal hall and pulled out the piano stool, ruminated awhile and pressed the different keys in a doleful way. It sounded fine. One day she wanted to be able to play *Clair de Lune* although that would likely make Mélanie swoon and attach herself onto Bitsy like they were conjoined. Perhaps if she ever learned to play it she would keep it to herself and to whatever piano teacher was lurking around in the far reaches of town. The crystal radio was on the fritz and the hall was ever so quiet and Bitsy was ever so restless, so she went to the library and took out a copy of the book by Marx and Engels and brought it back to the hall.

Again she sat on the piano stall and poked at the keys with the fingers on her right hand while dexterously holding and turning the pages of the book with her left. There were some real fancy words in there; words that Bitsy had never even heard of. But always they were followed by something that ruffled her: 'vanguard of the proletariat' by 'ascension to the ruling class', 'spectre of exploitation' by 'unite to revolt'. Bitsy was impatient with revolutions. When news broke in town during the War that the Bolsheviks had overthrown the provisional government Bitsy felt irritable for a day or two. She thought it was a lot of hullabaloo for them to do that. Perhaps in her heart she was too conservative and unostentatious by nature to believe that any of the ends justified the means, but not because the means were wrong - but because the means sucked.

Then night fell and Bitsy went to the Two Crows for supper. She ate potato dumplings and grilled sausage for her main dish. It came with walnut bread on the side but Bitsy's stomach must have shrunk because she was too full for it. Then she went to the Itch, drank four gin rickeys - two of which Mr Cricket provided on the house, though July probably wouldn't have condoned it - before swaying back to the beanery. Then she went to the kitchen and spoke to Elias Franke. Once upon a time Elias had smoked like a chimney but these days tobacco was practically in his very nature. He emitted fumes from his skin and floated on them. One might mistake him for a malevolent genie.

'How did you come across your profession, Herr Franke?'

'Ate some food and decided to make more,' said the taciturn Elias. 'As long as I have eaten I have known that it was my passion. And you? You seem destined for the realm of politics. It is in your blood.'

'I guess.'

'No?'

'I guess if I'm not destined for it then I've really wasted my life, right?'

'Trial and error,' suggested Elias.

'How did you know to come to America?'

'Lots of food in America.'

'But there's still lots of hungry folks though.'

'Wherever there's food there's hunger nearby. A cruel irony.'

Bessie Smith was singing on the gramophone. It was a little staticky.

Elias continued, 'I came also because of the music.'

'They don't have the record players in Germany?'

'Yes, they do. But the music is different. I prefer the soul.'

'I can take it or leave it,' said Bitsy. 'How does anyone know anything for sure?'

Elias sighed introspectively and gently hung his apron upon a hook in the wall.

'Germany is beautiful,' he said, 'the Black Forest is where I'm from; deep in the Rhine; a place called Baden-Baden. There they have thermal baths and rolling slopes and green and pink and red. The Wildsee is not far away and it is beautiful and peaceful and it is the only place that exists in the world to those who visit it and those who live there. Many nights I sat on the floating dock and dipped my toes into the water and thought of nothing but the water below me and the sky above. Never was I troubled and that is a feeling - or lack thereof - that often I miss. But in tranquillity there is not much soul. I have found in life that one must choose one or the other; I am yet to discover a place where I can truly experience both at the same time. I prefer the latter. Though I came here after the settlers had flooded the land I knew there was still a spirit lingering amongst them and their children. It is steeped in blood and land. Of course there are many other things steeped in the blood and land of this country, many abhorrent, but my selfishness and romanticism attracted me here nonetheless.

'Sometimes I go to the lake here and I sit on the floating dock like I did back in Baden-Baden. Only the lakeside here is alive with soirées and hoedowns and ding-dongs. The green and pink and red reflects off the water's surface and the music travels across it and is crisp as autumn. And I am not alone on the floating dock. A man is smoking a cigar while the bluegills nibble at his toes. A mother leaves the party to take her children home but they stop there awhile. We converse and she asks me my thoughts on the Kaiser and I resist speaking my piece about the Entente's expansionism, instead quickly decrying Wilhelm and receiving a warm smile in exchange. It is a small price. Then we speak about stocks or the New Woman or the talkies or Capone. And still the music plays and the lights flicker and twinkle on the water and I am filled with spirit.

'And I listen to Mamie Smith and Ida Cox and Ma Rainey and Jelly Roll Morton. I watch the lights and I meditate even though there is noise and brightness. I reflect on things but not the things of the kitchen; of the wider universe I ponder. The universe that I can see and the universe that I cannot see. The questions of my life - the questions that you have asked me tonight - these one finds answers to without thinking. These are inalienable facts of our being and they will one day be discovered. I ate a sausage and now I am a chef. A girl watches her father die of the fever and she becomes a physician. A boy gets hit in the head with a baseball bat and he becomes star pitcher for the Red Sox.'

The way he spoke was so nonchalant and yet a more sober Bitsy might have been torn to pieces by his words.

'So I have answered your two questions in one answer, albeit a rather long one. I came here because of the soul of the place and it is in moments of the soul that I find my answers. Not the answer to my profession however - that was a sausage. I can't explain that too well.'

For many hours that night Bitsy knelt by the bed with eyes closed and hands folded. Her knees blistered. She was feeling hopeless. Was it impossible for her to feel as Elias did; to have moments like he did on a floating dock? He wasn't even a poet or a philosopher - he was just a chef. Then Bitsy grew so tired and pained that she figured she might as well give it her best shot and hope for the best.

'I am selfish. That is all.'

(iii)

News of Bitsy's big day cautiously filtered through town over the next week. Once it might have spread like wildfire, but this time there was an atmosphere of wariness that accompanied it because everyone was afraid something might go wrong. There had been a great many delays to this exciting moment and no one wanted to be let down again. Once the message was passed on from one person to another the topic was swiftly diverted. Then it would remain dormant until the listener met the next listener. And so on and so forth. It was the talk of the town and yet it was mostly silent. It was very peculiar.

And then on Monday afternoon - the day the papers were being stocked - the inevitable happened. Screams were heard from the Pig's

Itch and a nervous crowd flocked to the scene, though an advised distance was maintained from the front door. Sunrise Livingston came running out and she was the one frightened.

'Orangutan!' she shouted, diving into the crowd. The old man Walter Hale who she attended to followed her out drunkenly, stumbling wildly in a daze of agitation, finding balance in the many arms of the throng. Some people began looking to Bitsy. Murmurings and shuffling feet had replaced violent screaming. Something about murmurings and shuffling feet unsettled Bitsy far more than violent screaming did. It meant that people were waiting. It meant that something had to be done. So she dropped her shoulders and trudged into the Itch just as Mr Cricket and Mr Hoyt tumbled out, neither with much grace.

In the barroom July was crouched behind the velvet couch and stealing glances at the chiffonier on the opposite side of the room.

'I'm guessing it's the jockey?' Bitsy said.

'Hell yeah it's the jockey.'

'Sunrise said it was an orangutan. Why the hell do you have a gun? You're not going to shoot the thing, are you? Are you mad?'

'No, I'm not going to shoot the monkey,' said July. 'It's to frighten the bastard away.'

'You think it knows what a gun is?'

'Look at how I'm holding it! What else would I be using it for?'

Eventually they chased the jockey out from underneath the chiffonier but it was at the expense of a couple of warning shots. The first was an accident and July blew a hole into the ceiling and through the mirror in the bedroom directly above the parlour. It frazzled them all - including the jockey - to such an extent that July did not hesitate in firing a second. Screams echoed from around the front. The jockey had been jumping from tabletop to tabletop but was now so agitated that he had to sit down on one of the chairs. He rubbed his ears and Bitsy felt her own ringing. In a new quiet the three of them kept still in repose. Then the jockey lifted himself up and trudged away, arriving at the open window and hauling his dainty body through it. July followed suit towards the window, peered out composedly and waited awhile.

It was getting dark as Bitsy and he returned to the people outside. Alma Bridger was there but no one had seen her because she was sat behind the crowd in a collapsible chair of her own. Bitsy grinned like hell and waltzed over to her, offered her a hand and pulled her up. Like her brother Willie she was arthritic. Big, brown, magnetic eyes on a pasty face and wispy grey hair on a delicate scalp. Bones everywhere and not an ounce of fat to be found, nor a squeeze of muscle. Yet the whole world was safe now.

'Hello, Alma,' said Bitsy, and heads began to turn.

'Hidy-do, little one,' said Alma, with a voice like moonlight on still water.

'Oh, it's a delight to see you.'

'Let's not make a to-do about it.'

They embraced shallowly and then released. Everyone was watching and everyone was silent and everyone wanted to hug her but they knew that only Bitsy would receive such a reception because Bitsy was special to Alma. Bitsy was as close to Alma's daughter as Alma could ever find, and in that moment of quiet when the final sprinklings of sunshine lifted away Bitsy saw that Alma was looking at Florence-Louise instead of Bitsy. They had always looked alike and now Alma could see what her girl would be if she had gotten to grow up. Bitsy straightened up and smiled as handsomely as she knew how. Then it was over and Alma acknowledged the sea of smiling faces. Mr Cricket appeared at the front of the crowd and bowed.

'Welcome back to the Pig's Itch, ma'am,' he said. 'I live on a bedroll on July's balcony. I done heard so much about yourself.'

There was a tutting somewhere off to the side and Bitsy assumed it was July.

'I gather it's an occasion of some kind,' said Alma.

'That it is,' said Mr Cricket.

'Is my brother around?'

'He won't be missing this,' said Bitsy. 'And it's night time now, look. He'll be stirring.'

Inside everyone stood on the balls of their feet and teetered from one foot to the other. It was difficult to resist stealing a glance at the quiet and yet mercurial Alma every now and then. Bitsy just kept on smiling. Hampstead was there with his mother and he nodded feebly at Bitsy, who pulled in her lips and gently curled up one corner of her mouth to show that she was sorry. There was no doubt in her mind that Hampstead would understand what the expression meant. Then he would watch Doc Bellingham and she would watch him and they wouldn't do anything about it. Bitsy respected them for that.

Charlie Bellingham kept with Hattie and Elsie on one side of the room. Maggie Bellingham kept with the queer Mr Grant and Doc on the other. Everyone had drinks now and Elias had brought the gramophone.

Eventually a sleepy Willie emerged from the outdoors and he knew that Alma was there long before he saw her. They hugged and Bitsy, who was nearby, heard him say:

'I've so much to tell you.'

And Alma nodded back at him and there they were. And as if on cue the door swung open and a tied newspaper was held triumphantly aloft. It was here! Confirmation! Vindication! Bitsy usually had no time for egotism but perhaps today she was soft. Her heart swelled and the cheer that followed Sidney's grand entrance made her want to swoon. As the boy edged through the shuffle of people the paper remained raised and seemed to float over heads. He got to Bitsy and he handed it to her and everyone and everything in the universe was silent. But Bitsy couldn't do it. Maybe this was her moment. It terrified her.

'Would you like me to?' said the most comforting voice in the whole wild world. Willie's hand touched her shoulder.

'Please, Willie,' she said.

As she blinked tears from her eyes she watched Willie take the newspaper and pull off the elastic band that bound it up. One collective breath was held as he opened it up and, hands shaking, turned to the correct page. He licked his thumb with every flick. Then he read silently to himself and the colour drained from his face. Willie looked helplessly from newspaper to person and his jaw hung open dumbly.

'Read it, Pop-pop,' said Doc.

And he commenced to read aloud:

ANOTHER UNIVERSE SEEN BY ASTRONOMER

Dr. Hubble Describes Mass of Celestial Bodies 700,000 Light Years Away.

For years astronomers have speculated as to whether various nebulous formations in the heavens belongs to this universe or were "island" universes of their own, immeasurable distances away. Some of the white patches were known to be true nebulae, composed of luminous gases, or star clusters that dissolved before the telescope. But others were puzzles, no telescope being strong enough to separate them into their component parts. Some astronomers suggested that they were universes of suns so far away that they appeared as one mass.

Evidence that another universe really exists is offered by Dr. Edwin Hubble in a study published today by the University of Chicago in the Astrophysical Journal. Dr. Hubble describes this universe as containing bright and dim stars and nebulae in heavens like our own, and offers photographs and definite measurements of the mass of celestial bodies that compose it. He found that this external galaxy, similar in many ways to our own, although entirely outside of the earth's galactic system, is 700,000 light-years away, in astronomical measurement which carries seventeen figures when reduced to miles. According to his computation it is 4,000 light-years across.

The galaxy's general appearance was described as like that of the Magellanic clouds, a mass of nebulae like the Milky Way in the skies of the Southern-Hemisphere.

Eerie silence followed and Bitsy wondered how a place so full could ever be so quiet. Even the world outside seemed to stop as a collective shock gripped the hall. There was tangible discomfort amongst the brothers and sisters of the town.

'Well,' said Alma finally. 'I don't much like the sound of that.'

A great many people nodded or murmured in agreement.

17

Whereas in other places there might have been something of a brouhaha over such a revelation, in town there was only a feeling of infinite smallness in the moment that Willie put down the newspaper. It was as though the collective had had its shoulders shaken by a giant's hands and then been socked in the jaw. The flickering kerosene was a gentle drumbeat; an ominous rhythm that encircled the tense throng and kept it from dispersing. A gulf emerged between each individual and suddenly there was an aching space in the crowd despite that toes touched heels and skin felt breath. Both Alma and Willie were there and yet uneasiness swept through the place in spite of them. The clear night outside somehow looked primed for a cloudburst, or worse.

Tucked into July's waistbelt still was Luella's Steyr. Under the canopy of discomfort in the Itch the gun was something to caress and feel better because of, so July draped the tips of his fingers up and down the barrel and also gently over the trigger. He saw the cat that had been mysteriously gifted to the Itch by an unknown provider - a tabby that Mr Cricket had swiftly and comically named Toto. And Toto the cat quietly leapt up onto the counter and perused its contents, his haggard little walking legs the only movement of any living creature in the Itch - except for July's curious fingers. After all the earlier business with the monkey jockey Toto had vanished upstairs awhile. Gunshots and screaming and monkey howls were bad news for a cat, but now that the world was more silent than it had ever been he was back to investigate. Toto didn't understand the implications of the newspaper article. Toto could keep believing that his world existed in town and in town only, whereas this was not a luxury that anyone else could afford.

Willie Bridger finally cleared his throat and July quit touching the gun.

'Some drinks, I think,' said Willie.

That was a honeysound to July.

'Mr Cricket?' he said, and Mr Cricket shoved his way through the crowd and stood to attention. 'Let's get the barrels.'

And so the anxiety was quenched by moonshine for hours to come, with no shortage of custom and certainly no reluctance to partake. It was all there was to do although it did not expel the tension in the room; rather it only numbed those present to the pain of it. Little talk was had and the few moments of optimistic distraction were always brought to a halt by mutterings like, 'Could it be that we are one of many - even countless - universes?' or 'Perhaps a mistake was made by Mr Hubble is what it is,' or 'Maybe short selling on Ford wasn't the best idea after all...'

And then a moment that hurt July even more than *The New York Times* had. For the evening thus far he had avoided even the sight of Mélanie, which had been made very possible by the news of this new-found island universe. She had scarcely crossed his mind as it had wandered through the vastness and probable horrors of outer space. And yet those horrors were minute in the world of torment to which he was born when Mélanie's husband Lester arrived stinking of saltwater and seaweed. Held aloft in his muscular, hairy hands was a bloody harpoon to which he had attached a small flag of the Confederacy - he was native to somewhere in Lafayette - and it was pristine and he was holding it with a bewildering pride.

'Heck, it's sour in here,' he said, wincing. He found Mélanie, put one arm around her and kissed her, the harpoon still held above his head. Everyone stood watching attentively and envied the sailor. July felt sick.

But Lester had no desire to keep the people waiting. He said, 'I have something to show you all that will bring smiles to your faces and fire to your bellies. For we will all be eating well a long old time. And let it be known clearly that I am no socialist; that I am no charity, but I will be giving with what I have made on my voyage!'

Everyone but July and Toto followed him out. There was an energy now and it was infesting the walls, even after the room had been almost entirely vacated. The lights flickered more violently and the stampede reverberated through the floorboards long after it should have. Toto looked uncomfortable and let out the gentlest of hisses, facing no one in particular and seemingly done in response to whatever song of evil that July was hearing too. He could not block his ears from it. He felt the gun again and this time closed his fingers around the grip, releasing a heavy moan as he did and feeling the muscles all the way up his arm tense and spasm. Outside he heard shouts of excitement and delirium. Whatever it was would create such a heightened joy simply because it was a distraction.

In July's distraction he found himself on a flowerbed in a valley in the north country. Tall trees with leaves of waxmelt-gold and magma-red spotted the banks and spurs that ravined the river close by. The sky was constant and bright blue and the sun fashioned ribbons of orange and purple to compliment it. In the flowerbed with him were two beautiful flowers which were Lune Solaire, and they were growing close by just as they had done all those many years ago, and it was still impossible that they did that. It was so impossible that July's heart soared and his fingers tingled and his legs shook and his eyes leaked. He was momentarily in Eden and he felt that God was close by.

But close by also was a whistling gale. At first it sounded distant but that was because July was knelt down and kneading the stems of the flowers, stretching and moulding them with such concentration that the whole beautiful world around him might have passed him by if it were not so sinister. And then the whistling came again and this time it was louder and more violent. It kissed the back of his neck and he knew it was a fall gale, but that was all he thought until it wrapped itself around him and made him shiver. Suddenly it was very alien and disconcerting but it was also familiar because it was the same noise he had known on the day Mélanie had left him. It sounded as though it wanted to speak to him; to warn him of something; or perhaps just to bring him down. Now it was at his throat and in his lungs, and his eyes were watering because of the cold and not because of joy. He tried to push back against it but it held him and pinched him.

Then the door swung open, Toto hissed and fled, and July was back in the Pig's Itch.

'A monster!' he discerned among the rabble of folks flooding back in. July drank some more and his chest became tighter. Usually this was a symptom of a hangover but on this night the hangover had met the drink and the two had coupled in some malevolent partnership. He could feel the coldness of that imagined wind on his skin and yet he found himself sweating. Mr Cricket was so excited that he did not notice.

'Mr Monroe's done killed a pilot whale in the Pacific!' he explained. 'But his ship done sunk in the battle. He got to the coast in Chile and dragged the carcass to the nearest town and sold it for a small fortune! Then he made himself a chuckwagon. Turns out he's a carpenter as much as he is a jack tar! He drove the thing all the way through one continent and into the next! He's got the money inside it!'

July said nothing and poured himself another gin. He could smell the saltwater from in here and it was making him more and more irate, but Mr Cricket was so enthused that he did not notice his friend's chagrin. Mélanie was one of the lattermost to re-enter the Itch and July saw a look in her eyes that he had not done in a long while, perhaps ever: a look of passionate happiness. Perhaps there was a touch of pride there too. And July had never felt more envious in his life, for he had no memory of causing such a gush of emotion on the angel's face. It had been beyond him. So this was Lester's pinnacle. His pride.

But Charlie Bellingham appeared between Mélanie and July and the latter was enraged despite that his previous vista had been troubling.

'What in God's name do you want?' July said. 'If you want a drink then ask me for one. Don't stand at me looking at me like I'm some crippled son of a bitch, you hear?'

'Don't want no drink,' said Charlie.

'Then quit staring, gibface.'

What sounded like a gunshot outside was followed by an echo of green glitter that fell through the window and then vanished almost instantly. Then the process was repeated and July knew that it was fireworks. Lester Monroe had found a way to celebrate that would provide yet another surprise for the people of town, who once more cascaded out to bear witness to the sailor's might. Charlie went too but Willie and Alma had stayed behind and approached the counter for drinks of their own. Alma looked worriedly at July and Willie didn't look at anything. Next to one another they were very similar.

'Are you here to mind me?' said July.

'You don't look well,' said Alma. 'Bed, perhaps?'

'I've got the spins.'

'Ah.'

They stewed without talking for a few moments more and July continued to drink. The fireworks commenced uniformly and the green shades of the earlier ones was followed by bright yellows and blood-reds. July could not resist stroking the gun more. Even with Alma watching him closely he lost himself to the coolness of metal on the back of his knuckles. The fireworks were only red now and the beige of kerosene was concealed by a scarlet hue that filled every corner of the room. More and more fireworks, more and more red.

'Let's go outside,' said July, downing the rest of his drink quickly and tucking his shirt back over the Steyr.

But July did not watch the sky for a second. It was as much to shirk Alma and Willie as it was anything else; July knew they'd ogle just like every other sucker in town. They were all lecherous for this idiot thug and July was sick to death of it and he was filled with blood. He sought out Mélanie and Lester and the crowd didn't seem to notice him. Perhaps some caught sight of the violence with which he tore through but no one stopped him, and soon enough old July could see the couple, their arms wrapped around one another's backs as they watched the display. Red was everywhere.

For a brief moment July caught himself and swayed on his feet. There was nothing good to come of whatever it was that he was about to do; no release to be found but for a short burst of adrenaline that would surely follow. All would be permanent and nothing would be undone. It was not worth it, he knew. But then Mélanie was being kissed passionately on the lips by her husband and the look of pride and excitement had gone from her face. Her eyes remained open while Lester's hammock eyelids kept his in the darkness as he absorbed the beloved's mouth. Then July knew that the action was already done, so he pulled the .32 from his waistbelt and cocked the hammer as he marched towards them.

In Mélanie's peripheral she saw July and pushed Lester away from her as she screamed. For a second Lester was dumfounded and furious but then he was clear. But he was not scared. He laughed at the approaching July even with the barrel pointed clumsily at his face, but July was in no laughing mood and nor was he to restrain himself. His index finger quivered over the trigger and then it pulled back and the whip-like *crack* rattled the earth. But as it did July felt impact on his outstretched arm and he was thrown off-balance by it. He stumbled as a result of it and his drunkenness and dropped the gun, then felt a heavy blow to the face which knocked him unconscious.

(ii)

Pop-pop had found Doc and Pa outside the Itch and stood with them awhile to watch the fireworks. Then Doc heard Pop-pop murmur something in Pa's ear and point discretely in the direction of July, and in a terrible moment Doc could see the outline of July's pistol pressed up against his tucked shirt. Pa, who was not typically light on his feet, darted quietly towards July as July readied to fire, knocking him over with one helluva shove just as the bullet left the gun. A few screams rang out and then Pa socked July in the side of the face so hard that he was simply asleep and likely would be for a day or two. Perhaps he would be slow for the rest of his life. Perhaps he was killed upon impact or would die of internal bleeding in the days to come. This was why Charlie Bellingham had once referred to his hands as his sleepers.

Sunrise was the first to make it to Mélanie and saw that she was unharmed. The same went for Lester, who loudly reassured everyone that the bullet had skewered wide of him thanks to Pa's tackle. Someone asked Pa how he knew to do so when everyone was entranced by the firework display and Ma shouted in response that Willie had told him that there was trouble afoot; that it was Willie that had saved Mélanie, Lester and July all. It was the end of the night and nobody knew what else ought to be done but leave, other than a few thanks which were distractedly thrown Pop-pop's way as they passed. Pa kept with July and picked him up in his big arms, then carried him through to the Itch and set him down on the counter. Doc found Toto meowing behind the bar and wrapped her long arms around him, lifted him up and petted him as he began purring.

When July came around the following night he was struggling to talk and that was because he had torn open his tongue after the punch. Dr Wagner sewed it back up right then and there and then gave him a saline solution to wash his mouth out with five times a day. He also told him to stay away from oriental or spicy foodstuffs. Sunrise watched attentively and said she would keep an eye on July so that Wagner could get his rest, but not before requesting that she get a copy of the medical transcript that Wagner would write up upon his going home. She revealed to Doc that she had been visiting Dr Wagner pretty frequently for some weeks now, perusing his records - much to his chagrin - and observing his work. She was fascinated by it and was beginning to contemplate medicine as a line of work. Dr Wagner might be reluctantly willing to take her on as a student, she said.

Pop-pop had stuck around too but Pa had gone home, pleading to no avail that Doc do the same. There was sleeping for him to do before he began the final stretch of construction on the planetarium. Meanwhile Doc and Sunrise had dragged a mattress from Sunrise's room down the stairs shortly after dawn while Mr Hale had shouted directions so that they didn't tumble and fall. Then they put it under one of the tables and kept each other warm as they slept awhile. Pop-pop had fallen asleep on one of the chairs and was now complaining about how badly it compared to his collapsible one on the hill.

July's eye was black and blue and swollen.

'Some whack,' he said, bringing a finger to it and wincing. 'This'll be some doozy of a bruise. What the hell?'

'Charlie stopped you,' said Pop-pop. 'He had no choice.'

'Sounds like a to-do,' said July.

'If the cops were here still you'd be back in the jailhouse before the week was up. As it is I've got no idea what to do with you.'

'I'd rot in a cell and come out sorer than when I went in.'

'Good job there ain't no cops anymore then. You can thank Charlie for that too.'

'So what then? A reprimanding? Probation?'

'You'll just have to get out of town the second you're well enough. We can pack your things for you and we'll figure a bill of sale for the Itch. Maybe the town will buy it or maybe we can find some dandy from elsewhere. No one will trust you anymore, July.'

'Even if I did what I did for love? Does no one have a heart anymore? Am I the only one in this stinking world with a heart? God, what I'd do to get rid of it.'

'Yes, even if you did it for love. You gave into your wicked temptation; your anger, July. And love is not violence,' said Pop-pop.

'Of course it is,' said July. 'It is the great evil of mankind. It is the greatest high known to man and yet once felt it can only be taken away. Of course it is violence. It is immaturity. It is infantile. When you are happy in love you act like a devil-may-care little pickney. When you are broken in love you act the vengeful, immature, self-pitying little girl. And to lose love that you didn't deserve in the first place, well, that's a whole other ball of wax. I've regressed into a child because of my love for Mélanie, and there is nothing more upsetting than a lonely child.'

'You think a court would hear that? You think a judge would listen?' asked Pop-pop calmly.

'Whatever.'

'Where will you go?' asked Sunrise.

'Where is it you come from again?'

'Rockwell.'

'You've turned out real fine. Perhaps I'll go there.'

'Do you not remember all the things that happened to me and Mr Hale when we were there? It's filled with ghosts and lonely people.'

'Ghosts follow me around wherever I go. And as for lonely people, well, I was a lonely child, I'm a lonely man, and I expect I'll die lonely. I don't think it's coincidence that my first thought was to go to a lonesome town. It's written in the stars. I'm defeated, and I blame the vagaries of fate. I'll give it a try at least, then east if it ain't working for me. Then maybe across the water. There's plenty of world out there, ain't there? And even beyond, it seems. Fancy that. Say, Willie, I thought you was planning on building some kind of fighter aircraft for the stars, weren't you? You reckon you could fix me up one of those before I pack my cases? If I am to leave town then I guess there's no stopping me; no boundaries; no bobwire; no rope; no limits. I might as well see these island universes.'

'Well, you'd have been able to at the planetarium had you not just tried to kill the sailor.'

'It's just gonna make it harder for everyone else to leave, that planetarium,' accepted July. 'Maybe I'm lucky.'

'Maybe so.'

With that Pop-pop was too tired to discuss the matter further. He told them that he had to sleep awhile before he could think about gathering July's things, so he bade them good evening and went up to the hill to sleep under the velvety night for the first time in many a year.

Doc had an itch.

'I would like to play the piano again before I leave,' said July. 'I would like it back here in the parlour where it was before I gave it to Bitsy. I want to play it in here.'

'Where is it?' asked Sunrise.

'Municipal hall.'

'Could we get someone to deliver it?'

'To me? Hell no,' said July. 'No, it'll have to be stolen. I mean, it will be less stealing and more borrowing because I intend to return it before I enter exile. This is not a twisted slice of revenge intended as a parting gift. Actually it is a parting gift, but a parting gift to myself. It is a chance to envelop myself in my glorious past before the future eats me whole.'

Doc still had an itch.

'How do you intend to drag a piano across town by yourself?' asked Sunrise.

'I don't,' said July plainly and implicitly.

'Not a chance.'

'I will help!' shouted Doc, itch cured. 'I will help you steal the piano with these mighty arms of mine! But July! Please take me with you when you go. I don't want to be here anymore. You two are my only friends besides Pop-pop, and it is my guess that Sunrise won't be hanging around forever after you've made tracks. I'd rather take *three* licks from my pa than have to stick around here with spittoons all night long. Please don't leave me alone here.'

July laughed.

'Do you think your parents will allow me, a man they saw trying to commit homicide, take care of their daughter indefinitely?'

'No, I doubt that very much. But -'

'So you are suggesting I kidnap you?'

'Look, I ain't thought it all the way through, but I'm savvy and I can figure a way around it. There's a parochial prep school up in Seattle - a prestigious school for smart kids. Sunrise told me all about it and how it might be the right place for me. Now, I reckon I'm smart. I'm sick of never admitting it. Hell, I reckon I'm *dead* smart. I may be a weird-looking mulatto gal with arms out the wazoo, but Doc Bellingham is smart as hell. I can make the cut for that school. And then I can get what I need to go to Boston.'

'What's in Boston?' asked Sunrise

'The Boston School of Zoology,' said Doc.

'Frogs?'

'*Amphibians*. I would like to study herpetology there.'

'Can you get a reference for Seattle?' asked Sunrise. 'You are a truant, don't forget. I don't imagine you're too popular among the staff at the schoolhouse.'

'Mélanie can do that,' said July quietly.

Doc turned sharply towards him.

'She can?'

'Yes.'

'How?'

'She's an excellent mimic in both her manner of speaking and her handwriting. And she's smarter than old Doc apparently is so she can feign knowledge about whatever subject you want her to. She's well-read. And she loves Doc for some reason unknown to me.'

'Is that consideration in your voice?' asked Sunrise.

'No. It is a musing and nothing else. What about for rent? I suppose you want me to transfer my skills from here, don't you. You want me to be brewing watered-down chartreuse for the rest of my days. I won't do it, Doc.'

'Listen, you'll have to do that with or without us,' said Doc.

'Us?' said Sunrise.

'Well – I – I,' Doc stammered. 'I assumed you'd want to come too.'

'What about Mr Hale?'

'Why not him as well?'

'Jeepers creepers,' said Sunrise.

'Why, this is just getting ridiculous,' said July. 'Let's start a merry orchestra while we're at it!'

'It's either this or we all go our separate ways!' cried Doc. 'And our separate ways are down lonesome roads, July. You know it!' she turned to Sunrise: 'Sunrise, you said that you were looking for Eden for the benefit of Mr Hale. It isn't here, is it. This is not Eden. You will leave soon.'

'I guess I will,' admitted Sunrise.

'And then you will go on from place to place, searching for the rest of your lives in vain because there is no place like that. The only one that comes close is the place where we are all together.'

'It doesn't come close,' said July.

'It's better than anywhere else!'

'And you, Sunrise,' July pressed. 'What will you do in Seattle?'

'I believe I can get a reference - a real reference - from Dr Wagner. Perhaps I could apprentice at a surgery or a dentist up there. And if not then I guess I will join the bootlegging industry. Why not.'

July was quiet and so was Sunrise. Doc breathed out loudly and tiredly, then lowered her voice to a soft breeze and smiled melancholically, glistening eyes wide and resolve in her posture.

'I don't want to be a *lonely child* ever again,' she said.

'You manipulative hussy -' began July, shaking his fist.

'You've got life in you yet,' said Doc. 'Let's start anew, yes? What do you say? Sunrise?'

'Yessum,' whispered Sunrise, the tips of a smile creeping onto her lips.

'July?'

July said nothing but did not refuse any longer. Doc had done it.

'Hell, let's go steal a piano,' she said.

(iii)

When the witching hour came the three of them stole away into the shadows and broke into the municipal hall, which had been locked since Bitsy had last used it. The piano did not have casters and they found that the three of them were unable to lift it off the ground for longer than a minute without the sound of someone's back cracking or their feet slipping. So they resolved to take inspiration from Lester Monroe. Of course July was keen to steal Lester's chuckwagon. They prowled through town and trundled it - with great trepidation - through streets of blankety quiet. July was sad to see that Lester's money had been moved someplace safe.

By dawn the piano was back in the Itch and July slumped onto the mattress in the parlour. He was a little dizzy and his head was throbbing, he said.

'You are a tremendous friend, July,' said Doc.

'Shut up or I'll give you a lick like Charlie gave me. Let me sleep and come for me later.'

'And you too, Sunrise.'

'*Thou know'st the mask of night is on my face, else would a maiden blush bepaint my cheek,*' recited Sunrise, hugging Doc and heading off to her room to sleep. Doc limbered home and collapsed into bed, finding the warmth of a sleep that one only finds when she is in the depths of promise and optimism; when extraordinary fatigue meets visceral hopefulness and there can only be one outcome, and that is a deep, dreamless slumber.

When Doc awoke it was dark out but the sun was creeping upon town. She had slept for twenty hours perhaps, and now she was hungry. She decided to make breakfast for everyone, even her whippersnapper sisters. Doc had no idea how to cook or fry or bake but she knew that heat and oil were involved. It took all of her growing alertness to fix up some bacon and eggs, which went wrong a couple of times initially, but by the time of her family's waking she had five plates set out and a dribbling, choking sandwich on each. Even the ketchup and mayonnaise and other miscellaneous sauces and condiments had made it to the table.

'Doc, why do you smell of fish?' asked Hattie, the little brat, eyeing Doc up and giving her an untrusty whiff as they all gathered around. It appeared that aroma from that Chilean fishing village had made its way all the way up on Lester's chuckwagon.

'I stopped by the fishmongers,' said Doc.

'Why?' asked Pa.

'I wanted to make breakfast for everyone and my first thought was fish. But then Mrs Sykes explained to me what to do with this fish to make it edible and I thought, no way.'

'What fish was it, Doc?'

'Erm...' Doc thought long and hard and nervously. 'Sall-monn.'

'Uh-huh.'

Ma and Pa exchanged a look that told Doc they planned to get Mrs Sykes to corroborate this clearly imaginary tête-à-tête, but Doc hoped she'd be long gone before truth will out.

'Well, this looks good, Doc.'

'Yessum.'

For a while the family bumped gums like usual. But then the conversation turned to the other night's events and a little heat rose despite that the plates had cleared. It began when the wellbeing of Mélanie was mentioned; what had been something of an afterthought in the wake of the shooting. But Pa kept quiet but for his deep and vexed breaths.

'What's eating you, Pa?' said Doc.

'I don't wish to rage, but I am rather sick of hearing that this woman is an angel. I hear it a lot of your friend Sunrise too. Are they not fallible like the rest of us? If they are angels then so are my daughters. What do they have that my girls don't?'

'Likable personalities unlike the cases of Hattie and Elsie,' said Doc. 'Mélanie is the cat's pyjamas. Look at her, Pa. She's got a little slip of sunshine in her eyes, and when she's sad she keeps it in her pocket. And Sunrise gives you a feeling. It's hard to describe, ain't it, Pa. She gives you a feeling that everything's gonna be okay.'

'And how!' said Elsie.

'Not me,' said Pa.

'She might be my best friend,' said Doc.

'Well, that really is swell, Doc,' said Ma with earnestness.

'I think this a load of baloney,' said Pa.

'Watch your mouth, Charlie.'

'Can't you see, Maggie? Or has your privilege gotten the better of you too? I notice that it was your old man to whom you gave the credit the other night despite that it was I who stopped July from killing that bellbottom. I was the one who put myself in harm's way, if you recall.'

'Of course I recall, but Charlie, it was he who alerted you to the situation, no?'

'Yes, he did, but I had already got my eye on July. I had been watching him from the moment the article was read aloud. He gave me the heebie-jeebies all night. When Willie nudged me I was readying to make a move anyhow.'

'Why didn't you say something?'

'Because I know how important it is for this town to have Willie in his illusive shroud; for them to be able to reassure one another that he watches over them and keeps them safe. Without it the sight of Eden is shown to be a mirage and everything learned crumbles. It is the same for Alma, I believe. Her shroud has remained because she seems impervious to weakness or disease, but we have seldom seen her in many years, so of course we cannot know how she has been in the meantime. And Willie's prowess is upheld only because we blindly ascribe all that is good and messianic to him. Whilst sin and suffering are absent it will be because of Willie. The only good that can come of their reappearance will be that perhaps the penny will drop; the clock will resume ticking; the earth begin to turn again. Willie himself knows it and I did not have to tell him, but he knows like me that we must suffer this falsity because it is too problematic to do otherwise. And he said that one day I will be recognised and that it will be hard until then.

'I got the rangers out of town, *me*. Willie and Alma oversaw the paperwork and reformation, but I caught the scars,' he pointed to the long white streak below his eye and the faint red rope burn on his throat. 'I did Willie's building. I saw July grow angry and I reached for him despite that he was armed and angry. And I am willing to do all of this and more for the benefit of this town. But one day they will see that Willie is old and he is tired and that they cannot keep pretending to themselves that he is their god. Then the town will face a decision and it will be upon this that they are judged. I think the people of this town are a good people, but they are ignorant, including many of the coloured folks. Have any of you girls yet read *The Negro Problem*?'

Doc, Elsie and Hattie all shook their heads.

'I ask that if you are reluctant that you read only one essay -'

'Du Bois's,' they all said, having heard about it before.

'Yes. Educate yourselves. You are all smart girls. Doc, you are of intelligence way beyond your years and yet you attribute these holy qualities onto your friends simply because they are your friends. One day it might hurt you. A nice white woman is not an angel, she is just better than other whites. But she is fallible like every human being and it is crucial that you all remember that as you go on about your lives. No one can save everyone, not even the beautiful white woman can do that. And while we keep telling each other that they will the plight of the Negro will persist indefinitely, for always we will be the secondaries and never the heroes. Margins might fill with our names overtime but that will be because the main bodies will fill with theirs. Never will the Negro be called upon to be heroic because always the white man or woman has been designated as such. I am so upset because this is all ignored, and the tragedy of this ignorance is that it is accidental in the cases of so many.'

Charlie breathed and lowered his head.

'I love my family. I love Willie. I love them all. I long for betterment. I am very tired.'

And though Pa had talked of Du Bois and the Talented Tenth a hundred times, Doc had never listened properly. Not until today, and that was because it made her realise something. It would mean that she needn't lie about her prospective endeavours. It would mean that perhaps Pa would allow her to go north for the opportunity of superior education. And Doc would repay him by minoring in philosophy or economics or sociology when she went to Boston. And then her dreams would be fulfilled and she would make her hero proud. Everything was in place and she held her father very tightly all morning. They sat together by the window and Doc told him everything that she planned to do with July and Sunrise and Mr Hale. Pa was quiet and contemplative. His chest rose and sank with heavy breaths through his nose. When Doc was done he remained quiet still, but he pulled her in just a little more closely.

18

One thing was bugging Doc and she wanted it resolved before she left with July and Sunrise, and that was the matter of why Hampstead left her those comics in homeroom. There was no doubt that it was him; no ten-year-old boy in the whole wide world had strips from *Little Orphan Annie* apart from Hampstead - and maybe his pal Hector - and one day the emasculation would catch up with him. So now it was up to Doc to finally reach out to the weird kid because she knew full well that he would blow any chance he ever got to talk to her again. It had been one shambles after another. The flagpole, the bellybutton, the soirée, the comics, the *New York Times* announcement... Doc held little hope for interaction at the planetarium opening. If she could corner him at his house and maybe threatened him with a whupping then he might explain what in the hell he had been thinking this whole time.

So Doc arrived after school and wiggled her naked toes nervously on the portico. The dog Goose was asleep and she'd had to tread carefully over him on her way off the sidewalk. She noticed that the ball of her foot was a little sore and pulled out a big old splinter just as Hampstead's momma opened the door.

'Oh, hidy-do, ma'am,' Doc said, wincing.

'Hello, Miss Bellingham,' said Hampstead's momma, who knew of Doc through Pa.

'Is Hampstead in?'

'Not at the moment. He's at the Outpost.'

'What's the Outpost?'

'I'm quite sure I don't know.'

'Oh, that's a shame. Never mind.'

Doc nodded, a little defeated, then turned back to the street.

'Wait, Doc,' said Hampstead's momma.

'Yessum?'

'Were you going to ask Hampstead to come out and play?'

'Nome.'

'Then what?'

'He left me some comics to read in homeroom a couple weeks back, but he never mentioned it,' said Doc. 'I just wanted to scare him into admitting that he's got a crush on old Doc.'

Hampstead's momma might have laughed if only to conceal the tears that grew in her eyes. She looked as though a thousand anvils had been taken off her shoulders.

'Would you like to come in, Doc? I'm making Oysters Rockefeller.'

Doc hummed for a second, then decided that she was hungry and that pursuing this manoeuvre would open up the door to seeing Hampstead's bedroom, and that was a door she couldn't ignore.

'Sure!' she said.

After chewing the fat awhile with Hampstead's momma on the subject of why Hampstead was such a whippersnapper, Doc finally got to eat. And she ate until she was nearly sick. Then she fell asleep for maybe an hour and when she woke up she saw that Hampstead's momma was no longer in the kitchen with her. Doc checked the pantry and she wasn't there either. Then Doc searched the whole house and couldn't find her, but boy did Doc luck out! Hampstead's room was - of course - signposted with his own name scribbly written in red chalk across the middle. And it opened without creaking. Doc went in and giggled like crazy.

The place was filled with knickknacks and crayons and books and teddy bears and chemistry sets and yoyos and tiddlywinks. And his clothes were strewn everywhere along with his linens. Doc wondered if she might get an infection in her foot just by walking across the bed-room, but she endeavoured to do so anyway and made her way to an upturned cardboard box at the bottom of one of the bedposts. Spilling out from it were the comic books and Doc saw *Gasoline Alley* and *The Gumps* and then *Little Orphan Annie* and Doc laughed her ass off.

'Doc?' came the voice of Hampstead's mother from downstairs. 'Doc?'

'I'm up here!' called Doc, taking one last sweeping look of the stupid room as she darted out of it, long legs lurching over obstacle after obstacle as though she were playing hopscotch.

'I was looking for you,' Mrs Hampstead told her. 'I was sat on the porch with Goose while you slept. I came to check on you and you'd gone.'

'That Oysters Rockefeller practically killed me,' said Doc.

'Well, bully,' said Hampstead's momma, before a wry smile formed on her face. 'Say, did you find anything interesting whilst you were up there?'

'Naw, I ain't very eagle-eyed.'

'I see. Would you like some coffee?'

'Do you have any cigarettes?'

'Sure, I reckon so. Hampstead's father used to smoke like a chimney, I reckon there's some hidden away somewhere.'

'Thanks, ma'am.'

Then Hampstead's momma sent Doc on her way with three Lucky Strikes and a small box of matches to boot. She fancied seeing Pop-pop and wondered how in the hell it ever got to be like this. She'd gone from school to Hampstead's and now she was going up to see Pop-pop and she didn't even feel like murdering someone. Never had she had this kind of social stamina before and it felt like she was running a race and out in front and no one else had a prayer. Perhaps she would holler at Pop-pop from the bottom of the hill so he knew that she was in a good mood, but then Doc passed Mademoiselle Celestine hauling a chuckwagon and breaking into a glamorous sweat as she went, and that was enough to fix Doc up. She wasn't going to look a fool in front of the mademoiselle, who scrubbed up good even in a bind.

'Hello, Doc,' she said.

'Hidy-do, Mademoiselle. What you got going on over here?'

'Someone stole the wagon, but only to drag it halfway across town.'

And then Doc remembered that it was she, Doc, that did that.

'Say, that's one helluva mystery.'

'Sure is.'

'How are you, Mademoiselle?'

'Me?'

'Yes, after you nearly died.'

'If I'd died I wouldn't be being forced to do this.'

'That July sure is a goof, ain't he, trying to shoot that Lester guy like that,' said Doc.

'For sure.'

'Did you hear that he will be leaving town?'

'I did. Lester was very pleased about it,' said the mademoiselle.

'How do you feel about it?'

'Oh, *comme ci, comme ça*.'

'I might be going with him.'

'For real?'

'Yes, perhaps.'

Mademoiselle Celestine looked a little dumbstruck.

'Doc, I will miss you,' she said after a moment.

'And I you. But I will be back often and I will write home all the time.'

'Do you have plans?'

Doc proceeded to explain to Mademoiselle Celestine every little detail of the life that she had planned out and again wondered how in the hell she ever got so sociable.

'But I need your help,' she concluded.

'You do?'

'I need a reference and July said you're good with a pen, and hell, I know how smart you are. Would you impersonate a teacher for me so that I can get into the prep school in Seattle?'

Mademoiselle Celestine burst into laughter.

'Could I ever get found out?'

'I will never, ever tell,' swore Doc. 'I swear I'll cut out this tongue before they make me talk!'

'Then yes, fine,' giggled the mademoiselle. 'You are quite something, but yes, I will impersonate a teacher for you. You know my address. When you find where you're living and what kind of recommendation it is that you need, write to me and I will write back with it.'

'You might be the finest angel to ever walk the earth,' said Doc. 'Thank you, Mademoiselle.'

'I want you to do something for me in exchange; a favour as currency,' said Mademoiselle Celestine. 'Will you look after July for me? He needs someone to do that for him.'

'I absolutely will. He is my best friend, after all,' said Doc truthfully, and then she began her ascent up the hill as the sun went down. Pop-pop was rousing and he beamed as he stretched, making note of Doc's waltzing gait and remarking that he hadn't seen her so enthused in a while.

'Me neither!' she said, before her awkwardness shattered entirely and she talked a blue streak for maybe an hour about what she was going to do with July and Sunrise. And often in her ramblings she stopped to remind Pop-pop that she couldn't bear to think of leaving him but that she had to do it and that she would still see him in the not-long. All of her excitement poured out of her and her passing words tasted like honey on her tongue and became music as they entered her ears. Never had she been so impassioned. And when she was done she gasped for breath and almost collapsed into the dirt seat and she saw that the stars were out in all their majesty and that the night was as pretty as any that she had ever seen, or maybe she was just imagining it.

'I love you, kid,' said Pop-pop.

'What, warts and all?' panted Doc.

'For sure, Doc. Warts and all.'

(ii)

Hampstead was all in a frenzy. Goose too was sensing a ruckus and was boldly following the boy around.

'She was in here?!' Hampstead said to Momma.

'Sure.'

'In my bedroom?'

'I guess so.'

'Why in the hell did you let her do that, you crazy hussy?'

Momma's jaw dropped and Hampstead's eyes widened. By his own brazenness he was taken aback.

'You are ten years old,' Momma said quietly.

'Nearly eleven,' whispered Hampstead.

'And if you want to go to the planetarium then you best take back what you just said, you hear?'

'I don't want to go to the planetarium. How many times do I need to tell people that that place gives me the heebie-jeebies?!'

'Hampstead, drop that tone! You're frazzled because Doc was in your room, fine, but you do not speak to your own mother like this.'

'Yes, yes, okay,' groaned Hampstead.

'Hampstead! Do not ever yes yes okay me, you hear?'

'Hell, I'll yes yes okay whoever the hell I want!'

'*Hampstead!*'

The room shook and Goose fled the scene, leaving Hampstead as the whimpering, hangdog pup.

'Yessum?' he whispered.

'Go to bed.'

'Yessum.'

The next night was a Saturday night and the planetarium was opened. It was ahead of schedule and everyone seemed pleased for Willie that he'd managed to do it in such a squeeze. Hampstead was pretty sick of having to interact with the whole town after the soirée and then the island universe announcement; he'd rather have been doing Book Club or Book Debate Club or anything really. Why was he always having to dress up and talk to sad-looking grown-ups? They gave him sadness like it was the cooties. But this was the last bunfight for a while to come, Momma promised him, and anyway it was punishment for being so dang rude to her. Hampstead accepted this with grace and scrubbed up quite nicely, though Momma had to fix his collar and shine his shoes again after he was tempted into going out wrestling with Goose.

'Look, Momma, there's Charlie Bellingham and his big shoulders,' said Hampstead when they arrived.

'Hush, Hampstead, he's a married man and I never said anything about that.'

'Sure thing, Maw.'

The dome was fixed onto the floor in the centre of the main aisle and a ladder had been nailed to the platformed loft up above. The loft was small and non-obstructive and was raised high enough that a tot would be able to reach up and touch the roof which the starlight would be painted on. A sturdy-looking fence with three rails made it safe. It was a neat little addition and Willie himself had been physically involved in some of the joinery, such was his desire to see his youngest granddaughters Hattie and Elsie get to go up there. As for Doc, well, she could probably reach the roof if she stood on her tiptoes, fifteen feet or no.

Before the fire was lit under the dome there would be insufferable mingling. Hampstead stayed close to Momma but then he caught Mr Bellingham again, snooping around the dome with scrupulous eyes.

'Hidy-do, Mr Bellingham,' Hampstead said.

'Howdy, Hampstead.'

'How you feeling today? The place looks swell, it really does.'

'Thanks, kid.'

'You still thinking on building that school for the Negro children? Now that the planetarium is done I expect it's next on your agenda.'

'Oh, I'm dead set on it.'

'Fantastic.'

'You ain't got the heebie-jeebies from this place no more?' asked Charlie.

'No, sir. Well, maybe a little.'

'I think I got them, you know.'

'Why's that, sir?'

'It's too soon, you know. I don't think we should've rushed opening this place.'

'I'm sure it will be a roaring success. I trust you.'

'I ain't sure I trust Willie's judgement on this so much,' admitted Charlie, and Hampstead left presently, unhappy to hear such worrisome words coming from the man who was, above all, a monolith of safety. But then his anxiety worsened tenfold because he caught Doc's eye and his tongue got caught in his throat, or maybe it was his heart that got stuck there. Either way he couldn't move anything except his eyelids, which blinked dumbly. Doc smiled cosily from across the room and then reached into the waist of her skirt, withdrawing from it a small, folded sheet of paper and a pencil. She scribbled something awhile as Hampstead watched. People milled in between them but somehow the connection was never lost. Then Doc folded the paper again, removed her shoes, stuck the note and pencil in one of them and then ambled away with the saunter one only gets when they are barefoot.

In all his life Hampstead had never moved so quickly. He flew across the room and nearly tripped a good three times before he got to the shoes. After throwing his arm in the first and finding nothing he realised he had gotten the wrong shoe. The note was in the other one.

To Hampstead - 1) Leaving town for good soon. 2) We can kiss during the display if you like. Or you could put your head on my shoulder or something if you prefer.

Hampstead felt that lump again and his tummy began to whizz. He reckoned he would need the bathroom pretty soon and he had no idea which end of his body he would have to place over the lavatory. He felt shaken to his very core and yet he wanted to keep hold of that feeling and he couldn't quite work out why. Beneath the physical torment he was suffering was a burgeoning optimism that was somehow part of it; an intangible tingling that had swept through from the small of his back to his fingertips and back again. Point 1) of the note had left his mind completely because of how absolutely incredible Point 2) was. But then he caught himself with a deep breath and re-read the note. Now he felt bittersweet.

With the pencil he wrote with a trembling hand on the other side of the paper:

1) Aw shucks. To where? 2) Kiss sounds swell.

And he replaced both pencil and paper in the shoe and walked away, forgetting that he ought to make eye contact with Doc to let her know it was done. But anyway he couldn't see her presently. He reunited with Momma and she remarked on how quiet he was and then how handsome he was. *Perhaps I ought to be shaken up more often*, Hampstead though to himself, very much enjoying such high praise.

Then Willie clambered up a few rungs of the ladder and thanked everyone for being there and yadda-yadda-yadda'd awhile. Hampstead had heard all his shtick a million times and he was not going to give Willie the satisfaction of his listening again, no matter how much of a godlike genius the old man was. Instead he sought out the shoes by the wall and saw Doc there again, subtly removing the paper and reading his reply. Again they caught eyes and again Hampstead felt terrified and exceptional. And as Doc was writing the fire was lit by Mr Bellingham and Maggie and Mary and some other grown-ups and the dome sprung into life and the roof was painted with Willie's masterpiece: the bright music of the night sky.

For some time everyone was dumbstruck and Hampstead included. The kerosene lamps had all simultaneously been extinguished and for a second the entire barnhouse was cast into a velvety darkness and impregnable silence. Then the dome worked its magic and suddenly the sloping roof was caked in the colours of the night; like looking down upon a rainbow snowfall. Hampstead wanted to stretch out and touch them. Momma's fingers interlocked with his and they both squeezed and it was as though Willie had brought that terrifying and beautiful cosmos within reach, and suddenly no one was afraid of island universes anymore. No one was afraid of anything, not even witches.

And in the splendour Hampstead wanted to make sure that Doc was feeling it also. With impressive restraint he pulled his gaze from above and scoured the inky, dark underbelly for the sign of a skinny creature with frizzy hair and crazy arms. She was near Willie now, helping some of the little children onto the ladder and holding it secure as they clambered up to the loft. Hampstead wondered why she was bothering, wanting her to feel as he was. Though perhaps Doc had spent enough time on the dirt seat on the hill to be excited by a projection of something she was so familiar with. Perhaps nothing could compare to the real thing. Or perhaps she just wanted to help the others.

Up at the loft the little rabble grew and hands were raised and some were on arms long enough to caress the lights and the kids bounded about it in celebration. It looked like Doc suggested to Willie that they were over capacity by this point but Willie was so caught up in the atmosphere that he told her not to worry. Doc offered her hand to a half dozen more and then they were all up there and all their hands were reaching out and it was almost as beautiful as the display itself. Hattie and Elsie reluctantly accepted the assistance as they made their way to the top, much to Willie's pride. Hampstead even saw rickety Hector up there!

Another lump caught in Hampstead's throat and this time there was no current of optimism flowing beneath it. He wondered where it came from and he felt cold and sweaty as though feverish. His legs ached. And he realised that it was because a terrible noise had found his ears; a quiet noise that undercut the splendour of the moment and whispered a warning from all corners of the room: *something is wrong*. And the sound was a grating or a grinding or a rasping or a grazing or something. It came from the loft and the eyes of children slowly lowered from the ceiling to the loft's floorboards beneath their feet, and then part of it gave way and collapsed.

Because of all the dust and darkness and commotion it was impossible to know for sure if any of the children had fallen with the timber, but it couldn't have been more than one or two if so. The most of them had scampered to the fencing or the beams on the wall at the opposite side. Everything fell silent but for the whimpering of one or two of them. The night sky became a mere backdrop for an impending tragedy.

'Children?!' someone shouted. 'Did any of the children fall?'

Everyone stared blankly but Doc, who stood closest. She threw herself into the wreckage to find out. And then there was more creaking and before anyone could sense the danger more of the loft collapsed above and Doc was shrouded in wood and dust and she was no longer visible. And no one could get to her because there was more groaning and rasping from the structure above and all of it looked ready to fall in and parts of it did. It was raining timber upon her and it seemed initially that no one could rescue Doc. But Charlie, Charlie would. It scared him none and he faced the danger despite the screamed warnings from behind him as he dug through the rubble, coughing and spluttering on dust as he went.

Sidney meanwhile had reacted swiftly and had got to the top of the ladder and was frantically pulling kids over his shoulder and sending them down the ladder, at the bottom of which a number of grown-ups were flocking. Hampstead saw Heck descend. He saw surely as many children go down the ladder as went up it, and all the while Charlie and Doc were lost in the storm of billowing dust beneath the loft. But then a shadow emerged and it was the silhouette of a mighty man.

'Everyone outside!' Willie shouted.

Hampstead was pulled by Momma but he stumbled and flailed because his body felt broken. The throng flooded out into the evening and it was hot and humid. A circle formed and Charlie staggered out into it with Doc hoisted over his shoulders.

'We've got all the kids,' Sidney said. 'We've got all the kids!'

Charlie gently laid Doc down on her back and Doctor Wagner emerged from the crowd with real grit in his eyes and stride.

'She must have been knocked unconscious,' murmured Charlie. He handed her over to Wagner, who turned her over as Charlie continued breathlessly, 'Yes, the rubble must have knocked her -'

And then the injury sustained to the back of Doc's head was revealed as Wagner examined it and everyone knew then that Doc was dead. Her skull was mangled a little at the crown and blood had seeped through her hair and down the back of her neck like a scarlet waterfall. It would have been done in an instant. When she was turned back over her eyes were wide and vacant and rolling.

Hampstead didn't remember much of what happened next but for three words that Willie Bridger said maybe a minute or maybe many hours later:

'I did this.'

19

There were a few quiet days in town following the collapse. Everything was black in colour and in sound. Bitsy, Mélanie, Lester, Sunrise, Alma, Mary, Jon, Elsie and Hampstead helped pull down what was left of the planetarium and it was delivered piece-by-piece to the carpentry store. Where there had been grass before there was now just a mesh of ash and yellow straw; a requiem to the tragedy and an ugly memorial to old Doc. Her body was kept in the morgue with a couple other recently-deceaseds, each taken many decades later in life than Doc had been. No one especially liked the morgue and so she didn't get many visitors. Mostly she just lay quietly and her arms kept falling out from under the white linen.

Hampstead stopped by two afternoons after the collapse and wore the fanciest homburg he could find. He trimmed down his father's old herringbone trousers and even dug out his pocket square. But Hampstead didn't feel much like a gentleman. The lady at the morgue said that Doc looked very peaceful and that Hampstead wouldn't be too distressed by the sight of her, so Hampstead asked that she pull back the sheet, then he looked at her on her back. They had cleaned her up real well. Hampstead's breath caught in his throat for a moment as he stared down blankly. It wasn't easy for him to know what to feel, but there was an ache in his stomach and suddenly moisture in his eyes.

'Her limbs were all out of whack,' he said. 'She would have made an excellent spider.'

'She was certainly unconventional to behold,' said the morgue lady.

'But unconventionally beautiful,' Hampstead said. 'You can pull it back over her now. Thank you.'

The morgue lady pulled the linens back and Hampstead shivered.

'Would you like to stay awhile?' she asked him. 'There are chairs.'

'I guess I will. Are these fellers going to stick around?' Hampstead asked of the two other trolleys lined up equidistantly across the room.

'They ain't go anywhere, I'm afraid,' said the morgue lady.

'I suppose.'

She patted Hampstead on the shoulder and left him to it. Hampstead looked around and scratched his nose. Never had he seen a dead body before and now he was desperately outnumbered by them. He had never even seen his father's because his mother had thought it would be too traumatic for him despite his protestations. Still to this day he wished he could have seen his face - even his cold face - just once more. Something to say goodbye to that was more than a memory.

After taking a deep breath Hampstead peeled back the linen once more, just enough so that Doc's face was on show but nothing below it.

'Far out, Doc. You scrub up better dead than you ever did living. There ain't a speck of dirt on you. How about that.'

Then his shoulders fell and he sighed plaintively.

'I'm sorry that I didn't ask you out, and I'm sorry that you didn't get to kiss me in front of the whole town. That would have been one helluva moment, Doc. And I'm sorry that I showed you my bellybutton that time. Say, we could call it even right now if you wanted to? How about that?'

He took the corner of the sheet and whipped it back, instantly regretting it. Having forgotten that breasts existed the sight of Doc's tiny ones wiped poor Hampstead clean off his chair. He breathlessly tried to compose himself as he scampered back to the trolley and threw the sheet back over Doc so that she was no longer exposed.

'Sweet Jesus,' Hampstead gasped.

'Is everything all right?' the morgue lady said, re-entering upon hearing the clatter.

'I just got a fright,' said Hampstead, picking up the chair with one hand and holding his chest with the other. 'Must be all the ghosts in here.'

The morgue lady left again.

'Sorry about that, Doc,' said Hampstead. 'I ain't ready for grown-upping, clearly. Grown-ups don't lark around like that. I guess we're easily even now though, right?'

Finally he caught his breath. The irony of the whole thing was that this was the first conversation that he and Doc ever shared. Some might argue that Hampstead talking at a dead body was no conversation, but many times had Hampstead got a similar if not worse reception from some that he'd fancied bumping gums with. Talking to Doc right now wasn't so weird. It felt as though she was listening.

'I'm also sorry that I got you in trouble those few times. I know you figured out that I was the one leaving the comics and the umbrella lying around, but I still feel really bad about the whole thing. While you sleep I'll keep living as though I'm trying to make it up to you. That's when I'm at my best, I think: when I'm trying to make things up to people and myself.'

Hampstead scratched his nose and twisted his tongue around his teeth.

'You see, Doc, I think the notion that I wanted you as my sweetheart is quite flawed. Some of my buddies at school reckoned that was where we was headed, but I never saw it. Sure you're funny and you're lonely and all that, and I like those things in a person. But I don't know that I ever wanted you to be my sweetheart. Look at how frizzy your hair is, for starters: if you were to put your head on my shoulder I'd have to apply an ice pack afterwards. And you're two whole years older than me. It's basically Montagues and Capulets. I don't know what I wanted from you really. A grown-up would understand. Pa would've have understood. I bet Mr Bellingham knows too. It's a shame I won't be seeing him much around anymore but I guess I will at the funeral. There I'll be seeing you too. See you round, Doc.'

He replaced the sheet over her head and stood up. Slowly her long arm slipped out from underneath and so Hampstead fixed it up for her, keeping it in place by tucking the sheet under her back and keeping it secure. Then he went and did the same on the other side. He straightened up and nodded at the trolley.

Then Hampstead remembered the note.

In him a fire burned so brightly and bittersweetly it might have been hot and cold all at once. He knew that there would be peace in Doc's writing if nothing else, but he also knew that in order to procure said peace he would have to do one more daring act of Hampsteadyness. Of juvenile tomfoolery. Of monkey tricks; clownery; mischief; horseplay; shenanigannary; high jinkery. Hell, of being a dang kid. And he knew deep down in this burgeoning blaze of his that Doc would let him off this once.

So when night fell and the kerosene lights of the Bellingham household dimmed and then fizzled out altogether Hampstead crept up the drainpipe and faced Doc's bedroom window, his feet steady on the portico roof. It creaked a little. With him he had the trusty carpenter's crowbar that had served him well on so many occasions when breaking into the schoolhouse to steal arts and crafts for weaponry. With a gentle thrust and jimmy he pranged the window open and slipped inside, scoured the dark room for signs of Doc's shoes but to no avail. At least they were even now - again - in that they had been in one another's rooms. He tiptoed through the house and hoped to high heaven that those bratty sisters of Doc's were heavy sleepers.

On the bureau in the parlour room was a cardboard box with DOC'S THINGS written on it. It was tiny enough but then again Doc had always been famously footloose and never a hoarder. Hampstead edged towards it and then covered his eyes with the palm of his left hand out of fear of having his heart broken again by the sight of Doc's oddments. The right hand he plunged into the crate and fumbled around for the leather or the strap of a Mary Jane, which eventually he caught hold of. And tucked away at the very toe of the thing was everything that Hampstead could have hoped for.

Seattle. Will see you in the not-long.

Hampstead could hold onto that at the very least. A satisfying resolution on the strange dischord of Doc's life. Of all the people that Hampstead had *never* known - and he reckoned that was most of the world's people - Doc was the swellest.

He didn't see anyone on the way home. Usually he would have had a peek in through the glass at the candy store but Hampstead reckoned even the sight of the plastic wrappers would make him nauseous. The night was still so hot out that Goose was asleep on his back in the yard, but he stirred when Hampstead opened the gate, then approached him with drowsy abandon. Hampstead stroked his snout awhile before throwing the soft ball for him to run after.

(ii)

There was an obituary for Doc in the paper the day before the funeral. Charlie, Alma, Bitsy and July wrote it up on a sultry afternoon when the snatches of the cool breeze was not enough to drag them from the porch shade. They had invited Willie but he had been up on Velvet Hill digging the grave and carving Doc's headstone. No one had spoken to him since Doc's death except Alma, who got a rejection of her invitation and a plea to be left alone. Charlie paced the floorboards with his left hand holding his right wrist behind his back. Alma took the rocking chair and was coughing and sneezing a bit. Likely she had caught the flu off Sunrise, whom she had spoken to at the planetarium. July sat on the floor and Bitsy rested on the steps with her head against the post. She thought it curious that she was invited to help but was eager to do so anyway.

As the hours passed the words drifted too into existence. No one took the lead and yet no one was silent. Because they had all experienced very different sides of Doc there was no reason to disagree over any detail; they all accepted that what was said was right and fair. Alma's relationship with Doc had been through Willie, who had often described her so colourfully and tenderly that it was as though Alma knew her as well as anyone. July had employed Doc out of pity and as a favour to Willie and knew her in a professional capacity. Bitsy believed that Doc was headstrong and philosophical. She never knew her that well.

'And you are the most honest person I know,' July said to Bitsy, 'so we ought to believe it.'

Bitsy vowed in that moment to stop writing Hampstead's obscenity around town. A twinge in her stomach told her that she ought to come clean, but she reminded herself that what she said about Doc was what she truly believed. It had never occurred to Bitsy until now but Doc would have one day made an excellent protégé to Bitsy.

By sunset the obituary was done and Bitsy delivered it to the stenograph office where she had once grown up. She re-read it as she walked, twice tripping over the curb and once on her own laces.

Doc Bellingham: An Obituary

Burial: August 6th, 8pm. Up on the hill.

Winifred 'Doc' Bellingham liked a great many interesting and strange things. Mostly she liked the pictures and looking at her arms, but she also partook in cosmology, wrestling, amphibians, truancy and the occasional dance. In her life she had done all that she loved. Doc died on August 1st in an accident, surrounded by all the people whom she had charmed in one way or another. She was 12 years old.

Despite Doc's tendency to avoid her lessons she was astoundingly bright and had no difficulty in finding success. She got a job at the Pig's Itch without the need for an interview. She was hoping to study herpetology at the Boston School of Zoology. She knew the 88 different celestial constellations in the night sky and could point each one out on command. One time she helped a friend move a musical instrument a great distance.

Ultimately, Doc was a budding genius, an excellent security guard and a tremendous friend. She leaves behind three frogs and some people who will miss her.

Doc was dressed in a silky prairie dress and button shirt before they put her in the casket. A bonnet was put on her head and they kept her barefoot, true to Doc. Half the town followed the procession from the morgue to the hill, where Willie Bridger had spent the last few days digging up the dirt seat that Doc liked to sit on when she was stargazing with him. It seemed that even Willie had forgotten how spindly Doc was because the hole was only narrowly long enough for the casket to be lowered into. It had to be pushed a little the final few inches before it settled a full six feet down.

Reverend Kingsley read aloud a psalm for the mourning as the dirt was thrown back into the grave. Willie Bridger watched from afar and smoked a cigarette - a rare sight indeed. Bitsy saw that Hampstead was fighting an onslaught of tears with little success. Moments ago he had decided to buttonhole Doc's father but old Charlie had told him something in the vein of 'not now', and so Bitsy approached the lonely boy with a hand for his shoulder, which Hampstead didn't really know how to deal with. He straightened his back and told her thank you for the comfort and that was that. Charlie read aloud *So, We'll Go No More a Roving* while the Aeolian harp hummed aside. Then some more passages were read by the miscellaneous members of the clergy, most of whom Doc had no relation to and who probably didn't know a thing about her other that she was a child and that she was dead.

Then the stars were out and it was over and Bitsy decided to go home, but first she wanted to speak to Alma.

'I've been thinking about getting the hell out of town,' said Bitsy.

Alma's rivered face transformed into one that was pulsing with optimism.

'You do it,' she said. 'Too many children die in this town.'

'I ain't a child, Alma.'

'I'll miss you.'

'I've hardly seen you,' said Bitsy.

'You should be glad. It hasn't been pretty.'

'Are you sure that I should go?'

'Absolutely, where are you going?'

'I expect D.C., or maybe Los Angeles. There's plenty of influence that needs pushing on the heavy hitters, and I ain't able to do much of it from here. Here it's just cuss words and -' she paused for a moment, 'monkey business.'

'I'll miss you,' said Alma again.

'I'll miss you too. I'm worried about July's place. Once I've gone there will be nothing to stop the Prohibition Unit taking him and the Itch. Pa will unlikely support a place like July's when I ain't even in the same town.'

'You want to affect greater change than just keeping the government out of our gin mills,' said Alma, 'and I think whatever happens to the Pig's Itch will be a worthy price to pay for what you do out there. He'll be O.K. in the end.'

'I don't know about that.'

'And Mélanie?'

'What about her?'

'You aren't worried that she'll miss you?'

'It's Mélanie, she'll be okay. There will always be people falling over each other to get her favour.'

'See, I think that's just the reason that she'll miss you.'

(iii)

July was sat outside Room 3 thinking about old Doc when Sunrise came out and looked a little startled to see him.

'I was coming to find you,' she said.

'Why?'

'Today is a lonesome day.'

'Indeed it is,' said July.

'You are still here, though.'

'I will stay in town as long as no one kicks me out. I don't think anyone is that bothered anymore about what I did; it's a distant memory because of what happened. And everyone wants alcohol now more than ever and the organisation of a sale would put that on hold for a time.'

'Then help me make sense of this before I go.'

Sunrise handed over a folded letter and July read it to himself. It was from Mr Hale and he had left her for the railheads already. There were myriad reasons explained for his leaving in the letter - Sunrise's reminding Hale of their old home, his shame at his own despair, his wanting to protect her from himself, et cetera - but also was there a nervousness and uncertainty. He asked how he might feel two contrary things at the same time: a wish that Sunrise be a rose of happiness without a worry in the world, but also that a tinge of sadness often remind her of him. He wanted her to be led by the roads and rivers of her life to the Eden in which she was already an angel, but he wanted her to look back.

'Say, would you mind if borrow some of these lines?' said July, thoroughly immersed.

'I cannot leave the letter with you so you should scribble them down now before I leave. But why would you want them?' said Sunrise.

'A sorrowful man will always play the troubadour, though perhaps I should avoid being derivative in the future,' July acknowledged. 'Keep it from me. It's from him to you after all.'

'All right,' said Sunrise.

'And where are you going now?'

'I don't know. Maybe back to Rockwell. Maybe hundreds or thousands of miles away. I have a reference from Dr Wagner, so I'll make use of it.'

'You won't stay?'

'How can I? I persuaded Willie to go ahead with the project; it's as much my fault as his that Doc died.'

'I think for once people are more inclined to blame him than they are somebody else.'

'But I am not,' said Sunrise. 'I have to leave and I have to imagine that I was never here.'

'I think we could all benefit from doing that,' said July.

'What's to stop you now?'

'I never kept in town because of Willie, Sunrise. I'm one of a rare few.'

Sunrise sighed.

'I know,' she said.

It was evening and it was warm and they ought to have gone and sat outside with their lack of business to attend to. Mr Cricket was working the bar downstairs with the help of a new boarder called Samuel. July could relax as long as he wanted. But neither he nor Sunrise wanted to leave their little spot outside Room 3 for a time, so they sat awhile in the quiet and smoked and drank and breathed. Then Sunrise patted July on the shoulder and told him that she was going to the bathroom. In her absence July darted on the tips of his toes through the Itch, past an inquisitive Toto and out the back door. Then he ran all the way across town and rested on the boardwalk outside the bodega on Bell Avenue. There he knew that he would not have to face up to a goodbye from Sunrise. She would be long gone by the time he returned to the Itch.

20

July finally caught the heat not long after Bitsy left for D.C. He was playing the piano on a humid September afternoon and the sun lingered on his fingers. Chords of light on chords of music. What he was playing was not interesting to him. Perhaps something honkytonk. Perhaps it was *Scarborough Fair* or perhaps it was this *Petrichor* ditty that maybe never even existed. It felt as though he ought to play a requiem for the earth on its final day but none of that sprang to July's hands. His mind was elsewhere and nowhere. There was a hullabaloo outside and the racket spread into the bar despite that it was near-empty. Another bootlegger might have concealed his reserves but July was a lazy bum and now the embodiment of indifference. He passed his time by breathing, eating and sleeping. No longer did he cry or moan or drink. Never did he wake up in the witching hour with a tightness in his chest and a throbbing in his temple.

So despite the warnings from those around him - Mr Cricket was extremely panicked - July kept playing and simply nodded in acknowledgement of his clientele's tip-offs. Stamping boots reverberated through the floorboards and through the piano pedals and still July played. The sound of the door swinging open behind him roared through his ears and still he played. Barrels were dragged out of the room and arms wrapped around July's shoulders and over his arms. If he had had Luella's gun then he might have shot himself but not because he was sad; it would be because he no longer had anything better to do. Prison would likely be a bust. Outside of prison was a bust. Death was just death. But he would have shot himself in the stomach or perhaps the femoral artery. Sure it would hurt like hell but he reckoned it would give Mélanie just enough time to run in and cradle him as he passed. Even in the good times he liked the sound of that. Gee, he thought, ain't it funny.

And then there was shouting and rope and dragging and he was on his way out of the Itch. His whole body was limp and lethargic and he did nothing to assist his arresters, though neither did he resist.

'You're almost good-looking,' one of the cops mocked. 'They'll have plenty of fun with you where you're going.'

'You think he looks forlorn now,' another one said. 'Wait till he's through a couple nights. He'll look like they hooked his lips to his feet.'

There was dust everywhere outside, gritting the boards of the veranda like snow might. In fact it was falling like snow because of the stampede of people that had followed the Prohibition Unit from their automobiles. They'd risen the dirt up and now it was drifting down and choking the air. But July squinted and cocked his head to keep as much out of his eyes as possible, scanning the throng for signs of her as he was pushed down the steps and onto the road. The jolt of movement he made allowed him to struggle free momentarily, so he tore hell for leather towards the crowd and looked everywhere, desperate and afraid.

'Mélanie?'

He found her and he fell onto her shoulder, letting his chin set for a moment and wishing his wrists unbind so that he might embrace her once more and tuck her hair over her ear. In hoping for as much contact as possible he pressed his body into hers and they were conjoined through gentle touch momentarily.

'*Au revoir*,' came her soft voice, and it was a honeysound to July; one that he would take with him to the bowels of incarceration.

'*Je t'aime*,' said July, feeling strangers' arms on him again. And then he was removed from her and he could see her face again and it was empty and lonely and celestial. She was of another world and he would not see it again, he knew. He said again, '*Je t'aime*,' and Mélanie kept watching him, her face becoming smaller and smaller as the distance between them grew to a gulf. July would not free himself this time. Once more he said, '*Je t'aime*,' and then he knew she would not hear him again. He had tried everything that he could and there was a strange peace within him suddenly. It was a peace that he carried him to the jailhouse and would nestle beside his grief and act as its curb over the coming months.

At trial July was told by his attorney that the judge would likely put him on probation if he privately agreed to begin supplying the district attorney's office with moonshine. There would have to be some quality checks and July would likely be instructed to perform a taste-and-swallow-test on every batch before it was delivered. They would also want permanent access to his distilleries and a small percentage of his profits. There would be a set of distilleries for the new clientele and one for the town and both would be manned at all times by non-uniformed agents assigned by the DA. They would provide the wood alcohol, carbolic acid and Coca-Cola for the town's smoke supply. In the DA's distilleries there would be good whiskey and good gin and nothing else. Other than that everything would likely be hunky-dory. The attorney spelled the whole thing out like it was set in stone. Ninety percent of the his bootlegging clients had had such luck, he said, but it transpired that the judge in question was a veteran who had once had a drop of whiskey at Flanders just before the Germans came over the top. It made him throw up and he had abstained ever since. July got twenty-two months in Folsom. Eligible for parole after twelve.

(ii)

While in the jailhouse July was sent Agent A.C. Jensen's 1921 Folsom inspection report by someone who did not give their name. It came in a large envelope stained by lemonade and also included a couple of strips from *Thimble Theatre*. It was very mysterious but July read all thirty-two pages of the report in an hour and stewed over the photographs included. He cried awhile as the fear bedded itself in his gut. The report said that the New Cell Building had natural light and ventilation but the Main Cell Building had neither and nor did it have running water. July was too panicked in the moment to rightly convince himself that he, being a prisoner of low concern, would unlikely end up in the latter. Then he read the comic strips and felt a little better.

Upon his arrival he was photographed and had his prints taken, then was bathed, shaved and measured. Then he was put in the appropriate scrubs and asked for a medical history. They gave him a rulebook and he was directed to the New Cell Building and put in a cell with two other inmates: an old cowboy called Clyde and a Mexican feller called Jose. Turned out the two of them had fought side-by-side during the Indian Wars but were part of the San Pedro Massacre about a decade ago. They were due for parole around the same time that July was but they still bemoaned their sentences, which really got under July's skin from the start.

They were served supper that first night in the Mess but July had his plate taken and his wrist fractured in a beating by some crazies from the Klan. It was sore and swollen for a while after. There was a helluva lot of old cowboys hanging around. Most of them were way over the hill and paid July no mind apart from when he got sent more comic strips. Fortnightly he got them without fail from this mysterious benefactor, but on the sixth time he received a note - littered with errors - to boot:

Mr Slade

Forgot to write a note on any of the last enveloaps so I figured you don't know who I am. It's me, Hampstead. From Boot Street. Hope you like the comics. I bet you're wondering where I found that report. I told Bitsy's pa that I helped with her politicks and that I could use a favore. Doubted it would work but Bitsy must have talked me up real well because he sent it right along. Anything else you're needing?

Hampstead.

With nothing else to do with his time July decided to write back to and thank Hampstead for his thoughtfulness. But talking to an absent guardian made him think of Mélanie and July's language verged on lustful and so he scrapped the whole thing and swallowed the paper. Then he had a thought. Clearly he needed to articulate his thoughts on Mélanie in some form or another and apparently writing to this boy Hampstead might provide an avenue for such a release. So he requested help:

Kid

Thanks for the strips. Real fun. Two things: 1. What's town like since I got pinched? 2. How literate are you?

July

He asked the warden to have it returned to sender and a few days passed. Then a very long note written in relatively frantic handwriting by a likely excitable hand was fed through the gates of the cell. Jose collected it and July asked him to read it aloud:

Mr Slade

Howdy, hombre! When ma told me that you wrote I told her it was a load of phonus balonus. I still ain't convinced! Town is lonesome. I am working as a salesman and technician at the photography emporium. Every day sum [crossed out] *someone wants to buy a kodak and I'm less of a goof about talking to people now. Also I can read and write real well. Why do you ask? Do you need some books to make your time more easy passing?*

Hampstead

To which July replied:

Kid

Hey. Let's not be daisies about this but I want you to help me write a poem. I ain't too good at words but I figure if you fetch a thesaurus from the library we can work as a team to get this poem done. Sound good?

Mr Slade

The gaps between Hampstead's replies became increasingly short despite that July only ever wrote him once a fortnight at maximum. One time Hampstead's reply came back within two days and the warden had to check it because he figured it was conspiratorial for someone to write so determinedly. Then he laughed his ass off at July for corresponding with a kid about poetry.

'Don't be such a bluenose!' he said, seeing July's scowl as he passed through the letter. 'Goddamn dame, if you ask me.'

Mr Slade

Howdy, 'buckaroo'! I heard that comes from a Spanish word. No need for a thesaurus. I'm a words kinda kid. Ain't good with numbers or nothing but I'm one hell of a writer. Send along your work and I'll fill it out no problem.

Kid

July sent forth the makings of a crude poem, twelve lines long and without any rhyming couplets or meter. Resisting that temptation made July pretty pleased with himself. The warden made a point of holding the letter back from delivery so that he could read it aloud at supper and July caught another beating. His eye was blue and he lost one of his canines. It would have been worse but Jose and Clyde got in the way and July didn't know how to feel about being saved by people like that. He chose not to think about it. Then a reply came two days later and July became irritable because the more frequently that Hampstead replied to him from then on the more frequently July got biffed about. And when July resisted the temptation to reply quickly Hampstead would simply send a follow-up note and it made no difference. So July resolved to match Hampstead's keenness so as to make the most out of it.

Then one day July was satisfied with the poem and he sat down on his bunk and breathed. He scribbled a penultimate note to Hampstead to tell him of this and asked to be apprised once more of the goings-on in town. A letter and three strips from *Take Barney Google, F'rinstance* came back a few days later. July had recently requested a greater influx of comic strips from Hampstead because he traded them with the locos in exchange for his meals and general well-being.

Mr Slade

Glad you're happy with it. Me too. But I'll probably make a few adjustments here and there till you get back. They're building a wheelbarrow store where the planetarium was. No one went near the site for a long time but now they're building a wheelbarrow store there. I was writing a novel but I gave up on it so that I can focus on my song, 'What's This Bug That's Got Me All Shook Up?' Sidney's gal hasn't replied to his telegrams in a while. The Snake Ranch bobwire fell again but this time the cattle all escaped. And the Pig's Itch is just a regular old boarding house now. Me and Heck officially recognised Tuna as the leader of our posse after a lot of dilibirating. I have learned to whistle. Got lots of ditties but Tuna don't let me play them much during Book Club or Book Debate Club because he reckons it's distracting.

Also Madamwois [crossed out] *Madamuase* [crossed out] *Miss Celestine has gone away. Might have been to find Lester but last we heard he was out in the Pacific again so that's unlikely. Everyone got up late the day after she left and they had to get a new knocker-up. I reckon even the roosters crowed a little later than usual. Doc's parents renewed their comitments to each other at marriage thanksgiving. That was swell. I was the photographer. Mr Bellingham looked happy and sad but it was a happy sad. He's going to start a new school and name it after Doc. Reckon I'll try a semester or two there. I'm glad things worked out for them. Not much else. Town is quiet. Mr Bridgers moved his chair up onto that big pile of rocks and he's kept it there with his ass in it. Not sure why he did that.*

Kid

To which July replied:

Kid

No more letters now. Thanks for your help. Just comics.

July

(iii)

And Hampstead was not the only literary maverick contributing to the Folsom literature circulation because Fitzgerald released a new novel during July's stint behind bars. It was a pulpy, uninspiring little yellow-back thing, but it made the rounds very quickly and Hampstead's comics became obsolete awhile. One could judge how engrossing the new Fitzgerald novel was by how dusty Spark Plug was. And for a few weeks after the first few copies of *Gatsby* filtered their way into the contraband sphere there was plenty of dust on all the comics. This was despite July's persistent decrying of the novel's quality and his assertion that it would not stand the test of time. The only thing that pulled on the strings of his narrow imagination was that curious motif in the valley of ashes: the oculist's billboard. And July consulted with Clyde and Jose and they both agreed that there was something particularly queer about it, only they were disquieted by it whereas July was comforted.

The strips had dried up by the time July got out but thankfully the judge changed his parole from twelve to ten months because of a ranch war in the Sacramento Valley. It had brought thirteen new inmates to Folsom. Hampstead had been sending some tatty reruns of *The Bad Dream* and *Old Doc Yak* and they were often covered in dust and stains. Still July got a kick out of them but he also got sick of them sometimes when he remembered that motion pictures existed. There wasn't much that he could remember of any of the pictures - even *Nosferatu* - but he could remember the feelings he got from them. That was enough to drive him crazy.

So on the bus south from Folsom July asked to be dropped off in Laguna. There he purchased a paper from the newsie with a tumour in his neck and scanned through it. There was a headline about the silent era being over as a result of a new picture called *The Jazz Singer*. July thought that that sounded like a load of baloney but decided to go and see it anyway. The picture wasn't much but July enjoyed that they included the Irving Berlin song. He hummed it on the bus all the way from Laguna to town and then he stopped humming and could barely get his legs to move. It seemed to take him a year to walk the length of the bus. He spent more time getting from seat to door than he had spent in Folsom.

The bus seemed to shake him off as he stepped out. He stumbled around as it rumbled away and then he composed himself, patted down his old clothes, put his luggage on the boardwalk and looked up at the hill. Willie was asleep in the collapsible chair. It was summer again and it was a hot one so everything was yellow or beige or orange except from the blue sky and a curious new piece of 20th century furniture that had appeared on the foot of the azure. An optician named Kingmaker had moved into town and had clearly been reading *Gatsby* as well, what with the looming billboard quite recently put up and painted with his giant brown eyes. Each had irises two or three feet up and across, just like in the novel. Only these, unlike Eckleburg's, were unfrowning eyes; considered and decadent and paternal, performing a watchful, careful vigil in the perceived absence of town's own Willie Bridger, whose own eyes were the mnemonic signposts of his old safekeeping. Anything could be commodified, July realised, even longing. God had abandoned the valley of ashes and now had abandoned this little settlement too, and Kingmaker was quite possibly the shrewdest man to ever exist on this side of the state.

It occurred to July that there was nowhere for him to go anymore; or at least for him to stay. He wasn't too keen on boarding at the Itch and goddamn him if he ended up having to stay with the Hampsteads. But nonetheless there was business to attend to, and also he wished desperately to distract himself from the eyes of the optician. The photography emporium was where he went first and there he met a small black boy who had grown several inches and was covered in dirt.

'Hidy-do, sir,' said the kid. 'Interested in something we got?'

'Hampstead, it's me.'

The kid stared awhile.

'Hell, if it ain't Mr Slade,' he said.

'That's right.'

They chewed the fat about prison and the emporium awhile.

Hampstead was now getting paid but was on probation still. They had a laugh because July was also on a probation of a kind. Then July asked for the finished poem and Hampstead was so excited that he momentarily abandoned his post without hesitation. Then he remembered that he was on probation and told July that he would have to keep on another hour or two and would July mind hanging around for him to be finished. So July went and sat and smoked and reflected pensively. He even slept a little because the heat was so. It was so quiet around.

And within the promised hour Hampstead finished up and led July to his house. There Hampstead's mother made him coffee and sang his praises for a time because she found no end to her gratitude for his providing the town a mill such a while.

'Good to have you back, Mr Slade,' she said, watching Hampstead and him searching through Hampstead's many books and papers for the poem. 'Though I don't know if I missed you or the chartreuse.'

'I miss the chartreuse,' said July. 'Say, Hampstead, where are all your comics?'

'Hell, I sent them all to you. Have you brought them back?'

'The Ku Klux Klan has them now,' said July.

'Here it is, the poem!' said Hampstead.

'Ah. Read it to me, will you?'

So came to me, and for my sins, a dream,
Which did provoke a longing all men feel:
Beneath my brow, a lonesome fall; a stream,
That surged and curved from high, and long concealed.
A happy time. My heart will hold it tight,
So short it was, reduced to melting snow –
'twas summer's close that I first knew that light
And summer's peak that saw me let her go.
Look back and love, to hide one's pains to dark,
Then fondness meets the dreams that paint her trace.
Whilst beauty fine - beloved still, a spark
From fires that burned so true: that distant face.

To see the swathes of time that we must traipse,
Alone, apart, and bound by ghostly shapes.

'Huh,' July said blankly.

'Do you like it?'

'I don't recognise it too well.'

'I ain't gonna lie to you, Mr Slade, but I done bought myself a thesaurus in the end. Then I done acquired some vocabulary help from the lady from the library - I got a lot of credit there despite my skin colour - and one of my misters at school helped me write it up. It's called a sonnet. Look here, it's got a meter, couplets, quatrains, the whole shebang. Mr Ratzenberger even showed me *Sonnets from the Portuguese* before we did it, so you know it's tip-top.'

'It's true that poets are the only true pedagogues,' said July. 'Is this even my poem anymore?'

'Well, sure. You see, it's all your thoughts and feelings and your story but they've been packed into fourteen lines by someone who can write better than we can. It might have needed some help coming to life but that doesn't mean it ain't yours.'

'I s'pose so,' nodded July.

'Would you like to purchase a kodak?' asked Hampstead.

'No one to take photographs of.'

'Gee, ain't that always the case. I sure wish I could have gotten a picture of old Doc before she died.'

'Yeah, that would have been real swell, kid.'

It would likely deliver him little more than pain but July had an unrelenting desire to see the Pig's Itch again. He had asked Hampstead in some of his early letters for updates but Hampstead had felt too mournful to visit it. In fact the greatest tribute to Doc was that the Itch was, according to Hampstead, going bust due to a lack of custom. This had nothing to do with July being gone - if anything the place was as welcoming as it had ever been. Someone had left a review underneath a spittoon and it said that it was a real swanky place. Never had

July heard someone call the Itch swanky while he was the proprietor. No, the struggles at the inn were as a result of the sadness that Doc's absence brought the guests. The most lonesome girl in the world and no one would be without her. Or so Hampstead reckoned. He was just a kid with a thesaurus, after all.

When July arrived he saw that it was no more dilapidated than it had been before he got put in the can. But that was still pretty dilapidated. He sat on the veranda, ate some of Mrs Hampstead's peanut butter and blackberry jelly sandwiches, smoked a cigarette and sighed. Then he played with his thumbs awhile before plucking up the courage to go back inside for the first time in almost a year. Perhaps he would weep. Perhaps he would cower. Perhaps he would feel nothing at all. But he had no time to feel any of these things because Mr Cricket was there to ambush him with a hefty punch in the ribs and a headlock to boot.

'I didn't expect to see you for a while yet!' he said, finishing the noogie and releasing his old friend. 'How are you? You smell like azaleas. I'd have cradled hellfire to have you back but a day earlier, I swear.'

'What the hell are you still doing here?'

'I live here, don't I.'

'You live here?'

'Sure,' said Mr Cricket.

'Why?'

'A plethora of reasons. I got my own room now, though I miss the balcony real and true. Oh, come with me,' he beckoned for July to follow him up the stairs - each creaking more than the last - past the ghostly memories of Room 3 and into the new abode. Indeed the interior was decorated as though it had a permanent resident. Everything was a shambles and July tutted and scowled as he followed the walls around. He caressed the splintered woodwork and breathed in mould. The air felt damp. The linens on the bed were discoloured and the summer outside only kissed his skin as he walked past the long windows. For such a quiet place it felt alive with disrepair. Suddenly July felt very paternal over it.

'So, what are your plans?' asked Mr Cricket, rustling around in the chiffonier for something unbeknownst to July but clearly of some importance.

'Ain't got none,' said July.

'Fancy being a boarder like me?'

'*Eh.*'

'Ah! Here we are.'

Mr Cricket pulled out a tiny vile filled with beige seeds, held it aloft.

'You recognise these?' he asked.

July's heart sank and a resigned tear brimmed in his eye. He gulped and took the vile, getting as good a look as his misty eyes would allow.

'Lune Solaire,' he said.

'Hell, that's it!' said Mr Cricket. 'I figured it was something like that. That angel mademoiselle left some for you. Did you know she kept them? That's one helluva pretty name - *Lune Solaire.*'

'Where did she go?' asked July.

'No clue. She left not long after they took you. Doubtful she went to find Lester; we reckon that's a thing of the past now. Could be she followed Bitsy east?'

'Doubt it. Why would she do that?' said July.

'I guess. She said you might want to try your hand at those bastards again. Although she said it a lot more delicately than that. Listen, I figured you'd be cut up about this and your face ain't telling me otherwise, but perhaps it's a good thing that she's gone for good. Out of sight, out of mind?'

'Sure.'

'You got them to grow last time, didn't you, them seeds?'

'Two in the same bed,' nodded July, wiping his eyes with his sleeve.

'You reckon lightning strikes twice?' asked Mr Cricket.

But July just shrugged and invited him out for a cigarette.

CPSIA information can be obtained
at www.ICGtesting.com
Printed in the USA
BVHW061346231222
654910BV00013B/1417